Valerie and

Colin Insole lives in Lymington, on the edge of the New Forest in England. He has contributed to a number of anthologies, including tribute volumes to Bruno Schulz, William Blake and Emil Cioran. His novella 'Bluebells I'll Gather' was recently published in 'Darkly Haunting' by Sarob Press. Colin's first collection of stories, *Elegies and Requiems*, was published by Side Real Press (Newcastle upon Tyne) in 2013.

colin insole

VALERIE

and Other Stories

THIS IS A SNUGGLY BOOK

ISBN: 978-1-943813-67-4

The story 'Valerie' is original to the present volume. The original publication history of the other tales, is as follows:

'The Hill of Cinders' was originally published as a stand alone volume, L'Homme Récent, Bucharest, 2015; 'The Binding' *A Tail for all Seasons Volume 4*, Priory Press, Isle of Man, 2015; 'The Slaves of Paradise' *Infra Noir*, Zagava and Ex Occidente Press, 2014; 'Dance for a Winter Moon' *The Gift of the Kos'mos Cometh*, L'Homme Récent, Bucharest, 2015; 'A Blue Dish of Figs' *Sorcery and Sanctity: A Homage to Arthur Machen*, Hieroglyphic Press, 2013; 'Salammbô and the Zaïmph of Tanit' *Transactions of the Flesh: A Homage to Joris-Karl Huysmans*, Zagava and Ex Occidente Press, 2013; 'Dreams from the Apple Orchards' *Sacrum Regnum II*, Hieroglyphic Press, 2013; 'The Abdication of the Serpent' *And the Whore is this Temple*, Mount Abraxas, Bucharest, 2016.

CONTENTS

VALERIE

and Other Stories

THE HILL OF CINDERS

July 1940

WHEEZING and out of breath from hard running, James Bulverton almost missed the entrance to the lane that led to the Hill of Cinders. But some sliver of memory from nearly thirty years ago guided him and he slipped out of sight, into the tunnel of overhanging vegetation.

Soon, he felt the soft, red ash under his feet, that swallowed the sound of his footsteps, and inhaled the earthy, burnt smell of the soil—more reassuring than treading lawns of thyme or chamomile. The path snaked around the back of the hill and he climbed easily now, resting finally in the saucer-like tier, close to the summit. Here, as from the gods of a great theatre, he could view the panorama of town, sea, school and the rolling downland of Southern England. In the twilight, the contorted white flowers of bindweed, streaked with unhealthy yellows and greens, as if they'd sucked up and absorbed the chemicals in the ground, seemed like the soft lamps in the gallery, before the actors emerged. Even the cobwebs, strung along the bushes, had a metallic glow, as if slaked with lime or sulphur.

He was rewarded with a sunset of gold and crimson, and the flicker of salmon-pink waves on the English Channel. For all its beauty, he anticipated most the hill under moonlight, as the night sky merged cosmos and the mutant red shapes on the wasteland of cinders.

In the playing fields below, a whistle blew, signalling the end of cricket practice. The boys headed for the pavilion, like docile sheep, returning to the fold. 'Poor little lambs, who have lost their way. Baa! Yah! Baa!' he muttered. A runner, circling the track, known in the school as 'The Turf', sprinted indoors. Faithfully repaired daily, by the groundsmen, the masters would never allow the red dust to rise, nor submit to the title of 'Cinder Track'. At a balcony, he recognized the bony silhouette of his old house master, straining and heaving with the blackout curtain. And on cue, in all the windows of the town, like little puppets in a display case, the good citizens acted out their duty, snuffing out the lights. His compulsion to experience again, especially on this night, the glories of the red desolation, was overwhelming. Perhaps he too was bound by the same innate mechanism of custom and ritual as those who obsequiously obeyed the regulations of school and war.

His first and only previous visit, was in the summer of 1912, when he was eighteen and a senior prefect at the school. The Hill of Cinders was forbidden; to trespass there meant immediate expulsion and shame. The sanction had never been necessary for it had had a squalid and tainted history, without romance or sense of adventure, to tempt even the most daring or rebellious pupil. In the eighteenth century, its strange red soil prompted a rash of mining speculation. A group madness descended on the town. Fortunes were invested and squandered as theories of valuable mineral deposits were investigated. Agriculture and trade were neglected as men, women and children exhausted themselves in fruitless digging and excavating. Huge engines churned the soil and the townspeople crawled into labyrinths of tunnels and caves. Noxious chemicals and gases were pumped into the chambers in the hope of releasing precious metals. They found nothing but disease and misery, for long exposure to the claggy ash caused tumours and malignancies. Children were born deformed and deranged. When sanity returned to the population, the hill was abandoned and shunned irrevocably. For years, the town was a place of poverty and deprivation. Only the school's arrival, in the early 1820's, revived its fortunes. The hill was never visited and its isolation enhanced its reputation as a place of danger and forlorn desolation. It was rumoured that chasms, pits and mine shafts remained, rendered more perilous by the cover of diseased vegetation. From afar, it appeared that heavy artillery had shelled the entire protuberance. During daytime, it seemed merely oppressive, an industrial slag heap that marred or obscured the beauty of the downs. But under the light of the moon, with its unnatural soil and colouration, it seemed a piece of cosmic debris or detritus, spewed out by some poisoned star in its death throes. It was an affront to the serenity of the night sky—a derangement of planetary order and symmetry. Both town and school were embarrassed by its presence for its legend lingered in the national consciousness. A young man, joining his regiment or university, who committed an indiscretion, would be branded contemptuously as a 'clinkerboy'—the byword for reckless folly.

It was the only taboo that the school enforced. Surprisingly, it showed an indulgence and understanding, remarkable for its time, towards weaknesses of the flesh. A senior prefect, who had blown his brains out in his study, spurned by the pretty housemaid he had become infatuated with, was remembered with affection by the masters. His photograph still adorned the lobby. Another boy, who had contracted disease from a lady of the town, received not only expert medical treatment, but sympathy and concern. Drunkenness, rowdiness and violence, committed in the town's night quarter, were punished with token beatings and fatigues, but never expulsion or disgrace.

The school functioned as a nursery for empire and the exploits of former pupils were remembered and hailed as examples for current students. Their efforts in quieting a province and opening up railways and trade were chronicled in lessons and assemblies. Detailed maps followed their progress as they carved their way through desert, forest and swamp. Postcards from these glittering alumni, depicting conquered tribesmen and curious native customs, were framed and displayed in the halls and classrooms.

But for one day each term, the school gathered for a sombre conference and reflection on 'The Two Men of Ignominy'—former pupils who had knowingly brought ruin upon themselves and others. The school had nurtured its share of rogues, thieves and murderers, but only treachery against country, family and caste, marked out those individuals for especial notoriety.

In the days of tension prior to the Indian Mutiny, Captain William Charles Detchant had goaded and provoked native troops, engineered quarrels amongst his superiors and incited outrages, committed by both sides. He had played the two cultures against each other, as a jaded rake might set two yard dogs at each other's throats, for amusement.

His actions culminated in his wilful desertion of a garrison town, which was being held against the rebels. Considered a safe haven, it was crammed with women and children, who had hastened there from more isolated outposts. Feigning a change in orders, he led the guard to another location, leaving the town exposed and vulnerable. The inevitable massacre occurred. A plausible and convincing liar, Detchant was able to conceal his actions for over a year, even returning home on leave. And it was in England that his crimes, secret and insidious, were gradually pieced together.

He was seized by fellow officers, whose families numbered several of his victims among their members. Court-martialled and condemned, he was hanged on the parade ground, in the presence of his regiment. The execution, on June 23rd, 1859, was photographed and the dozen prints formed a major part of the school's instructional lectures.

No details of the cruelties and horrors suffered by his victims, nor the humiliating rites and customs of the hanging, were spared the boys. A whole morning, with illustrations, diary entries and contemporary accounts, was devoted to recounting the story. Layer upon layer, it instilled into them the perils of treachery.

The afternoon was devoted, in turn, to the case of Victor Albert Chirk, who undermined, in the early 1880's, the administration of a crown territory in Africa, allowing a rival colonial power to seize the advantage. Many troops, including former pupils from the school, were lost in skirmishes. And a tribal people, sympathetic to British rule, suffered huge casualties, with entire villages burned and massacred. The government, beleaguered by a scornful opposition and an outraged sovereign, was forced to mount a protracted relief campaign to restore order. Chirk's deceit, practised over many years, was carefully hidden. Like Detchant, he was arrested in England. But to pacify local anger in Africa, it was considered expedient that he should be delivered over to the justice of the tribe, where he was put to death, on January 10th, 1883.

Again, the school was obliged to pore over a library of letters, documents and photographs, chronicling his ruin. The masters spoke quietly and eloquently, allowing long periods of silence for the impact of the images to take hold. The slow pace of the whole day, remorseless and inexorable, was modelled on the hellfire sermons and meditations delivered by the Jesuits to pupils in their charge.

There was no doubt that these two cases had a salutary effect on the school. The boys were more reflective and subservient; slackers and idlers reformed and studied with renewed vigour. The documents and photographs were always accessible, in the archives of the school's reference library. Together with many of his peers, James Bulverton had studied the two men's histories, with morbid fascination, analyzing their features, handwriting and interests in dread of finding common flaws.

But in his senior years, he began to question the righteous condemnation levelled at the two men and saw instead a contrived hypocrisy. Their lives seemed like staged ceremonies. The photograph of Detchant, stripped of his uniform and insignia, his face distorted to a mask by the canvas bag as he sucked in laboured, frantic breaths, resembled an effigy, a Guy Fawkes figure on a bonfire, the perennial image of treason. The school needed these scapegoats. It welcomed and rejoiced in their rebellion. During the seminars, he watched the longing in the masters' faces—a hungry fire that needed to be stoked and satisfied with sacrifice and ruin; the zeal of pagan priests around a stone table. And he noted that the photographers who captured the horrors, both in Africa and on the parade ground, belonged to the same firm that took the formal portraits of the boys, to embellish the halls and lobbies.

As they discussed the Chirk case, he watched his house master pause and scrunch the joints of his knuckles, one by one, with calculated effect, before delivering Kipling's line, with polished rhetorical flourish.

'And the women come out to cut up what remains.'

They wallowed in the treachery and its potent cocktail of horror and glamour. He suspected that the boys were being teased and tested—taken to the edge of a precipice and dared to tread too close to the cliff face.

During his junior years, as an unthinking conformist, howling and yelling in the scrum of the other boys, the red mound held no allure. The dormitories of the younger classes were situated facing downland and towards the manorial estates. But when he became a senior prefect, with his own study, the crimson devastation of the mound began to draw him in. After a long shower of rain, a mist or fog rose from the hill and swirled around the canopy of trees in lurid shades of tangerine and flamingo pink. In the summer, it seemed to smoulder under moonlight and he felt compelled to leave his window and curtains open to absorb the glow. Coils of inky darkness spiralled down. He felt as if spores from the black trees on its summit were dropping onto his bed, like flakes of ash. If he listened hard, he could hear the drip of water in the abandoned quarries, inviting him to explore their banks and peer into their chasms. As he lay awake, it seemed that the moon, the stars and the hill were aligned, part of the slip and drift of the cosmos, whilst he remained below, cut off from its magic.

One evening, a moth the colour of charcoal, as if it had fed on the nectar of soot and clinker, alighted on his pillow. Tiny specks of vermilion dust, attached to its wings, dropped onto the white linen. Crushing them under his finger, they seeped into the fabric and spread, forming a network of veins and filaments, like a secret map etched in blood. From the Hill of Cinders, a black cloud funnelled into the canopy of the trees, divided and broke, before settling on the hillside. And he longed to wander and explore the grottoes and caves of burnt soil, where at night flocks of black moths heaved and twitched.

In the next room, the coarse voices of two fellow prefects were celebrating a house cricket triumph. Heffer's career on the family's tea plantations in Kenya was long planned in advance and Sebdon was destined for administrative duties in the clusters of Pacific islands. Already they called themselves 'great men', and as avid readers of *Stalky & Co.*, were singing the refrain,

> 'It's a way we have in the Army,
> It's a way we have in the Navy,
> It's a way we have in the Public Schools,
> Which nobody can deny!'

Waiting for them to separate and for the sound of snoring, he pulled on his clothes and shoes, negotiated the stairs that led to the kitchens, and slipped out into the night.

Every step was an act of rebellion, of unpardonable treason, and several times he nearly turned back. But the hill glowed under a full moon; a dark cauldron enticing him on. Occasionally, a light from the summer meteor shower fizzed and danced before its vapours were extinguished. In the stillness, he sometimes heard the slight hiss of its brief descent. And he pictured the fall of Lucifer, the bright angel, plummeting through the skies; his wings scorched black by fire, wind and retribution.

His climb to the summit was slow and ecstatic. As he gripped tree roots and branches to secure his footing, the red dust smothered his clothes. He had expected the nauseous, harsh smell of chemicals, turned toxic and decayed by time. But it had the subtle aromatic perfume of old incense, or the soft powders on the clothes and cheeks of young women he had danced with. As it seeped into his skin, he felt immersed in the musk and sweat of a lover, experienced and sensitive to his youth.

Much of the old industrial machinery remained—ghost shapes of twisted metal and wood, curled with tendrils and creepers. On a wall, isolated human faces were depicted, chiselled into the surface of the brick and coloured with the soil. Perhaps they were idle daubs, executed by the miners during their periods of rest, or commemorations for the dead, lost and suffocated in the tunnels. But weathered by time and damp, and grotesque with tumours of fungi, they resembled cave paintings from prehistoric times. The site had an ancient grandeur and silence; a lost city, abandoned thousands of years ago. The images seemed more moonlight and starfall than human memory. The beauty of its emptiness and futility contrasted with the ugly spread of the school and town in the valley below. The feverish and ill-planned excavations of the eighteenth century had collapsed. Tunnels plummeted into chasms of exposed earth, where layers of differently coloured minerals glowed in the moonlight, sickly and unwholesome. Ladders and bridges balanced precariously in the ruins, or lay flattened, like duckboards, across a swamp of cinders and mud. A few years later, in the battlefields of Flanders, he was to recognise the similarity and feel a strange sense of affinity and ease with the wilderness of no-man's-land. Fellow officers admired his calm and sang-froid, never realising that he positively embraced the scenes of devastation and the brutal clarity of human misery and folly. It was there that he learned, with indifference, that Heffer had fallen to a sniper's bullet at the Somme and that Sebdon had perished through his own regiment's misdirected artillery barrage.

In his initial excitement at climbing to the first tier, he had turned around to survey his progress and seen something large, moving in the bushes, behind him. Assuming it to be a deer, or a dog turned feral and scavenging for food, he had forgotten its presence. But gradually he became aware of the creature, carefully skirting into cover to avoid him, as he investigated the landscape. He had not entertained the idea that it could be human.

From the summit he had a panoramic view of the meteor shower. Patches of bare chalk, on the downs, shone like bone under the moon, and he imagined that each white scar had been scorched into the landscape by the vapours of their expiring lights. The hills stretched to the horizon; rolling undulations where sheep grazed and the smoke from isolated cottages and farmhouses rose to the sky. Landscape blended and merged into the cosmos and the night.

He had no knowledge of astronomy or the names of the constellations. But one cluster, sinuous and slender, climbed with the head, body and tail of a serpent. Around its mouth was a void and he pictured a lost star, red and venomous. Millenia ago, it had festered and glowed, before exploding; its debris, scattered across the firmament. And here on this hill, like the ash and soot from a great chimney, the red dust had fallen; a soft rain, sombre and melancholic. It endured, beyond the base clays and silts of this earth. The ice sheets could not freeze it and it grew, sullen and rebellious, against the landscape of ice and tundra.

He had planned to spend the night on the summit, watching the moon's changing light, its shifting colours and perspectives. But a summer storm arose, with soaking relentless rain, forcing him to seek cover in a deep stone shelter, once used by the miners. Hurrying inside, he glanced up and saw the silhouette of a man where the path narrowed, over a treacherous gorge. The figure, shabby and dishevelled, moved tentatively, slowed by the danger, before dropping out of sight. He felt no fear. Perhaps it was a vagrant or an outcast from the town. He felt a bond with the stranger. The man had both maintained his own privacy and also respected the solitude of the interloper. He had understood the silent courtesy of pariahs.

At first, he was engulfed in unremitting blackness; without moon, stars, or the flickering lights from the school and town. He felt cocooned in stone; in communion with the night, the earth and the gathering clouds above, that overwhelmed all human endeavour. The rain hammered the roof of his shelter, gushing down the hill, and he could hear its fall into quarries and unseen mineshafts.

When the thunder and lightning came, it lit up the splendours of the wasteland on the hill and he could glimpse, far below, the tawdry little classrooms. They were dwarfed by the majesty of the storm. All the rituals and formalities of school life—its assemblies, sports and relentless busying, parodied and mimicked the futility of the old miners as they delved, toiled and died in vain. All was reduced to darkness, lit occasionally by a brief image of empty rooms and the drawn curtains of the studies, where they snored and dribbled onto their pillows.

In his stone shelter, he felt the vanity of being in the engine room of the storm—the still point at its centre. He alone was exempt from the common tide of humanity and allowed access to visions and truths. From each flash of forked light, he counted the seconds; his body convulsing, believing that he was delivering the blast of thunder. Nearby, hidden in bushes and shivering with the rain, a man watched him; this absurd little figure, covered in red dust, capering and grimacing. He understood each gesture, each spasm of hubris and conceit. And unwilling to intrude and pry any more, he edged away to the far side of the hill.

As the thunder subsided, James Bulverton's sense of exaltation remained. In this hut, where night and cosmos were one, was the void, after his red star had burst. At its fall, came the blackness and the thunder, as tidal waves engulf and smother the land, when the sea bed is shaken by an earthquake. The occasion warranted a ceremony, solemn and unseen. Searching in the darkness, he found several sharp lumps of granite or flint, and on the stone wall he formally inscribed his name and the date of his epiphany—as a supreme being might signify his power and authority to those who crawled and squirmed in awe of him. It was an act of defiance, announcing his rebellion to anyone who dared come to this forbidden place. He hacked and carved blindly, guided only by touch, with vigorous bold slashes of the flint, sealing the work by rubbing the red soil into the gashes.

When the rain eased and the moon returned, he left the blackness of his shelter to prepare for the return to school. Quietly negotiating the descent, he was about to step into the lane when he heard voices. His bravado vanished— replaced by the sickening fear that his truancy had been discovered and that masters from the school were waiting. Crouching low, he hid in the undergrowth until it was light, listening to the soft murmurs and whispers. Finally, there was a scuffling of branches and raised voices followed by silence and he guessed that his pursuers had grown weary of their ambush and retreated.

The disturbance had delayed him badly. He'd intended to slink back at dawn, before most of the school were awake. Only the caretakers and kitchen staff, under the cook, 'Old Beef and Dumplings', preparing the huge vats of steaming porridge, or frying the masters' kippers and bacon, would be about.

But already he could see shapes moving, lethargic and sleep-heavy, at the windows, as the studies and single rooms stirred. He broke cover from the lane and it seemed that a hundred eyes gazed and noted his shame. He ran bent double, in that ridiculous gait that the junior boys, flushed from cover after smoking in the rhododendron bushes, imagined would hide their identities.

His clothes, face and hands were covered in red ash. Under the tap, by the cricket pavilion, he washed himself down hurriedly. But the cinders seemed to cake and solidify, sticking to him in clumps. Only by sluicing himself in water, could he free himself from their clagginess.

By backstairs and dodging voices, he gained his study without challenge. There, he tidied and brushed himself, but still his hair and fingernails were smeared with red dust. Checking his appearance in the mirror, he seemed to have been caught in the night's thunderstorm, for his shirt and trousers were sodden.

Someone knocked loudly at his door and he expected his house master, stern and silent, ready to accompany him to the headmaster's study. But it was Sebdon, who eyed his appearance with detached scorn.

"You incontinent little beast, Bulverton. Something's up. The head's wrathy—flapping about like an old washerwoman. Someone's in for a licking, or worse."

Soon, news filtered through that a special assembly had been called; the entire school summoned to attend. It would be done publicly, he thought. He would be humiliated in front of them all; beaten, expelled and frogmarched to a waiting car, to the catcalls of his peers.

There was a palpable sense of tension and outrage in the masters' faces on the dais. The benign softer ones dared not meet the gaze of the pupils as they filed in and took their seats. The others stared, cold and hostile. The head waited for the nervous coughing and shuffling to subside and rose to his feet. James Bulverton was sure that he singled him out with a look of loathing and contempt.

"A boy from this school, a senior prefect no less, has committed an act so heinous and treacherous that he joins the small rank of 'The Men of Ignominy'." There was a pause and he seemed to study James Bulverton, waiting for him to break or run. "The police notified me this morning that Edward Colkirk, deputy head boy in 1881, whose exploits in business and commerce have been recognized in our lessons, was arrested on the outskirts of the town, within sight of the school, and charged with the Lombard Street murders. You will all be aware of the case, which has considerably worsened this country's relations with our neighbours in Europe."

James Bulverton shook and fidgeted with relief. The case was notorious and had led to a damaging miscarriage of justice. Two years ago, senior partners at an international trading firm in the city were murdered. The evidence against two men, one Austrian, the other German, had seemed overwhelming, and both had been hanged, to riotous scenes of malicious celebration by the London crowd that rivalled Mafeking night. Subsequent events had proven their innocence, but relations between Britain and the other two countries were severely damaged. Any lingering goodwill, between nations already increasingly hostile to each other, had been compromised. It was dubbed the 'British Dreyfus Case' and in subsequent years many said that the incident had helped precipitate the Great War.

The head concluded, "In due course of law, your former prefect will be put to death, between heaven and earth, being unworthy of both."

The assembly ended and the masters, gowns swirling, swept from the hall. But James Bulverton's house master stopped and took him to one side.

"Clean yourself up. You look as if you've been out all night, rolling in a sand pit."

It seemed a casual offhand rebuke, fair and justified. But there was something in his voice that was charged with a secret knowledge and a sly smirk was exchanged with the head. In Bulverton's last weeks at the school, the masters accumulated the documents and photographs that chronicled Colkirk's life. A wealthy sybarite and the companion of beautiful women, he exuded glamour and mystique. James Bulverton reflected on his fall and capture, on the very morning of his truancy. The identity of the stranger on the hill intrigued and puzzled him. But never once did he associate that ragged and forlorn solitary with the suave elegance of Colkirk.

In the holidays, before James entered university, his father reflected on the case, one morning when they read, in the daily newspaper, of Colkirk's execution on September 9th, 1912.

"He gained nothing from the murders—no financial reward—and there was no woman involved to muddy his wits. It was an act of calculated folly—a macabre game. Do you remember the treason of the first Thane of Cawdor, in *Macbeth*?

> 'He died, as one that had been studied in his death,
> To throw away the dearest thing he ow'd,
> As 'twere a careless trifle.'"

The blackout had been rigorously observed. He watched the shapes and colours of churches, pubs and cinema blur into a grey, amorphous mass. It was a dead little town, its inhabitants wrapped in darkness, or hurrying into the damp of the air-raid shelters when the sirens wailed. It seemed a vast sepulchre, in which the shrouded bodies were stacked and shelved in compartments—a great hive of flaccid, sickly things, sweating and coughing. In the morning they would emerge, tired and blinking, into the sunlight, to scrape and slave in factory or ration queue. Even in high summer, their skins were white and damp, as of subterranean creatures exposed by the lifting of a stone or clod of earth. Their lives echoed the unknown dead from the Hill of Cinders—the countless fools who had toppled into mine shafts, been buried under an avalanche of clinker or overcome by gas.

Occasionally, on the promenade hedged with barbed wire, shadows moved. They were the sentries of the Local Defence Volunteers, known contemptuously as the Pump Corps. They guarded a hinterland. Beyond them was the sea, violet and still, with its great, hidden forests of weed, undulating and shifting, where great fish glided and teemed. Light played on its surface, brightening and fading, as clouds drifted across the moon. The night seemed to shine with patterns of colour, with the perfume from the sea and the trees, and the red beauty of the hill, now crimson and glowing under moonlight. Only the town was moribund. Those old men, armed with kitchen knives strapped to broom handles, were the gatekeepers between the living and the dead.

Although he had never returned to the hill, the memory of that first night of rebellion, with its bright fall of meteors and the ensuing darkness of the storm, in all their symmetries and cadences, sustained and comforted him in the troubled years after the Great War. Sometimes he would wake before dawn, knowing that in his dreams he had walked, solitary and proud, in the serenity of the red dust, or had sheltered in the hut, with the rage of the night and the cosmos resounding around him.

But recently he had been visited in his sleep by vivid and disturbing visions. He was on the summit of the hill. Red dust was dropping from the star he had pictured thirty years ago. And the star had grown, a monstrous swollen thing—a bloated parody of the moon. At first the fall came in gentle plumes, sweet and aromatic, that collected at his feet, like autumn leaves. But the star was fragmenting—rotting and decaying like rancid meat on a butcher's hook. Gradually the sky darkened as the fall became a deluge of ash and soot, silent and relentless. The debris rose to his knees and his steps became laboured and precarious. In the darkness, he was overcome with vertigo, conscious that he teetered on the edge of the summit, afraid of plummeting to the earth or sea below.

The hill, the night and the cosmos were one; merged in a choking and perilous cascade of dust. Blindly, and gasping for air, he veered in the direction of the path, but the ground gave way beneath him and he tumbled into a chasm. The fall always woke him as he tried to remember whether he had dropped into one of the old mine shafts or quarries, or plunged onto the pebbles of the beach. The dream puzzled and intrigued him but his resolve had hardened. Thirty years ago, he had stood in the stone shelter, his body pulsating with the revelations of the storm, imagining that he had invoked the tempest. But this night, he had conjured something more tangible. He would rain down fire and thunder on them all.

His nocturnal visit to the hill, all those years ago, had never been discovered by the school. Instead, in his final days, as senior prefect, he was showered with prizes and honours. And later, his exemplary war record, with decorations for gallantry, was lauded and extolled in assemblies and lessons.

But his contempt and loathing for the school and his fellow countrymen, with all their certainties and platitudes, which had been nurtured on the Hill of Cinders, grew. If asked to explain his estrangement, he would have struggled to give plausible reasons. His old house master wrote politely, asking for his wartime reminiscences and descriptions of his acts of heroism. Dutifully, he replied in detail, but felt manipulated and played, as if an unwilling participant in some great plan or conspiracy. He felt gulled. Like the second murderer in *Macbeth*, he was one 'whom the vile blows and buffets of the world have so incens'd that I am reckless what I do to spite the world'.

A troubled and unsettled spirit, his work took him into the Germany of the Weimar Republic and Hitler's rise to power. With no particular sympathies or allegiances with the new ideology, he lingered on its fringes, amused by the upheavals and chaos. Business deals led to meetings with Ribbentrop and Speer, and he enjoyed their disarming cynicism and admired the way that the party had played the old German military and political elites for fools.

He returned to England in 1937, a wealthy man, with contacts in the Reich. He corresponded with them discreetly, by letter, feeding them little scraps of information about people he knew, and was given the means to communicate secretly, by radio, in the event of hostilities between the two countries. When war was declared, he fell silent, as open sympathisers were arrested and interned. His German friends were disappointed, regarding him as a mere flaneur or gadfly.

But one evening, at his club, shortly after the fall of France, a vital snippet of information was disclosed. By chance, he met Thrapstone, a former pupil at the school and three years his junior. The same old hierarchies endured and the man sought to impress Scragger Bulverton, his senior prefect and the cruellest exponent of the childhood tortures of Brush Drill, the Corkscrew and the Key. A pale, studious boy, who excelled at languages, Thrapstone had been bullied relentlessly, but nonetheless regarded his former tormentor as a hero and a bulwark of patriotism. Lowering his voice, but gushing with the pride of secret knowledge, he had confided that a special operation was being set up on the manorial estate, near to the school. With its separate lodges and houses, set miles apart, it was to provide accommodation for Poles, Czechs, Dutch and Free French, who would be trained as agents to be dropped into their respective occupied countries, as spies and saboteurs. Due to his linguistic fluency, Thrapstone had been assigned work there. And tonight, as James Bulverton waited on the Hill of Cinders, the agents would be gathered in one building, to be addressed by senior intelligence officers on the ground rules and operational procedures. Pompously, he had assumed his old role of authority and warned Thrapstone against openly discussing secrets, even with friends.

But he had quietly scouted the area, with his black Labrador to provide respectability if challenged. He knew the old coverts and hidden entrances. Visiting the estate had always been forbidden, but the masters winked at trespass and the gift of a rabbit or pheasant often softened the punishment, if the trespass were discovered.

The story was true. Regular army troops patrolled the woods. Their security was discreet but formidable. Lorries, stacked with provisions and equipment, negotiated the narrow tracks. Occasionally, cars driven by military personnel raced through, their passengers anonymous young men and women. Having travelled extensively in Europe, he could distinguish Slavic and Polish faces.

He communicated his findings and by the third transmission realised that he was dealing with senior German intelligence officers. It was arranged that on this night, when all the agents would be congregated together for their briefing, a group of bombers would attack the estate. His torchlight signal, from the Hill of Cinders, would guide them to their target. As an act of personal spite, he had implicated the school in the scheme, claiming that several masters there were acting as instructors for the spies.

Midnight approaching, he had settled down to wait for the bombers when a figure began climbing the path to the summit. He recalled the old courtesy of the dishevelled stranger on the hill, thirty years ago, and wondered if it was the same man. He'd thought often of that hermit or recluse, speculating on his fortune and genuinely wished him well, hoping that he'd found the solace of some quiet cottage or refuge from the world. But this one ascended in laboured jerks, furtively peering over his shoulder. He recognized the uniform. It was a boy from the school—a ropy, gangling child who kept stopping to adjust the glasses on his nose. The courage of this ungainly, fearful youth, uncomfortable with strenuous physical exercise, impressed him. He, too, was braving shame and expulsion to experience the ecstasies of the hill and its rebellion. James Bulverton decided to leave him to his visions and discoveries without disclosing his own presence. He ducked unseen into a hide of bushes and bracken, overlooking the sea.

He scoured the horizon for aircraft but soon drifted into a reverie, induced by the beauty and stillness of the night. Waves lapped at the shore, hissing on the pebbles, and he sensed his heartbeat adjust to their ebb and flow. The charcoal moths rose in clouds, feeding on the curious variety of berry that flourished on the hill. Even when ripe and black, their flavour was as sharp as lemons and there was a ferrous, metallic taste to them. The little creatures hovered in the sogginess and drop of the fruit, the air tainted with a chemical lushness. The two brightest stars comforted him. Arcturus, harbinger of storm, and Vega, the eagle falling on its prey, reassured him that all would be well. At the railway station he thought he was being watched and then followed through the town. His sprint to the hill eluded all pursuers, but now he was convinced his fears were imaginary. Straining his ears for the approach from the air, the distant sound of a rare motor vehicle, raised and disappointed his hopes. He speculated on others who had stood on this hill, invoking the cosmos for auguries and portents, before the mound's reputation became blighted. What visions and treasons had they seen and plotted, before the ice sheets came or the seas filled the Channel, under a younger moon and different stars?

The throb of the bombers stole up on him and their appearance in the sky surprised and elated him—his dark angels, riding the storm clouds with thunder on their wings.

He roared them home, punching the air with his fist, whilst his other hand directed the torchlight. His body convulsed in grotesque spasms, as it had done in the shelter when he was eighteen years old. The air-raid sirens were blaring and he pictured the school, scurrying for cover; fussed and chivvied by the masters. Let them burrow and squirm into their worm holes; a direct hit would take them all.

But something else was in the sky. He'd expected some desultory anti-aircraft barrage. There were no obvious military sites nearby and he'd assumed that the attack, swift and precise, would be accomplished before any response was launched. To his dismay, a group of fighter planes, from the east, was homing in on his bombers. They were Hurricanes, in night camouflage, and their presence indicated foreknowledge. Weaving agilely above their targets, they seemed like hawks swooping on suburban wood pigeons grown fat and cumbersome with a plentiful food supply. Without the covering fire of escort fighters, the bombers blundered and stuttered. The majority were hit before they reached land. Rolling and plummeting in their own fire, smoke and noise, they broke upon the stillness of the sea. Two eluded the onslaught, but their bombs fell in woodland or on the downs. And in the empty lodges of the estate, where the carefully fabricated facades had been built, all was silent and dark. Little Thrapstone had snared his rabbit. The barbed-wire fences and army patrols remained to deceive the enemy for years. But the men and women of Special Operations Executive were hundreds of miles away, in Hampshire woodland.

James Bulverton watched the aftermath of the fiasco with sullen rage. A boat chugged out into the sea to rescue one of the stricken pilots. His dark avenging angel floundered in the water, entangled in his parachute, and clambered on board with the aid of a sailor's hook. It was an humiliating and absurd image. He resembled an obese woman from a silent film comedy who had toppled over backwards into a boating lake, her skirts billowing like a sail.

During the aerial battle, he was aware that the youth had retreated into the stone shelter. He had heard his whoops of encouragement and sensed his disappointment at the outcome. Eventually, he drifted into a troubled sleep and woke in sunshine shortly after dawn. He could see figures moving in the town. There was a pronounced jauntiness and swagger in their step. The school seemed transformed, its fragility gone. Adamantine and enduring, its timeless rituals were strengthened by the night's actions. An early morning train crossed the downs, whistling as it picked up speed, as if to mock and taunt him.

The magic of the hill had leaked away in the night. It was no more than an arid mound of ash, dirt and clinker. The wind blew red dust, irritating and corrosive, into his eyes, and his lungs felt clogged with its stickiness. His skin itched, where his body had lain in contact with the soil. A port-wine rash was developing, with feverish little blisters. The earthy perfume he had breathed with relish was the stale stench of years of failure, the forlorn endeavours of all those who had worked and died there. It permeated into the soil, trees and bushes. Rising to his feet and inspecting the landscape, he peered into one of the quarries that had once enchanted him with its cascade of flood water. A stagnant blue ooze bubbled around the skeletons of horses.

The poor beasts had probably expired there, hauling the heavy machinery, when the mines had operated and their carcases had been tipped into the pit.

One last morbid call of nostalgia remained before he could quietly slip into the lane and catch the fast train home to his London suburb. In daylight, he wanted to examine the carved signature and the date of June, 1912, that marked his youthful epiphany.

The stone shelter seemed diminished under the sun—a dreary little hut, like a workmen's lavatory. And someone, in modern times, had bolstered the roof, with a sheet of corrugated iron, almost concealed with branches. Its walls were bound loosely together, in a rough mixture of large slabs and lumps of granite. But the rock he sought, in the depths of the chamber, seemed to have been hewn from the very bones of the hill. A huge wall of pumice-grey, it was pocked with strawberry-coloured blemishes and excrescences, like honeycombs or wasps' nests. The stone itself seemed diseased, as if a careless touch risked infection—a spread of calcified leprosy or scabies. The contagion spread across the entire stone, like the pattern of blood poisoning, festering and marring the skin on a human body. Its fevered design mirrored the constellations of the night sky—each star a distempered red pimple or pustule. It was a stone created in some ancient fusing of rock and mineral, of burning stars and falling red dust. In darkness was its sickness fused, where night, the cosmos and the hill were one. Perhaps this was the prize hauled from the tunnels, after decades of toil, sickness and death. Engraved on its summit, the letters weaving together and embellishing the deformities, were the words: 'Put to death, between heaven and earth, being unworthy of both.' And underneath, hammered into the stone and sealed with the red dust, like the inscriptions added through the ages on a family tomb, were the names and dates.

William Charles Detchant—June 23rd 1859
Victor Albert Chirk—January 10th 1883
Edward Colkirk—September 9th 1912
James Bulverton—November 11th 1940
Clive Arthur Staplow—

The youth Clive Staplow had hewn today's date, but already the colour had run and blurred his work. The red soil churned and fomented, as it would for years, until his treachery and fall reached their poisoned climax, here on the hill.

James Bulverton pictured them all, each in his respective generation, twitching and gyrating in this cave, in futile hubris and ecstasy, before returning, like the passing dead, to usher in the next treason.

Heading for the path and escape, the landscape spat him out. The hill's business with him was finished. The wind hurried him down, an absurd figure—a tattered heap of rags, flapping down the track. He felt as if he was descending a treadmill, paddling air, as the ground slipped beneath his feet. Nearly falling as he stumbled into the lane, strong hands seized, handcuffed and bundled him into the waiting police car.

THE BINDING

Ballaugh Village—Isle of Man—August 1870

CARREE LEECE set down her violin for she sensed a lull and weariness in the festivities at her husband Conal's thirtieth birthday party. She had played and sung for over an hour and her music had been warmly received. But she knew the applause was forced. Her mother-in-law had winced when she missed the integral high note at the emotional heart of the last song. Her voice was shrill and tuneless and she was conscious of its sounds drifting out, far into the heath. She hoped that no solitary traveller or farmer was passing close enough to hear. And her fiddle solos in the ballads should have soared, bringing tears to their eyes. But her playing had been humdrum and uninspired—dulled by the unspoken pity and blame with which her husband's family regarded her. At twenty-eight she was childless. "Barren" was the word she had heard whispered when she entered the kitchen unexpectedly. But they were kind people and they smiled and simpered as they shifted the conversation to her music and her cooking.

She knew the fault was hers. Conal's first wife had borne him a daughter in their first year of marriage, before polio carried them both away. The colour and vibrancy of the flowers he tended so diligently on the little grave at St Mary's added a further reproach. And he had played and romped so vigorously and desperately with the seething tangle of nephews and nieces, who swarmed over their fisherman's cottage, that her distress deepened.

In the evening, when their guests had departed, the silence was suffocating. The cottage was large and their footsteps echoed on the stairs and on the floorboards in the empty rooms. It had been her family's home for many generations, stretching back at least to the reign of Queen Anne. And there was evidence of earlier settlement on the site. Medieval silver coins and fragments of brick and pottery from even more distant times had been unearthed in the garden.

She lay awake, long into the small hours. Always, her body felt constricted; bound by invisible cords and ropes that smothered and stifled her. She remembered her secret, futile visits to the wise woman who dispensed herbs and charms from the neighbouring hamlet of Ballavolley. Daily she had sweated, her head over the steaming vapours of catmint, and she had even swallowed and retched on stinking arrach, that grows on dunghills and smells of rotting fish, or worse. And in bed, her husband, recoiling at the foulness of her breath, had turned his back and cradled his pillow, aloof and unresponsive.

The next evening, she sat in the garden, with the expanse of moorland before her, preparing a basket of mackerel for smoking. She worked quickly; her knife gliding with practised skill, and her fingers deft and nimble. The bright, fresh colours of blue, green and silver, on the skin of the fish, shimmered and merged with the twilight heat haze from the furze bushes and heather. Clouds of insects rose from the gorse, and flurries of feeding birds, noisy and clamorous, swept amongst them. Shadows rose and fell and she smiled to herself, for some seemed like the shapes of figures asleep by the mounds and bushes.

One in particular appeared like a green dress, decorated with dark blue flowers, in the cluster of vegetation growing up the trunk of an ancient yew tree on the borders of their property. Over the centuries, its main branches and heart had collapsed and new growth had sprouted from the dead wood, leaving grotesque hollows and contortions. Stones from the boundary wall had weathered and fallen into its remains, creating a strange union of stone, tree, flowers and earth. And hidden at first, amongst the songs and quarrelling of the birds, she discerned a tune, hummed very softly from the direction of the yew tree—a melody from her childhood that she had forgotten.

Squinting and concentrating hard, she gradually became aware of a woman, resting against the trunk of the tree. Her song finished, the stranger rose to greet Carree; her movements lithe and fluid. But the face was old, cracked and lined. Carree knew most of the villagers and those who lived in the isolated farms, and the woman's presence, as night drew on, seemed odd.

"I'm staying with my daughter, a mile or so down the track into the valley, near Ravensdale, to help with the gathering of the berries. Do you not remember visiting our modest smallholding when you were a girl? The harvest this year is rich and abundant. My name is Mabily," the woman said. "And yesterday, as we filled our baskets, your songs drifted to our orchard. We sensed a deep sadness and loneliness in your music."

Her gaze moved to the upstairs bedroom, planned and furnished as a nursery, where the once bright wallpaper peeled and flaked and dust gathered in the empty wardrobes. There was something comforting and reassuring about the woman's homely voice that made Carree want to confide in her. And she spoke of her childlessness and the secret visits to the wise woman.

"Many of the most potent herbs and remedies have been lost or forgotten," Mrs Mabily said. "At our cottage are infusions and distillations to cure your condition. They are far sweeter than stinking arrach. What happiness could come from scrambling for plants on the edge of some foul midden? Call on us, tomorrow, at noon, when the men are busy with their nets."

Finding comfort in solitude, Carree had walked the lonely track into the valley many times but could not picture the cottage the old woman described. But when she saw its timber frames, peeping out from behind the mounds of heather and green turf, she knew it had always been in her memory—as enduring as her own house and older even than the first church of St Mary's. The gardens stretched far into the distance, blending into the moor and gorse. They were lined with bushes of blackcurrants and blueberries, fringed with rows of raspberries. Dimly, she could see the shapes of people picking, bending and stooping; their skirts brushing the foliage as they worked. Wicker baskets filled with the fruit were piled near to the door and their perfume was heavy and narcotic, making Carree's head swim with dizziness.

Mrs Mabily, brisk and bustling and full of matronly good humour, was waiting for her and led her to a herbarium, cool and airy, where stone flagons of juice were being prepared with plants and flowers. Neat shelves were lined with bottles, their contents coloured purple and crimson; each one a slightly different tint and labelled by its year. Interspersed amongst the bottles were little human figures, made from twisted stems of barley and wheat and decorated with twigs, bark and leaves, to represent farmers, fishermen, their wives and children. Black strands of horsehair were tied tightly around their midriffs to hold them together. Crystallized flowers formed their eyes and they stared down as if wise and benevolent, rough creations of surprising artistry.

"A foolish hobby of mine," said Mrs Mabily, gently squeezing Carree's hand. "A simple treat for the children who visit. I remember you coming here, over twenty-five years ago, with your grandmother; your frock and fingers stained purple with all the berries you'd picked. I gave you a cornman—a mackerel fisher—and you said that one day you would marry him."

And now Carree remembered the day well: hurrying home in a sudden shower, protecting the little figure from the rain, under her dress. Its eyes had been made from marigold flowers. Drops of moisture had seeped through onto the petals and she had imagined that the figure was alive and crying.

Balancing a pair of spectacles on her nose, Mrs Mabily scrutinized the bottles and reached for one marked 1842.

"The year of your birth," she confided. "A year of great fertility. All is well."

And with meticulous care and show of precision, she measured and mixed powders and herbs on an apothecary's scales, before blending them with an extract from the bottle.

"Drink a teaspoon at nightfall, until the contents are drained," she said. Impressed both by her kindness and scientific integrity, Carree was reminded of a family doctor, wise and trusted. She fished in her purse for silver, to offer as payment but Mrs Mabily waved the money aside.

"My only condition for this gift is that I alone must act as your midwife. The country women and family members, well-meaning as they are, can be rough and heavy-handed, causing great pains in labour and even stillbirths and miscarriages. My skills will ensure a trouble-free delivery. And a year hence, to this day, your child will be born.

"Soon, when the harvest is complete, I will return to my own cottage, in the east of the island. But I will call on you, from time to time, to ensure that all is well. My daughter lives a secluded hermitic life during the autumn and winter, absorbed in her studies of the berries and their properties. She does not welcome visitors. But in your walks, you will see her light and the smoke from her fire.

"And keep our meetings secret from your husband. Men will scoff and mock. Their scorn and crude laughter will spoil the tincture. When your time is due, introduce me as an old friend of the family—someone who knew you as a child."

It was the truth, thought Carree, who hated lies and deception, as she walked home, the bottle hidden in her dress, as the cornman had been sheltered all those years ago. And she wondered why, throughout her childhood and adult life, she had entirely forgotten about the smallholding with its abundance of flowers, herbs and fruit.

That evening, as Conal smoked his pipe, Carree took up her fiddle. Never had she played so well. Her music soared with runs and trills, ecstatic and mercurial. And as the melody rose, she knew that it was heard with appreciation in the remote cottage, near the valley, where they were distilling the freshly picked fruit and twisting the corn and grasses to form shapes to beguile the children.

Mrs Mabily's promise was fulfilled. Snow was thick on the ground and there was a bitter east wind, but to Conal it was a day of unexpected rejoicing, when Carree confirmed her pregnancy.

The next day, when alone, she received a congratulatory visit from Mrs Mabily, who exuded encouragement, advice and folk wisdom. And throughout her labour, the old woman made occasional discreet consultations, which Carree found reassuring and timely.

Many times she walked the lonely track and made the detour to the lane, past the smallholding, finding its presence a further comfort. Its location always surprised her. The landscape stretched out, wild and empty. Particularly in winter, it seemed a bleak inhospitable wilderness, devoid of humanity. When she expected to see yet another swathe of windswept heath, there was the cottage and its gardens, slumbering in hibernation. Smoke rose from the chimney and through the shutters; she could see a fire flickering and sometimes even the daughter's shadow as she worked with her herbs and distillations.

When Carree's time was come, Conal's brother and his large family came to offer moral support. And Mary, her sister-in-law, piqued at being excluded from assisting at the birth, teased and frightened her with warnings about the excruciating pains of labour.

"The first child is always the hardest—especially for a woman of your age," she said.

But Mrs Mabily took charge, dispelling all terrors. Her manner was cheerful and firm, marshalling them to produce towels and hot water. She had made a preliminary visit, the previous day, charming Conal with old stories of the herring fleets and legends and superstitions about the sea birds that even he did not know.

Downstairs, whilst the children played in the garden, food was prepared and the atmosphere was relaxed and celebratory. For good luck, Carree took a thin gold chain, homely and unadorned, to the bedroom. It was an old gift from her grandmother and she intended to attach it around the infant's neck.

Alone with Mrs Mabily, Carree was surprised that she ignored the steaming jugs of hot water and threw the towels in a corner, like discarded theatre props. Instead, she made Carree drink a dark infusion and began a rhythmic muttering in a strange language. The words flowed in a soft, musical incantation. All her anxieties and pains from the imminent birth disappeared. She lay relaxed, immersed in a tranquil reverie, listening to the voices in the kitchen below, until gradually she was able to observe all that happened, believing herself in the room with them.

She saw the blue flame of the match that lit her husband's pipe. The smoke curled in wreaths and she breathed the bonfire aroma of his strong, black tobacco. A beer bottle opened, the liquid foaming slightly, and from the stove, bloaters sizzled and the butter browned in the pan.

The heat of the tea brewing steamed the windows and she imagined patterns forming in the glass as it misted. In the garden, in a haze of lavender, the children were dancing and chanting an old rhyme and she noticed the scab covering the graze on the eldest boy's knee. She smiled, for their movements were clumsy and their voices coarse.

"All is well,
Bitter and bad.
Courting Joanney,
Double myself."

Their cat, Kirry, sauntered in, tail in the air, enticed by the smell of the fish cooking, and clambered on her lap, purring and paddling. Her arms gripped the creature to stroke and nuzzle him, and a voice, distant and hypnotic, said, "All is well."

She was roused by the sudden cry of the baby that she squeezed tightly in her arms. But even in her joy, its voice was discordant and raucous— a rook's ugly call, drowning the song of a blackbird on a summer's eve. "Bitter and bad," came the chant from the garden. "Double myself."

At the bedroom door stood Mrs Mabily. Under her cloak was a bundle, wrapped in a white shawl, that squirmed and wriggled. The gold good-luck charm was hooked and gripped in a small fist. Briefly, she saw a face that mirrored her own child, but softer and fairer featured. Its cry, quickly stifled, was sweeter and more melodious than the ugly thing she cradled. Mrs Mabily seemed hurried, as if Carree had woken from her sleep earlier than planned. And in the woman's hand was something else, that shimmered with gold and silver strands, with black stones like eyes, and bound tightly with hair.

Placing her baby—a girl—on the bed, she struggled to her feet. But Mrs Mabily was gone. Slowly and painfully, she reached the top of the stairs and peered down. In the kitchen, the scene was exactly as she had imagined. Yet they seemed calm and almost drowsy, as if they had forgotten her.

"Where did Mrs Mabily go?" she called, raising her voice to rouse them.

"She's still upstairs with you," answered Conal, puzzled, as he clambered unsteadily to his feet. "No one's come down. We'd have seen them. Everything's been quiet and peaceful. Old Kirry had a turn though. He was sat in your chair, chewing his fish. His fur bristled and he hissed and spat at something. Swallowed a bone, I expect."

"Didn't you hear the two cries—one harsh and fretful and the other sweet and contented?"

"We've heard nothing," he said, scratching his head as, gradually, the impact of the birth returned to him.

In concern, he mounted the stairs, taking them three steps at a time, and they entered the bedroom together. The child was lying on the bed entranced, staring out of the window. Her hands reached out towards something seen in the garden that fascinated and enthralled. The moment passed. Whatever had gripped her attention was gone; the face crumpled in bitter disappointment and she howled, shrill and inconsolable.

The mystery of Mrs Mabily's disappearance and the loss of the little gold chain were quickly forgotten in the family's happiness at the successful birth. Carree considered confiding in them what she had witnessed, but shrewdly decided they would judge her a delusional hysteric— perhaps even summoning their local physician to sedate her. Instead, she kept her own counsel.

And when dusk fell and the visitors had departed, she dared not spoil her husband's contentment. She was moved by his delight and by the delicacy and gentleness, as he handled the child. Engrossed in his love, he was oblivious to the faint sounds that drifted through their open window. Far away, from the direction of the cottage on the heath, Carree could hear music, fierce and celebratory. And in its wild twisting frenzy, she knew that it mocked and triumphed over her.

Angered by the deception and treachery, she resolved to visit Mrs Mabily and confront her. Within a fortnight, when her fitness and vigour were restored, and the household had fallen into a benign routine to accommodate the child, named Creena, she took her in her arms and walked to the cottage.

When she took the side lane, past the mounds of green turf, all trace of the building was gone. Where the kitchen had stood, timber-framed, with trained roses arched over the door, were the twisted boughs of hazel trees. In a clearing, an ugly clump of leprous fungi, yellow and venomous, mimicked the chairs and homely table she remembered. A coil of pink and white bindweed flowers and the rough stalks of columbine, their seed pods brown and dry, nodded in the wind, where the glass bottles and potions had stood.

The long garden, with its neat rows of fruit bushes, was rough scrub land, filled with belladonna, henbane and black nightshade, their berries profuse and ripe. Draped over one of the hazel trees was a huge cobweb, recalling the white shawl that had covered her stolen child. Its shape was compressed to mimic the imprint of a tiny human form. Mrs Mabily's spectacles, which had conveyed the authority of a wise doctor, were echoed by two pebble-shaped snail shells, joined by a trail of white slime. The apothecary's scales, on which the powders had been so carefully mixed, were flat stones, shiny and black, and precariously balanced.

The landscape seemed to have been arranged to parody the things she had seen as her memory had been tricked into believing in the permanence and history of the cottage. She had been gulled. All had been an illusion. She had never visited this place as a child with her grandmother. From her infancy, the old woman had been bedridden, wracked with rheumatism and troubled with strange fantasies and delusions. And Carree knew that her child had been stolen by the secret people of the hills and woodlands; the vooinjer veggey—the old ones of the green mounds.

At first, Carree found it hard to love her child—a plain, stolid baby, who seemed permanently fretful and dissatisfied with life. Always her eyes sought the horizon, searching for something finer and more magical than the fisherman's cottage could offer. She would pout and sulk, angry at her own clumsiness, smashing and pounding the delicate wooden toys that Conal spent his evenings carving for her. At night she cried incessantly, a hoarse, wailing noise that jarred and irritated. Carree remembered the grace and fine musical voice of her stolen one and felt that she had been left with a discarded runt—something soulless, shrivelled and ugly.

But gradually, her indifference turned to genuine affection. She recognised a kindred spirit; one who, like her, had been tricked and deceived. A bond was formed, of the despised and rejected, against the subtleties and spells of those more artful and beautiful. Also, she was resolved to spare her daughter the neglect and contempt she had suffered from her own mother. Often wandering alone amongst the hills and mountains and babbling nonsense, she had died young, when Carree was in her late teens. There was a history of feeble-mindedness in the women of her family, once they became mothers. They became alienated from their children—invariably solitary girls—despising and rejecting them. The fathers grew lonely, drifted away, abandoning the cottage to the women. Carree was determined to break that malign tradition.

As a young child, Creena was plagued by the company of an imaginary playmate, called Morien, who mocked and humiliated her with snatches of songs and rhymes that she tried to imitate but could never master. She was taunted and made jealous by her companion's tales of adventures with a mysterious people who had wonderful powers. Carree was both intrigued and impressed by the names her daughter mentioned—Casnar, Saidi, Edern, Edlym, Addanc and Nudd. They sounded real—plausible names that the vooinjer veggey might call themselves—and she listened seriously to her daughter's tales without scorn and laughter. And there was one creature whose title could not be divulged, for it was secret. Morien was terrified of her and had been warned and punished by her for speaking to Creena. Finally, the visits ceased.

Out of defiance and a vain hope of seeing her stolen child, Carree walked often to the site of Mrs Mabily's cottage with Creena. Both sensed a wariness and hostility, and were troubled by the feeling that they were intruders and trespassers. On cloudless days, they would be buffeted with sudden squalls of angry rain. Thorns and briars whipped and scratched them unexpectedly, but their resolution and stubbornness hardened. And it was there, surrounded by the heathland, in the shadow of the green mounds, that Carree first taught her daughter the violin. Sometimes, as she attempted a tune, her faltering notes seemed to be caught by an echo that mocked and imitated her failings. They remembered Morien, the imaginary child, from Creena's early years and they discussed and speculated about her abrupt disappearance.

Three more children were born to Carree and Conal— cheerful, uncomplicated sons who absorbed their father's time and love. But Creena was her mother's favourite and when she reached puberty, Carree dared to confide in her, one afternoon by the mounds, what she had witnessed at her birth. The revelation was met with calm, thoughtful acceptance and an exchange of secrets. For Creena was convinced that one night, as she lay between sleep and waking, someone had entered her bedroom unseen and plucked strands of hair from her head. And by the morning, her body had felt cramped, as if invisibly wrapped in gentle swathes of cloth, as ivy creeps and engulfs the trunk of a tree. That feeling remained with her still.

Creena practised her violin with application and diligence and became a competent, if uninspired, musician. By the age of eighteen, she was a popular guest at weddings and feast days. Always, she took a particular delight in hearing new melodies and struggled hard to learn them.

At a summer fair in 1889, at Peel, there was a fiddler from the West of Ireland who played in a style unknown to her. There was a strange mixture of melancholy and fervour in his jigs and reels, of Sligo and Connemara, that evoked a landscape of mountains, lakes and barren wilderness. A kind and generous man, he was moved by Creena's interest in his music and spent an hour teaching her his bowing techniques.

Pestered by the boisterous good humour and banter of her younger brothers, she sought the place of solitude and remoteness by the green mounds to perfect her art. Rarely had she played with such passion and fire. Her fingers glided over the strings in a trance of movement, and the sounds resonated across the moor. As she rested, she became conscious of a figure watching her intently from one of the hillocks—a young woman of her own age who almost resembled her. But whereas her own clothes and features were plain and constrained by custom, modesty and temperance, the girl's face had a feral beauty that seemed, to Creena, both wanton and dangerous.

Her hair, which clustered around her shoulders, had the colour and fluidity of reed beds blown by the wind, and within its textures were tints of the surrounding landscape—the bright yellows of gorse flowers and the dark red shades of heather. It was adorned with sapphires, as large as cornflowers, but around her neck was a simple gold chain, almost humble by comparison. Creena's hair was coarse, dark and bonneted and she was conscious always that it carried the odours of the kitchen and the ever-present reek of fish.

"I know every dance and melody from this island—from the crude pipings of its first people to the solemn dirges of your churches and chapels— but your music is new to me," the girl said.

And with a superior smile, she produced her own fiddle, a delicate instrument the colour of hazel wood, and matched Creena's unaccustomed virtuosity, but with added flourishes, embellishments and trills.

"There are other pieces I've not yet attempted," Creena said, modestly. "I can't master the rhythm of the bow. I can only hum them."

"Come inside and sing them to me," the girl said, hesitating, as if afraid of someone. "My name is Morien and I am your twin sister."

A section of gorse seemed to flicker and fade, revealing a door to a wide chamber, luxuriously furnished and lit with pale yellow candles. Inside, figures sat weaving, talking or reclining.

She knew she was in the company of the vooinjer veggey, the secret fair ones of the hills and mounds. They had great beauty, grace and radiance but it was hazy and ill-defined, like viewing someone that glimmered behind a veil or a layer of gauze. Their shapes were elusive and equivocal and their hair and clothes resembled rocks, trees or the secluded pools and lakes hidden in woodland that travellers stumble upon but can never find again.

At first, they greeted her entrance with shyness and a fey reluctance, as if her presence amongst them was forbidden. But as their guest, she was received with courtesy and brought offerings of food and wine, in return for her songs. Fearing something illusory or enchanted to snare and entrap her, she sniffed it gingerly but it was wholesome and good. And all her fears of the legends of entering their domain disappeared and the warnings of the country people seemed staid and cowardly.

And yet, despite the wonder and magic of what she was witnessing, Creena had the feeling that she was in the presence of children or adolescents, showing off and boasting in the absence of authority. Some looked sheepishly towards the door, whilst others prodded, dared and goaded each other into disclosing deeper secrets and revelations.

Amongst the company of the vooinjer veggey, who seemed as ageless as the mountains and sky, were two women with faces that recalled her own family. Their expressions were nervous, as if they dreaded the future. One was withered, her skin darkened to the colour of a pickled walnut. Her hands trembled and reached out in senile frustration for the fiddle as her feet vainly sought the rhythm of the dance. In the distance, through a window of cobweb, Creena noticed a wide circle of tumuli, each one covered in flowers and grasses.

"They become angry when we age and decay," said Morien. "They blame us for our mortality. But they tend the graves of the stolen ones and whisper softly to those in darkness."

There was one object in the chamber that both fascinated and disturbed Creena. It was a tiny effigy of a woman, delicately crafted from gold and silver. Black opals formed its eyes. But around its waist, strands of coarse human hair, wiry and frizzled, like her own, were wrapped, as if to constrict and suffocate. As the light played on its features, Creena realised the resemblance of the object to herself, and from puberty came the memory of someone stealing unseen into her room at night to pluck strands of her hair.

51

Afraid of what enchantment or malicious game they had devised for her, she asked:

"Why have you made sport of me by creating that image in my likeness?"

Morien hid her face in her hands. Most of the vooinjer veggey smiled slyly and some offered her fresh delicacies as a diversion. But one of the youngest blurted out.

"Little fool. The effigy is not of you. Yours was fashioned many years ago. A golden gift for your mother, in exchange for her child of song. But buried in secret, away from her prying eyes. The image you see is of your own daughter, yet to be born. See the ties and knots to bind and make her barren until we break the spell."

"They need our music," Morien admitted. "Despite their mastery of nature and their immortality, there is a staleness and weariness about them. Human songs, with their desperate sense of love, loss and death, have the fire and vitality they crave. And so, some of us are stolen. The thief comes in the guise of a wise nurse or confidante. She calls herself Mrs Mabily—an ironic joke, as some humans say that Mab is the fairies' midwife. But her name is Luned and she has great magic and sorcery."

Before Creena had time to answer, there was a roar, as of a great wind scything the trees. Scraps of food rose and shrivelled like leaves and a figure loomed at the entrance, stately and imperious. Carree would not have recognised her as the benign herbalist and midwife. For this was Luned, Queen of the northwestern vooinjer veggey, who inhabit the lands, from the coast to the mountains, that humans call Ballaugh, Jurby and Andreas. She was quickly joined by other, older creatures. Her hosts cowered and shrank into corners, their beauty and elegance gone. Their faces were now lined with deep creases and wrinkles and their colour was a leprous yellow, as of old things living too long underground and grown malicious and conniving. The transformation reminded Creena of seeing her own features, twisted and ugly, in the distorting mirrors of a fairground booth. They seethed and writhed, a nest of rats uncovered by the lifting of a flagstone. For comfort, Morien grasped her fiddle, hiding her face under the sweep of her hair. Its shimmering colours and the vitality of her youth contrasted with the tangle of ancient, angry bodies.

"Which of you has brought this child, of all mortals, to our country?" said Luned.

"Morien invited her. She told her all our secrets and why we take their children. She spoke your name."

They clamoured together, united against Morien, their fingers prodding and stabbing, like sharp twigs.

Both sisters anticipated a violent revenge, of fire and thunder, or paralysis of limbs and speech. But Luned stepped forward and lightly touched Morien's hair, caressing and stroking individual strands. The creatures peeped out, leering and smirking at the joke. At first Morien did not understand the cruelty of the gesture and blinked vacantly. But one held a mirror and her face crumpled as she saw her hair, iron-grey, with bald scabbed patches, where the fingers had touched. Ragged clumps lay at her feet like dirty wool in a sheep field. In bitterness, she clawed at the jewels that clung to the patchy remnants and dashed them to the ground.

Creena realised that the older ones were conferring on her fate.

"Bind her alive in rock or in the roots of a tree," said one of her former hosts, who had smiled and plied her with food.

"And lose the music their family brings us? She must leave us unharmed. Fetch me black nightshade and thornapple. The juice of those herbs and my incantation will induce a forgetfulness and an ignorance of us all. She will remember nothing of me, of Morien, or the wonders of our land."

The older ones crowded around Creena and she tasted the warmth of their breath, both earthy and scented with leaves and the roots of trees. They gripped her firmly but there was restraint and gentleness in their touch. She saw her sister, haggard and desolate, her face and neck bare and stripped of all adornments. But there was also a look of defiance and rebellion. Creena felt a hand reach into the folds of her clothing and something was lodged in a pocket of her dress. Their gaze met briefly and conspiratorially, before the juice of the flowers was squeezed into her eyes. Luned was chanting, her voice soft and narcotic, and Creena slipped into unconsciousness.

Carree found her, ambling home late, awkwardly gripping her violin like a frying pan. She moved as if sleepwalking and set about her household tasks with a docility that worried her mother. Their mutual glances and whispered confidences were missing. Carree knew that she practised in solitude by the green mounds, and suspected mischief. That night, before retiring to bed, she entered Creena's bedroom and referred lightly to Mrs Mabily and the abduction. Her daughter stared back with vacant politeness and incomprehension. All the years of trust and the sharing of terrible secrets were met with a puzzled yawn. Pleading tiredness, Creena pointedly made ready for sleep. But as she removed her dress, a little package dropped at Carree's feet, which she retrieved.

It was a bundle of red vervain—the herb which banishes spells and enchantments—tightly bound in human hair, long and grey, with something glinting inside. Carefully, Carree untied the plant. And there, eighteen years after it had been hooked in the fist of her stolen child, was her humble gold chain. Whilst Conal snored, she worried, speculated and wrestled with doubts and fears on its meaning. But finally, she made a distillation of the herb, before tiptoeing into Creena's room, to soothe her eyes and head with its juice.

Hot and feverish, Creena slept until midday. Her mother was alone in the house, tidying her own room, when her daughter, solemn and pale, knocked and sat wearily on the bed. She recalled everything, her senses sharp and vivid under the influence of the vervain. She spoke especially of the effigies, buried in secret, that rendered the women of the house barren until the vooinjer veggey broke the spell to steal a child.

Her tale finished, she gazed desolately out of the window, at the yew tree on the hinterland between their garden and the heath. And a memory of despair returned, locked since the day she was born. Someone was passing out of her life, forever. By the tree, they lingered briefly, and an object, beautiful and shining, was hidden, deep within its wreck.

Carree also was reminded that she first saw Mrs Mabily resting by its trunk. The centre of the tree was full of holes and apertures. Together, they fetched rods, a spade and a rake. Cautiously, they levered out stones, bricks and the ossified remains of dead roots and branches. In the hollow they had excavated was a chamber. The rays of the sun shone into the gloom, revealing a nest of objects that glinted with gold and silver, and black gems.

As they pulled them to the surface, they recognised first their own images and then Carree's mother and grandmother. But still the eyes of black opal glittered in the chamber. Raking and hooking, the pile mounted, until they had counted beyond a hundred—generations of the women of their family, stretching back over millenia, whose children had been beguiled. The heap flickered and the eyes blinked in the full heat of the sun. And it seemed that a wind rushed through the holes that were their mouths and the hollows of their golden bones. They sang briefly with voices strange and sweet. The gold and silver withered and crumbled, turning to dry straw and grass, and the black jewels dropped as petals falling from a flower. And the heap began to seethe and rot. It stank of stagnant ditches and the holes and burrows of furtive woodland creatures. Creena felt the invisible ties and bonds around her body fray and snap like a tangle of old rope. It fell into the pile, which churned and heaved before subsiding into dust and earth. From the direction of the green mounds they heard a wailing cry, of defeat and despair.

"All is well," said Carree.

Creena knew that the vooinjer veggey valued Morien's music too highly to harm her further. But the next day, she took her violin to the mounds. The atmosphere was bleak and sullen but she made a promise to the secret ones. She and the generations yet to come would play for them, in that place, on the anniversary of their birth. In return, she asked for her family to be left unmolested and for the voo-injer veggey to restore the glories of Morien's hair. On the third occasion, the answering violin of her sister, wild and exhilarating, told her that her pledge had been honoured. Her children and their descendants heard it too, even until modern times, when the music became slower and more subdued, and finally was heard no more.

THE SLAVES OF PARADISE

October 17th, 1946

IN the mirror this morning, my face, thick with soap, seemed disembodied and mask-like. And each sweep of the razor created a deeper whiteness—a sickly pallor, more intense than the creams and chalky powders of the mime artistes. Steam rose and settled on the mottled, cracked glass, in grey flourishes and spirals, like letters and ciphers scratched on stone. A tiny cut on my earlobe trickled and spread—a thread of red silk around my neck. And I remembered that she had danced in the scene at the 'Café of the Red Throat' when we were film extras in Nice.

The newspaper vendor pointed to the photograph on the front page, smiled and spat. It showed the bodies of the Nuremberg dead, the ropes still around their necks, and some had little flecks of blood around their noses and eyes. I could draw their portraits from memory or invoke the death masks of collaborators and the host of spies and informers that gathered, when we were Children of Paradise, in Nice, in 1942.

But her face, I cannot remember. Its form and detail, ever supple and fluid, like quicksilver, always eluded me. I caught only the shadow, the ghost of her soul. My dull art, with the crude naivety of its charcoal scratches, could never evoke the fire and restlessness of her spirit.

Before the war, we had an apartment in the Marais, where she worked as a seamstress. At night, she danced in the theatre chorus, or toured the cafés—a chanteuse, singing the street ballads of nineteenth century Paris.

Our rooms overlooked the site of the long-demolished Boulevard of Crime and her talk conjured up the ghost outlines of its lost theatres, where crowds flocked to see the melodramas. And from the lofty balconies of the gods, for four centimes, they entered a paradise of ribaldry, raucous humour and the smells of oranges, cigar smoke and cheap scent.

Scouring the flea markets and secondhand shops for momentos, she had accumulated a collection of photographs, costumes and powders from the Théâtre des Funambules. Once a dark, suffocating cellar for performing dogs, it became the stage for the pantomime and vaudeville of dream, where the great Pierrot, Jean-Gaspard Deburau, performed his strange, ethereal mimes of doomed love and death.

On her windowsill, staring out at the memory of the streets of the 1830's, was a model of the death mask of Lacenaire—criminal, poet and anti-hero of the Boulevard of Crime.

"He veered between gallantry and cowardice, tragedy and farce," she said. "He committed two squalid little murders and wrote his verses, awaiting the guillotine. The phrenologists gripped and examined his skull, both alive and dead, for the fault lines of depravity. And he wrote, laughing at them all, 'I am ashamed I am only gross matter.'"

On her wall was a copy of Daguerre's 1838 print of the deserted Boulevard. It showed, in the foreground, a white building with an open window and the curtain pulled to one side. And I imagined her there, peeping out at the shifting pageants of people through the passing decades, and smiling to herself—her light, in that dark room, where I could never see her face.

✳

On the day before the Germans entered the city, in June,1940, loudspeaker announcements warned us to be meek and docile. Whilst the wealthy clambered aboard trains and taxis, hoping to escape the advance, most waited, clustered together, in a mood varying between panic and dull acceptance.

But as the sound of artillery drew ever closer, she surrounded herself with fabrics, thread and the costumes from her wardrobe of antique theatre. And when night fell, by side alleys and back staircases, we carried her work to the rooftops of the city.

From a skylight, we saw a dizzying panorama of stone and slate, with narrow catwalks spanning chasms of darkness. The parapets and fields of grey, stretched to the horizon, and distant churches, with their secluded cornices and secret carvings, hidden from public gaze, were caught under the moon. Most of the city slept, their troubled dreams muffled behind drawn curtains and blinds. But in a faraway attic, an insomniac paced the room, the smoke from his pipe curling under the open window and into the night.

With an acrobat's unfaltering poise and balance, she bore her art to a perilous chimney stack, its brickwork seeming to plunge into emptiness. She had fashioned an effigy of Lacenaire. Roped to his tower, he seemed a solitary king of moonlight, inspecting his deserted realm with amused disdain.

And the next morning, their victory parade passed, all swank and slow swagger. From its promontory, the effigy surveyed the pageant with the scorn and defiance of the condemned man on the steps of the guillotine. She had arranged its limbs so that they cast a dandified air of parody and ironic detachment. The figure both imitated and mocked the narcissism of brute power.

The crowd, who had stood passive and hushed, pointed and laughed. And the faces of the soldiers were briefly unnerved and hesitant, as if caught with their flies unbuttoned. Hours later, we watched them dismantle her tableau. The officer, overcome with vertigo, peeped from the skylight and yelled ineffectually, whilst two German soldiers edged and stumbled precariously towards the figure. Their invincibility was challenged. She had exposed their clumsiness and vulnerability. A little group of bystanders jeered. The soldiers reminded us of Laurel and Hardy—two clot-heads on a rooftop, attempting to attach a radio aerial. One, his arms flapping the air for balance, finally gripped and untied the scarecrow.

"He clasps it like a shy but eager lover," a woman shouted.

"It's how he embraces his mother," another said.

As he swung it towards safety, its head, of painted rags and sacking, separated from the torso and plummeted to the street below, bouncing and dancing on the rooftops as she had planned. And I saw that she had stitched in red cotton, across its mouth and throat, the words of Lacenaire.

"Let me sing my song of death."

✳

We travelled to Nice for the filming, where her contacts in the theatre and the resistance secured us work amongst the rabble of refugee actors. The entire Boulevard of Crime had been reconstructed and we thronged its pavements and theatres to watch the mimes of Deburau, the murder of Desdemona and the intrigues of Lacenaire. From the balconies of paradise, dressed in the clothes of the 1830's, I saw her dance a cameo role, and cheered and hooted with the rest.

The crowd swelled and passed in all their masks and subterfuges— Italian soldiers, Vichy collaborators, resistance fighters and spies; their faces blurred and merged together. And behind the facades of the mock theatres, in the dressing rooms and recesses of the film set, the plots and conspiracies were hatched. Faces appeared in door-ways or were reflected briefly in the long line of mirrors, before fading from view. Footsteps, confident and benign, would approach, only to disappear amongst canvas and scaffolding. And from behind curtains and cameras, there was a continual rustling and whispering, and the sound of stifled breath. Regularly, we were visited by politicians and writers—apologists for the occupying forces. And she would identify their faces for me—Darnand, Céline and Brasillach—and note the actors and film engineers they selected for confidential asides and private meetings.

One figure on the film set was accepted by all the cliques and factions. Gaston was a deaf mute who cleaned floors, removed rubbish and swabbed the latrines. He lacked the grace and balletic poise of the theatrical mimes and

Pierrots, walking with a clumsy stumble and communicating in grunts, squeaks and coarse gestures. His lumpen idiocy, unthreatening and guileless, made him tolerated and patronised by all. Pétain and Laval meant no more to him than Moses or the Man in the Moon. And he endeared himself to us all by stealing and sharing food from the film's banquets. He would enter the dressing rooms, engulfed in a huge black overcoat, in a flurry of legs, brooms and mops, to bring us hams, cold fowl and jugs of wine. His scuttling motion, his coat and his ability to locate and scavenge food, earned him the nickname 'The Cockroach'. He formed a friendship with the film's parrot—the stage prop of a street beggar who feigned blindness. Gaston pushed gobbets of melon and apple into its cage with a strange delicacy of movement, and the mouths of both gaped wide in unison.

Our lodgings, bare and ill-lit, and part of a warren of bedrooms and secret attics, were beset with the same spies. Our work with the resistance made us doubly wary and circumspect. Shyness and reticence dominated even our times alone together and we fell into a tacit chastity. I watched her body, as if behind glass, or obscured by the veil in a private theatre box—a privileged voyeur. Even our rare intimacies felt separated by distance and costume. And as the fire burned low and the candles were guttered, the disguises and subtle changes of her face faded and were lost.

The codes and messages she delivered were hidden in my sketches of the dancers and actors. But I was a mere scribe, disguising numbers and ciphers in art that was, at best, derivative and sterile. She had the protean ability to pass unnoticed, to travel unmolested and unchallenged into the heart of the occupying forces. She collected rumour and gossip from Nice, Monaco, even from Genoa and Turin. She never confided precise information to me, but I understood it concerned enemy plans to invade Gibraltar and aided the allied invasion of Sicily.

In our lodgings, we established a ritual of burning the coded messages. A constituent of the paper or ink made them glow in the fire, like golden letters, flickering briefly against the black grate.

"See the initials of the girl you'll marry," she teased. "Read your future in the fire and ash."

Her missions were given the codenames, 'Ragman', 'The Lonely Sleeper' and 'The Sandman', used by the spy, Jericho, in the film. And the messages were conveyed to the marquis in a waterfront tavern named 'The Café of the Yellow Moon', where she sang her ballads. It was decorated with scenes from the heyday of the Théâtre des Funambules. Pale snake-like Pierrots, their shapes rising to the ceiling, conveyed an atmosphere of mournful silence and the dreamlike melancholy of the mutes. Pierrot made futile love to a rose, its colours diseased and leprous; to the sickly yellow moon, its face indifferent and passive. In another tableau, his eyes stared, lovesick, at a street coquette. Overcome by remorse on Good Friday, but recalled by the bells of Easter to return to her debauchery, she left him forlorn and empty. In every scene, love proved unattainable, fortune was fickle and only death remained. One striking image showed him besotted by a rich society beauty, and killing the ragman in order to steal clothes to impress her. But at the wedding, the ghost returned to haunt and frustrate him. Dressed in black, Pierrot was carried away in his coffin. And at the graveside, folly and death were both antagonists and lovers, bound together in a perpetual embrace—a melancholy dance, on the edge of the chasm.

The café's proprietor, who claimed that his ancestor was once stage manager at the Funambules, resembled a Pierrot run to seed, bloated and obese. There was an unhealthy puffiness in the face of this whey-faced clown, known as 'The White Sow', that belied the elegance and adroitness of his movement. Occasionally, when her songs of death had silenced even the faintest whispers from the audience, he would dance, his flesh wobbling, with precise nimble steps and mannered gestures of hands and eyebrows. Holding the folds of his apron with pudgy cocked fingers of chalk, he twirled and minced, seductive and obscene.

He lived alone, with the companionship only of a caged monkey—a sooty black mangabey from Senegal. The poor creature was housed always within sight of the sea and its ships, and its face would mimic the contortions of the murals. It had an antique weariness, a despair that recalled the endurances and penances of the Middle Ages and the trials and martyrdoms of the saints.

"The beast dreams of its freedom, yet torments itself by hope," he said. "It must be punished until it can embrace the bars of its cage with contentment and resignation. Only when it turns its back on the sea and its dreams, will I release it from its torment."

He permitted me to sketch his customers and display my drawings in an untidy ever-changing frieze. I made the occasional sale, obtaining a few francs or exchanging them for wine and food. But she would move from table to table, displaying my folios and charming money from them all. Thus, the crucial coded messages were passed openly and without suspicion.

Even on nights free of missions and subterfuge, whilst I smoked and dozed, alone in our room, she was drawn inexorably to the café, like Kafka's dreamer, fascinated by the fresh mound of a grave in the distance, where flapping flags and banners marked a great celebration. At the graveside, the headstone was rammed into the soil, whilst an artist waited impatiently to complete his inscription. Only when the dreamer had dug with his hands, into the prepared loose earth and spun into the waiting chasm, did the artist mark his name, in elaborate flourishes of gold.

And in the café, on its rare busy nights, where the actors and extras—subdued like sleepwalkers by the narcotic pallor of the murals—conversed and celebrated in whispers and silences, she immersed herself, ever deeper, in the dreamscape of the Pierrots. Her ballads told of failed love and fortune, of embracing death and folly. There was a reckless bravado in her as she compulsively sought danger, trying to guess the allegiances of faces that stared back, mute and moon-faced. Often, the café was almost deserted, and in the emptiness, she would sing only to the murals and the monkey—a fool's serenade to the rose, the moon and the stars.

✳

On that last day in Nice, there was a fevered unrest, a collective hysteria, in which all the precarious strands of our deceptions and disguises were pulled tight around our throats. We filmed the final street scene, in which the carriage of the heroine, Garance, escapes the forlorn love-stricken clown through a festival of revellers. They, too, were dressed as Pierrots, white-robed and chalk-faced, as if in mockery of his distress. And flower petals rose and fell on the carnival of dancing girls and the swirling mass of powdered folly. In that pageant, we met and danced briefly together, before the spin of the crowd separated us.

And I sat, hot and light-headed with the dance, sketching the carriage and encrypting the message I had been passed, into the flow of the horses' manes. Screwed up into a tiny ball, it nestled in my pocket, ready for our evening ritual of deciphering the golden symbols and letters in the flames. I was joined by Gaston, carrying a dustpan and brush. He grunted and winked, and passed me a linen bag, which concealed stolen chocolate. And I pulled out my handkerchief to wipe the sweat from my face and something fell to the floor. But in my dizziness and haste to complete the drawing and hide his gift, the moment passed and was forgotten.

In our lodgings, I washed the chalk and paint from my face. Their flakes rose in the air, mingling with the dust in the plume of late sunlight through the window. She still wore her dress, fashioned for the reign of the Citizen King, and stray petals from the dance clung to her hair and clothing. Clutching my sketch of the escaping carriage, with its encrypted message, and laughing as I kissed her, she set out for the café, alone, hurrying in the confusion of oncoming rain and storm.

As darkness fell, the wind rose. Awnings and shutters were clattering, and from the window I saw the shapes of pedestrians, clumsy and bent double, or staggering as if drunk or sick with fever. I dozed fitfully, half-conscious of a task neglected, a lapsed ritual. There was a cold emptiness in the soot and ash of the grate. I had forgotten to burn the code message and vainly searched my pockets. I remembered the tiny ball of crumpled paper falling from my handkerchief amongst the dust and flower petals from the dance, and the swish of Gaston's brush. Outside, people were running and shouting, and I recognised many from the film set.

Pulling on a coat against the wind and rain, I hurried into the street and ran towards the Boulevard of Crime. The flimsy facades of the theatres were breaking under the storm, their paint and artifice exposed. The front section of the Théâtre des Pygmées, dark and ornate, had flopped like balsa wood, revealing a tangle of cameras and lights. From the balconies of paradise, modern tubular chairs teetered and fell. Discarded costumes, top hats and bonnets were entangled with workmen's overalls and pieces of plastic. The curtain of the Théâtre des Funambules had blown loose and swung like a ship's sail, revealing a line of motor cars. And in the mirrors of the dressing rooms, the scene seemed to play out with an increased energy, as if wood, metal and fabric were brought to life in a fury of animation.

Drowsy actors and stage crew, roused from their sleep, mingled in the wreckage with police and sightseers. They passed amongst the buildings like sleepwalkers between one world and the next, characters out of time and place. All the backstage bravados and hierarchies had collapsed. They drifted, lost children, strangers in a strange land. And in the mirrors their images flickered, faint and transient, dwarfed by the upheaval of the collapsing scenery.

Giddy and disorientated, I hurried to the café to tell her.

In the harbour, banners and flags flapped joyously in the wind and shop signs cavorted and danced in celebration. A figure in a doorway, near to the café, swept and poked with a broom, shoving an object wrapped in a white sheet like a shroud. In my delirium, I imagined it concealed the remains of the monkey, its face of despair faintly outlined. The café was in darkness—only the ghost faces of the Pierrots were visible through the window. They gleamed pale and yellow, under the corner street lamp—corpse lights from a freshly-dug grave. The door was barred and bolted but I heard voices whispering in the rooms above. For years, hiding behind lies and self-deception, I remembered nothing of the next hour, except that I imagined myself sketching in the small notebook I always carried. In the teeth of the gale, I was forming intricate letters of gold across the white page, my hand racing with spirals and flourishes.

I was found, several streets from the café, by two comrades from the resistance, their faces worried and haggard.

"Where's Paulette? The café's deserted," one said.

But I could not answer. And I stared at my notebook, the pages torn where my pencil had gouged and ripped its layers. They frogmarched me back to our lodgings, in the guise of a drunken reveller escorted home by his friends. And there, agitated and clamorous, I was given a draught of some narcotic—morphine or laudanum—and I fell into oblivion.

It seemed days later that I awoke, still drowsy and sedated, in a house unknown to me. My clothes had been hurriedly packed and my companions were anxious and watchful. They spoke in whispers, arguing and planning, treating me as a child or invalid. And finally, by back roads and tracks, we returned to Paris, in a succession of farm vehicles, motor cars and carts.

A Clown Chastised

At first, I was permitted to return to our rooms in the Marais. And I expected to find her waiting for me, cross-legged on the floor, busy with scissors and fabric, unable to speak clearly for the pins she held in her mouth. But there was only dampness, mildew and the dust of our years of absence. Mice nested in the innards of the rags, discarded for the effigy of Lacenaire.

At night, I dreamed I walked the streets of his Paris, scanning the crowds that surged towards the theatres, for a glimpse of her face. I saw her veiled in the window of a carriage or reflected briefly in the glass facades of shops. But always, the press of people hindered me. Some, sensing my urgency, deliberately barred my progress, affecting bows and flourishes in feigned apology. And I recognised many from Nice, who sniggered behind their fans, or bore their teeth in false smiles, before laughing together behind their hands. All shared a secret knowledge, baiting and gulling me to a particular street corner, like an animal lured into a cage.

As I turned into the Boulevard, I recognised the scene from her photograph. The street was deserted. A curtain twitched and I saw her retreating into a white building. The door was ajar and I passed into the vast, derelict network of the old theatres. Their abandoned labyrinths of corridors, private boxes and galleries remained intact, but the inner shells of all the buildings were exposed and could be accessed by passageways and spiralling staircases—the catwalks and pathways to a hollow paradise. Colour and light had seeped away in their years of neglect as if the flesh and life had dropped from their skeletons. It was an architecture of bone, of ash- coloured curtains and stage sets that appeared almost translucent and shadow-like. In the dressing rooms, lines of mirrors reflected only the masks and costumes that hung from the wardrobes, and little clouds of white chalk and colourless rouge shifted with the draughts from the chasms.

But in the distance, as if on a silent street, on a night of stillness and moonlight, I saw her briefly and recognised the faint echo of her footstep. I followed her to the small interior I remembered from her description, of the Théâtre des Pygmées. Lining the wall were rows of tiny, plaster puppet heads. Their limbs and torsos had been heaped together, as if in a mass open grave. I knew the faces—crude caricatures of Céline, Brasillach, Gaston, The White Sow, and all the actors, friends and spies from Nice. The colours of their glass eyes had drained and they appeared cloudy and withdrawn into an inner world, as if their blindness had given them an arcane knowledge of secrets and mysteries. Like those of a phrenologist fumbling to unlock the marks of vice and read the dreams of these death masks, my fingers explored the contours of each skull. But as I gripped hard, thinking I had finally deduced their allegiances and treasons, the plaster broke and crumbled, and the opaque eyes fell and were lost in the dust.

Through the recesses and corridors of the balconies I climbed, where the imprint of past revellers lingered in the stale memory of cigar smoke, cheap scent and the rot of oranges and decaying fish. In the theatre of melodrama, I gazed down at Desdemona's abandoned bed chamber. It resembled a frowsy attic, the sheets grey and frayed. The stub of an old candle had fallen and its wax had seeped into a handkerchief, staining it a pale yellow. A sword leant incongruously against the bed, but its paint had flaked, revealing its wooden shaft. And it was here that I caught the echo of her voice, singing one of her ballads of love and folly.

Following the sound, I came to a pale chamber where the walls had been decorated with murals depicting the adventures of the Pierrots. But they had faded into ghost outlines and their story was told in shadow. The room was cluttered with abandoned costume trunks, like coffins, cobwebbed and white with dust and flaking plaster. And from the empty stage came the last notes of her song. As it died, a trickle of red petals dropped from the ceiling, vivid and crimson in that grey room. As they fell, the edges of the trunks seemed stained with blood that oozed and congealed in a slow soft stream. And a hideous ululation began, a howling as from a caged beast, and I awoke, knowing that I dreamed again of the Café of the Yellow Moon and the noise was of my own making.

When I learned that filming was to be resumed, in Paris, in the spring of 1944, I declared my intention of rejoining the flotsam of fringe actors and extras, deluding myself that I would see her again. But my behaviour was becoming increasingly disturbed and I was a liability to my friends. I was nearly arrested in the Boulevard de Temple, clutching her photographs of its lost glories and hammering on the doors of residents, demanding admittance to the Funambules. One evening, as rumours of the allied invasion grew and my indiscretions became perilous, I was drugged and placed under the supervision of a doctor in the public ward of a Paris asylum. There, my dreams and rantings would pass unnoticed.

In the asylum, silence was enforced as rigorously as at the Funambules. In a ward of thirty or forty souls, of both sexes, we were clothed in loose, grey pyjamas. I faced a shabby row of grimacing Pierrot faces. Some, like the café's monkey, gazed beyond the bars of the window, their catatonic stares fixed on the flowers and trees in the hospital garden. Any deviance, whether of howling, rocking, weeping or night-time disturbance, was punished with an arbitrary and indifferent savagery. To cure my nightmares, my body was purged by cupping—that ancient practice where spoonfuls of blood were drawn out, or dried strips, like salami, were collected on the rim of the glass. Mustard poultices were strapped to my back whilst the nurses studied my agonies with an amused, detached curiosity. When I questioned my treatment, the doctor gripped my skull, smiled and said:

"You are punished for the lies and evasions of memory and for taking refuge in dreams. Pain and the spilling of blood will strip away your deceit. And only when the past comes back to spring at your throat, will you be free."

Most of the male patients were roughly shaved in their beds, the water and soap suds soaking the sheets and staining them a dull grey. But I was singled out by the pasty-faced orderly, who sat me opposite a mirror in the washroom, so that I could witness the emptying of my face, to see its pallor deepen.

He handled the razor with cruel, flamboyant flourishes, holding my head or twisting my nose and pausing to consider his next stroke with the fastidiousness of an artist. And it seemed he inscribed my name in the mirror in letters of dirty water and flakes of skin and hair. When I asked why I had been selected for this solitary ordeal he said:

"I merely scrape the chins of the other fools. For you, my Pierrot, I scour your dreams away."

The decor of the ward was spartan and tolerated no ornamentation. But when Paris was liberated, a huge bouquet of flowers, cut from the inaccessible garden, was displayed. Masking even the stink of sweat and the bed pans, which the orderlies nicknamed 'potages' or 'casseroles', the perfume filled the room. But the inmates recoiled from their brightness and held their noses to block the fragrance, as if rotting meat had been cast before them. They had been given a memory of home and beauty, reminded of times when they were young and happy, and they could not endure the pain.

I studied the arrangement of summer flowers with growing unease, struggling to recall the association. And at its heart, almost hidden by blowsy delphiniums, cornflowers and waxy dahlias, was a single pink rose, its petals about to unfurl. On the film set, from the wedding bouquet of Garance, she had stolen such a flower. And later, in our rooms, half-serious and half- teasing, she had fastened it to my shirt, her fingers lingering and seductive. She had quoted Mallarmé—"The one rose, with its perfect summer, gone into times past, yet then on into the future."

Flinging aside the bedclothes, I lurched towards the vase, my pyjama bottoms dropping like the pantaloons of a circus clown. And with all the grey, sodden intimacy of my thin thighs exposed, I tore the bouquet to shreds, my fingers cut and made raw by the thorns of the roses.

I once listened to the sly, insinuating voice of a prison warder who told of a man, his appeal for clemency denied, who destroyed the furniture of his condemned cell and scattered his food, water and the playing cards that kept his mind from the death chamber. And the guard had watched, amused and indifferent, until his fury had abated. He then laboriously collected and reassembled the pack and they resumed their game of cribbage, in silence, tapping out the dead hours with matchsticks.

And my jailors, too, studied my tantrum with folded arms, their smiles curled and ironic. When I returned from the punishment of a mustard poultice, prolonged to thirty minutes, a fresh vase of flowers, more intense and evocative, stood at the end of the ward.

One night, when the ward was bathed in a pale yellow, sulphurous light, I imagined myself back at the café. The faces of the patients opposite me, propped up in their beds, seemed imprinted onto the walls, like the Pierrots of the murals. And a door, leading to one of the hospital's secret chambers, had been left ajar, and a dark shape was visible, as if someone had fallen asleep on a long bench. Its outline, the shadows of the Pierrots and the window bars that resembled the monkey's cage, convinced me that it led to the inner sanctum of The White Sow, where sometimes we had sat, drinking brandy and dozing, until the small hours. I remembered my search for her on that last night of storm and chaos in Nice. Exhausted by the dance and by her mission, she had fallen asleep. A wave of relief swept over me and I rose to wake her. There were so many things that had happened that I needed to tell her. The years of our separation, with all their madness, pain and ruin, seemed crammed into minutes.

She was lying, wrapped in a sheet, and I lightly touched her neck, pulling aside the covering, before stooping to kiss her forehead. And I saw the shrivelled corpse of the old woman, whose coughs, convulsions and screams of dementia had filled the ward.

The doctor found me bent over the body and led me gently back to bed. But there were no more punishments. The war was over and other scores were being settled. My friends in the resistance now visited and spoke eagerly of fugitives brought back from Sigmaringen, and others who had fled or perished by their own hand. Of her, a voice from a distant country, barely remembered, they knew nothing. I was discharged and the days of my future were about to break upon the past.

There were new tenants occupying our apartment in the Marais. Sheepishly, I knocked and asked about her photographs and momentos of the Boulevard of Crime, but they shrugged and spoke of a new, post-war world, free of the old symbols and images. All had been burned or despatched to the rubbish tips.

Blunted by the asylum and the inertia of my self-deceit, my art lapsed still further into sterile parody and I resorted to repetitive part-time work. I copied the epithets and slogans for advertisements, decorated the edges of funeral cards with swirls and flourishes and chiselled out the names on tombstones, embellishing them with stencilled cherubs and angels. And from a cramped little booth, I caught the likenesses of tourists and theatre-goers. A charcoal line divided their portraits from the expanse of paper below and their displayed heads seemed to float, like death masks on a shelf.

I ignored the release of the film. Most of the scenes had been shot again. The storm had destroyed the set, and the actor who had played Jericho, the spy, had fled the country to escape the anger of the resistance. My memories of her came from a distant past, a far shore and another country that seemed more indistinct with every day. But finally, for a few cents, I climbed the stairs into paradise, intending to watch Lacenaire, Garance and the tragedy of the Pierrot, with aloofness and indifference.

Each scene and image sliced away at the lies and evasions that had cushioned me from the events of that last night in Nice, leaving only the rawness of my shame and guilt. Once, in a crowd scene, I swear I saw her, dressed as I remembered her on that night of wind and rain: rose petals on her hair and clothes and her skin, the colour of snow or alabaster, like Desdemona. I recalled the masks and make-up, transforming the faces of the actors. In the long line of mirrors. I had seen the pallor of Deburau, the blackening of Othello and the veils and disguises of Garance. They had sat down, all ease and banter. And under the paints and powders, their demeanours changed and they assumed their parts. But one character, a minor role, stood out. It was the beggar, who feigned blindness, having eyes and wits far sharper than the fools he gulled. His image swirled and merged with one who had passed amongst us, innocent and guileless—a deaf mute with delicate fingers that fed lumps of melon and apple to a caged parrot, and collected the dust and detritus of our lives.

The Café of the Yellow Moon was in darkness, barred and bolted. But there was a small side door ajar, in an adjacent alley, that we sometimes used to escape notice. I entered and heard voices, soft and silken, whispering in the room above. On the floor of the café were several trunks and cases, clothes spilling out from hurried preparation for a journey. The monkey's cage had been unfastened and placed alongside the trunks, and the creature, freed from the torment of its dreams of freedom, was asleep. From the walls, the grey fingers of the Pierrots seemed to gesture these changes, their mouths open to signal new horrors.

And from a hook hung a black overcoat, like the sloughed skin of a monstrous insect. Down the corridor, in the sanctum of the White Sow, where an oil lamp glowed faintly, I saw her asleep. She was lying on the couch where we smoked the café's foul African cheroots and drank brandy into the small hours. Uncovering the sheet that draped around her, I kissed her gently and saw the necklace of dark blood and the jagged gash in her throat. The knife, a serrated Moroccan curiosity for slicing lemons, a favourite of the White Sow, lay on a nearby table. Upstairs, a door was open and I glimpsed a shape briefly in the mirror, and from its mouth came impossible sounds. Instead of the familiar animal grunts and squeaks, came the oily drawl of an urbane sophisticate.

"The fool dropped it at my feet, like a dog offering a ball. All their codes and methods uncovered by his carelessness. Did you ever suspect her?" Gaston said.

"Not once. I believed her too unworldly for intrigue. But her fondness for the artist surprised me," the White Sow said.

"He was unworthy of her. His sketches caught only the moment—stilted and frozen. But those daubs killed her more surely than your knife. A hanger-on and a booby."

"The very word she used for him, as she tried to escape."

"Let her rot and perish and be damned tonight."

"Put out the light. I saw the handkerchief."

And they laughed loudly, as they quoted the scene from Othello shown in the film.

"Their Italian cell of agents is exposed. As we speak, arrests are being made here in Nice, in Monaco and in Turin," Gaston said.

"What about the artist?"

"Worthless to us, captured or dead. But he has the knack of betraying his friends. He's like a carrier of typhoid, spreading contagion to those he loves. Let him spread his poison. He will be watched."

And then they spoke of arrangements for disposing of her body, of their work in Nice being over and of their plans to travel north.

The fingers of the Pierrots pointed at me accusingly and their mouths gaped in horror. Shielding my eyes from their gaze, I staggered from the café and was found, streets away, by my companions.

"Blood-letting will strip away your lies. And only when the past comes back to spring at your throat, will you be free," the doctor had said.

And this white face, permeated and stained to the bone with the pallor of cowardice and deceit, must be purged of its cold treasons.

From my bed, on this late afternoon in autumn, the discoloured surface of my mirror appears like a distant headstone. My razor, with its plain handle, waits only for the artist's hand to carve the inscription in sombre letters, unadorned with spirals or flourishes of gold. Outside, caught briefly under the yellow street lamps, the revellers flicker and glow. And I see the faces of them all, as on that last day in Nice, dancing in carnival celebration, flinging rose petals in the air. The ground is thick with the years of their fall. Crimson fades to brown and the rising layers crumble and decay.

In the clamour and riot, I hear her song and watch her dance, faraway, as from the balconies of paradise. Muttering Othello's epitaph, I rise to meet her.

"I kissed thee ere I killed thee. No way but this.

Killing myself to die upon a kiss."

At the graveside, the dancers wait and cough impatiently. Stumbling, I dig with my nails into the loose mass of falling petals, grip the knife and drop into the chasm. And as I fall, I mouth the words of Lacenaire.

"God—eternity—man's soul—Nature. All is a secret. Tomorrow, I shall know."

DANCE FOR A WINTER MOON

Bosnia-Herzegovina—February 1908

USUALLY, Anna Lahmann looked forward to walking the length of the town in late afternoon, delivering powders and medicines from her husband's dispensary. There was a lazy good humour and banter in the exchanges with shopkeepers and stallholders, as they finished their day's trading. The main street snaked up the hill and from its summit she liked to view the entire settlement, tucked in snug against the boundaries of the forest and the distant mountains. Particularly in these winter twilights, the lights flickering from the remote farms and orchards, and the plumes of smoke from the shop fires were homely and reassuring.

Their decision, three years ago, to set up a medical practice in this isolated region of Bosnia-Herzegovina, twenty miles from Mostar, was scorned by their Viennese friends as a perilous folly and gamble. But despite the initial shyness and suspicions of the townspeople, they had prospered. The young doctor's diligence and zeal for his work overcame difficulties with the language and culture, and his reputation and clients grew. Open and confiding in manner, and tolerant of traditional remedies and folk wisdom, he made his patients feel co-conspirators against disease.

The town welcomed them into its social activities. They were honoured guests at weddings and christenings, where the doctor's ham-fisted fiddle- playing drew enthusiastic but undeserved applause. And Anna's informal piano recitals of Mozart and Schubert were welcomed and appreciated in the rough-and-ready salons and soirées. In summer, they boated on the lakes with friends or joined parties of the wealthier inhabitants for weekends at the seaport of Dubrovnik. They felt established and happy.

But today, at dusk, as she stacked her basket with prescriptions, her sense of composure and serenity was disturbed. Figures moved in their lane, by the doctor's laboratory, where its long windows already reflected a milky, insipid moon. The trespassers were six children, earnestly absorbed in a strange game of jumping, ducking and weaving amongst the bushes. After each child had performed their action, they strutted and swaggered before the others with almost comic formality.

"Six, for the six proud walkers," Anna muttered to herself, recalling an old piece of doggerel from her childhood in England. She knew several of them by name but they were oblivious to her presence as she stopped to greet them, blocking their view of the window. The spell of the game was broken and, without speaking, they slipped away, furtive and disappointed. And caught in the thin, sickly limelight of the moon's glow, she realised they had been dodging its beams, daring and testing themselves against its touch, as they might tease a dangerous tethered guard dog by approaching within inches of the reach of its chain. Reflecting on the incident, she recalled that the children's silence and sullen detachment had been mirrored in the past few days by a growing wariness and caution within the town. Friends from a nearby hamlet, who had planned to visit on the following night to celebrate the doctor's birthday, had postponed their journey, offering tenuous excuses. Anxious not to offend, they had promised to come the next week. And this afternoon, many of the shops already had their shutters up, as if the coming darkness held some fear or danger.

Her final stop was at the town's church, to deliver ointment for the priest's rheumatic knees. Adorned with frescoes that stretched to the ceiling, and statues of saints and martyrs in cornices and high perches, the building's art and beauty always beguiled her. And yet, many of the statues and paintings had been vandalized. The eyes, in particular, of the holy family and apostles, had been gouged out, exposing the bare plaster or stone. The damage had been done over a period of many years. In some cases, smoke from the candles and incense had almost masked the marks of knife and chisel, whilst other outrages appeared fresh and recent. It seemed a particularly sly and cruel desecration, as if the shells of their sanctity remained but the souls had been picked clean. She had remarked on the sacrilege to the priest.

"It was the Turks," he said, evasively.

The explanation puzzled her. A zealot, anxious to wreak ruin on a rival religion, would have despoiled the entire church, destroying all that hammer and pickaxe could reach. To bring ladders, climb precariously to the ceiling and meticulously carve out the eyes of selected figures, suggested a cold and devious design.

This evening, the vestry, usually a warm hub of cosiness, where the priest brewed tea and toasted oat cakes, smothered in butter, for privileged guests, was deserted and locked. But inside the church, a lantern glowed and she could hear voices, subdued and conspiratorial. Pushing open the door, she observed the town's fishmonger at the top of a ladder, which was steadied by his wife. With knife and trowel, he was scraping the aureole of nine stars that surrounded the infant Christ, and carefully emptying the blue dust into a canvas bag. Her presence embarrassed but did not deter them. Three stars were crushed and bagged before he clambered down, with the remark:

"Others will come for the remaining six."

At the priest's house, his housekeeper informed Anna that he had been called away unexpectedly and would return the next day. Her voice was hesitant and equivocal and Anna suspected that he had conveniently absented himself, anticipating the desecration of his church.

The incident had shaken her, upset her confidence in the stability and serenity of the town. The church's permanence, at the heart of the townspeople, was challenged. Empty and forsaken by its priest, it seemed a fragile redoubt in hostile country, abandoned to the onset of night and darkness. And as twilight deepened, the town itself seemed frail and vulnerable—a rickety line of wooden shacks petering out into the vast expanse of wilderness where the surrounding forests and mountains loomed, dark and pervasive, as if about to engulf the houses. The glow of lights in the outlying smallholdings, usually so comforting, might have been the fires of siege and destruction, as the blackness advanced, splintering and obliterating the farmhouses and scattering the flames of hearth and stove.

The feeling of unease was not caused by the season. Last winter, they had joined the throng who gathered on the ice and skated like dervishes, until they were giddy, exhausted and happy. But in the past week, those who braved the ice had slimmed to a trickle until the deep pond, which glittered invitingly, was abandoned. And last year, there had been walks and sledding excursions into the hills. The countryside had seemed to sweep onwards: a panoramic backdrop, suggesting a world of adventure and exploration.

She hurried home, the moon more prominent as night advanced. But its light was disfiguring, altering the perspective of the street and blurring the shapes of houses. Some buildings were accentuated, like monstrous white mushrooms, whilst others were cast into a void, more empty than mere darkness. She crossed the bridge over a river that flowed quickly in warmer months but was now almost frozen, its banks choked with ice and snow. Balconies and roofs were reflected—distorted and twisted, seeming about to topple into the water. And on the far side were the same children she had observed earlier. They were skirting the edge, like a little pack of terriers ratting in the reed beds, as they hurled stones onto the surface, watching the ice and lights fragment and delighting in the ruin and confusion of images.

She was unable to sleep, worrying about the derangement of the town. The almost full moon was out of sight but, even with the curtains drawn, she felt its presence, cold, grey and insidious, seeping into the bedroom. Furtive and dissembling, it seemed to hide in shadows, behind cupboards and wardrobes. Her husband lay still, saliva bubbling onto the pillow, his hair flopped to one side and his throat exposed. He seemed lost in some ecstatic dream of exploration and adventure, for he smiled as she remembered him smiling when he climbed the summit of a steep hill and saw the valley stretched out, green and golden, below. But tonight, his expression also reminded her of the Fool in the Tarot pack that had amused them in Vienna. Blithe and giddy he seemed, oblivious to the precipice that gaped at his feet as his eyes gazed at the sky and sun. Conscious that the gesture was absurd, she flicked the lock of hair across his forehead and covered his bare neck with the bed sheet, lest the light of the moon should catch him unawares.

Its latent menace, stealthy and unsettling, recalled a memory from her childhood. It was a late September night and the moon loomed through her window—an obscene thing, like a bloated face, diseased from within and mottled with pink splodges. Around it was an aureole of seven stars, forming a decoration, like a chintzy lace collar. Her father had pointed to them, as he visited her room, leaving the curtains open so she could admire the night sky.

> "Nine for the nine bright shiners,
> Eight for the April rainers,
> Seven for the seven stars in the sky . . ."

He had meant to amuse her with the verse—a piece of nonsense to remember—but she found the words sinister and knowing, like the poem about the "candle, to light you to bed". That was followed by the "chopper, to chop off your head". Always, it was accompanied by that sly little mime, with the hands, as if to copy the creeping approach of evil coming up the stairs. And as the moon's position shifted, there was the same echo of something intimate and shocking about its movement—the cloying grin and mincing tiptoe of a predatory stranger playing peekaboo. The next morning, a day of sunlit beauty and mellow heat, the feeling of malignance and imminent danger remained. The leaves on the trees, stretching down to the wood, shone with the reds, yellows and oranges of autumn. But in their fading colours and the reflections they cast in the puddles and garden pond, she saw the pink decay of the moon's face.

Her father was picking pears, his ladder wedged firmly in the soil as he probed into the topmost branches. Clusters of the best fruit were just out of reach and she begged him to leave them. But he laughed, head thrown back, confident and condescending, climbing higher than the ladder's top step. She knew that his fall was inevitable. He twisted backwards in a comic pirouette, landed on his head and broke his neck as the fruit showered down. His dead face was awry, with a foolish expression of surprise and coyness, as if he'd been caught in a game of hide-and-seek. His skin was pale but blotched in places with a puffy redness. And she understood the cunning joke of the moon. It had mimicked his death mask, and the stars, like grinning acolytes, had fashioned themselves to mock the way his shirt collar hung loose around his crumpled neck. In the days and months that followed, she had tried to rally her mother out of her grief but she was inconsolable. For years they remained—two women, utterly alone, in each other's company. Words and gestures were hollow and meaningless.

And now, in the bedroom, where her husband dreamed, the solitude returned. The moonlight had leaked away and she lay awake, with a feeling of the oppressiveness of night and cosmos bearing down on the little surgery. The stars offered no comfort, dimly glowing through the net curtains. They seemed part of the constriction—corpse lights in the gloom or emanations of gas, deep in tunnels underground. It felt as if the town had been smothered and they alone remained alive—lost travellers in a vast subterranean cave. She reached out to touch her husband and he groaned, as if wandering blindly in the darkness of forest or mountain. The hills and the memory of Dubrovnik were a universe away. Or perhaps that bright port too had been squashed between the forests, the mountains and the sea, its terraces and groves of plums and quinces concertinaed and toppling into the ocean.

The morning offered scant respite. It seemed to Anna that the danger had regrouped and was gathering on the fringes of the town, in the hinterland of woodland and mountain track. Sorties had been sent out to probe and scour the dreams of sleepers and under the vindictive power of moon and cosmos, misfortune would come inevitably the following night.

At midday, the doctor returned from his rounds, peevish and out of sorts, on his birthday. He had encountered an unexpected mulish obstinacy in his patients—an indifference to his science. His medicines and advice were dismissed as irrelevant and several ushered him to the door as an unwelcome guest during some secret crisis.

"Several houses have drawings, like five-pointed stars, above the thresholds," he said. "Perhaps it concerns our fishmonger's criminal eccentricities, or some folk custom devoted to a saint or patriot. Do you remember the line from the old song? 'Five for the symbols at your door'. My scholarly interest in the practice met with silence and a retreat into themselves. I anticipate a quiet afternoon, with no patients and an untroubled evening—which I welcome."

Smiling ruefully, he set off again on his duties. Whilst describing the strange behaviours she had witnessed the previous day, Anna had not confided her deepest fears to her husband. He would have listened with sympathy and understanding but reason and science would dismiss any supernatural auguries.

It was midafternoon before she noticed the priest's pony and trap negotiating the main street. She waited an hour and hurried to the church to deliver his medicine. Several doors had been smeared with a blue paste in a crude five-pointed representation of the night sky. Imprisoned in the centre of the pentagram was a jaundiced moon—a confection of dirty white powder, sealed perhaps with egg yolk. They were forlorn daubs, a childish mimicry of Passover, to ward off malign spirits and pestilence.

At the church, the fishmonger's prediction had proved correct. The entire circlet of stars had been chiselled bare and there were further desecrations. Depictions of the moon and cosmos, surrounding a representation of the Magi—a beautiful, subtle fresco of smoky gold and crimson—had been crudely hacked and removed. She found the priest in the vestry, piling logs on the fire. She reported the vandalism she had witnessed. He sighed wearily.

"Usually, only the eyes are taken. Many believe that the intense colours and power, inherent in the gaze of the saints or holy family, can cure a grave illness or prevent incipient blindness. The powders are either ingested or applied as a poultice. But currently, there is a feeling within the town of imminent threat—a premonition of great danger. As a priest, I should dismiss such fears as naive superstition. But when I studied in the city, there were nights when the carriages and wagons careered through the streets as if impelled by a strange madness and reckless abandon. An omnibus might topple from the cliffs or boats collide and sink in the harbour. A fever from the moon, the night and the stars, seems to take hold and entrap the unwary. Even in the city, where the cosmos is blurred or obscured by street lamps and its music is drowned by the clamour of human noise, some people, intuitive and prescient, perceive the dangers. They are the ones who abandon sea voyages or train journeys on the premonitions of dreams or curious auguries. Therefore, I refuse to condemn my congregation for their mutilation of the church. I turn a blind eye and make sure that the logs on my fire do not spit sparks onto the floor."

The main street was almost deserted as she left the church. An occasional figure, muffled against the cold and the coming night, muttered a greeting and scurried home. The doors and windows were locked and shuttered; the inhabitants huddled around their stoves and fireplaces. A pall of smoke rose from the chimneys of the town into the night sky.

She glimpsed them first—lit by the first stirrings of the full moon—in the freezing waters of the river, by the bridge. They were standing rigid and statuesque, their shapes overwhelming the familiar reflection of shops and houses. When they moved, it seemed she was gazing into a whirlpool of ice and struggling currents, where the images of stability and serenity fragmented and broke. The known world of roofs, gardens and balconies toppled and splintered in a moonlit whirl of smoke, wood, frozen water and distorted landscape.

The children were now twelve in number and arranged in a formal circle. They had chosen the derelict field behind the inn for privacy rather than secrecy for they were unmoved by Anna's presence. Nearby, another child, almost hidden by bushes—his dark shape, more tumulus than human—began to beat a slow, hypnotic rhythm on a toy drum. The circle moved in a stately pavane, like planets in their orbit, with graceful hand gestures and blank, empty faces directed upwards, as if imploring the night sky. In turn, each moved to the centre of the group. There, they gyrated and convulsed, with violent stabbing motions and their faces gripped in a rictus menace, their venom directed at the line of shops and houses. At the end of the sequence, one child withdrew and slunk silently away, unsteady on her feet, as if sick or drunk. Anna thought at first that she was sulking but this proved to be the pattern of the dance.

The others reformed and the drum beat grew faster and more intense. From somewhere in her memory, Anna recognized the rhythm of a tune she had once known but could not bring to mind. The dance resumed, at times measured and ordered but often with wild, careering kicks and arm slashes. They strutted like grotesque parodies of adults, in the throes of great grief and trauma, or swirled, gracile and fluid, like reed beds blown by the wind. It seemed that they were enacting scenes from a tableau, each with its own story, steps, atmosphere and malice. As each sequence ended, one withdrew, as if overcome with weariness and lethargy—old men and women, broken by misfortune. As the numbers reduced, the drum beat became more frenetic and disturbed until only one child remained. The noise ceased and the drummer slipped unnoticed from the field. Miming a silent howl of despair, the last girl rocked in a spasm of grief, twisted round and round, until falling giddy and exhausted on the ground, before lurching home, like the others, sullen and defeated.

"One is one and all alone and ever more shall be so."

The remark was made by the priest, who had discreetly watched the dance, with a mixture of awe and amused detachment.

"What were they doing?" asked Anna.

"It is a protection. Something similar has probably been performed since the first fires were lit on the edge of the wilderness and the early peoples cowered as the malice of darkness and cosmos closed in on them. The children sense the unease and tension of the coming night. Often a chant accompanies the drum.

"Twelve for the moons that wax and wane,
Eleven for the falling dancers,
Ten for the towers and beacons tall
And nine for the nine bright shiners."

And Anna remembered the strange counting song from her childhood, with its mixture of Christian imagery and forgotten pagan astrology.

"We used to sing of twelve apostles, the eleven who went to heaven and the ten commandments," she said.

"I'm sure there are many versions, as new Gods are embraced and the old discarded or discredited. But always it ends 'One is one and all alone and ever more shall be so'. I doubt the potency of the dance or the incantation. It's all show and flummery. At best, it exhausts them—withdraws them from the mischief of the night. They will sleep until noon. And their parents too will lie low, protected from the coming storm, as they watch over their children, who dream and cry out in their sleep."

Conscious that they were the only ones left exposed to the sky in the deserted street, they parted, hurrying away, dodging the light of the moon, like wayfarers caught beyond the hour of curfew.

After a muted birthday supper and celebration, Anna peeped from the window into the darkness. The street was silent and empty. Candles and lanterns in the houses were faint or non-existent, the inhabitants unwilling to draw attention to themselves. The town resembled an animal crouched in its lair, with predators sniffing and scraping at the weak entrance points. She knew that the peril would come from the darkness, some sly contrivance of night and cosmos, nudging and whispering together. All would be well if they stayed indoors, hidden from the moon and the stars.

Her husband read, first from a medical textbook and then a light novel. But he was unable to concentrate, unaware of the forces that threatened, instead blaming his listlessness on tiredness and overwork. A conscientious man, devoted to his patients, he never refused to admit the sick when they called late at night, and was willing to visit, in emergency, the bedridden, or those overcome with fever. A lamp shone at the entrance to their house as a symbol of his calling, welcoming the distraught.

Tonight, Anna feared such a visit, imagining the moon leaking a contamination of disease and infection that would catch him unawares. And quietly, she sneaked down the path and guttered the lamp, leaving the house in darkness and hidden from prying eyes.

To drown her disquiet, she played the piano—bold mazurkas, jigs and waltzes, to counter the soft malignancy of leprous moonlight. The tempo increased—a frenetic false exuberance—and she realised that she was mimicking the spiralling rhythm of the children's dance. As the loud pedal reached a crescendo of reverberation, she experienced a slight shudder of vertigo and remembered the giddiness and despair of the last child. She finished abruptly, and with the fall of the music came another faint echo that tripped and hid behind the din of dying notes: a distant rider, galloping hard and approaching. But the clatter of hooves died as she climbed the stairs to peer out into the night from the bedroom window.

A bright moon showed the main street, silent and asleep. With relief, she scoured the horizon, where the vanishing point seemed to blend landscape and starlight. All seemed still until the flicker of one orange star juddered and she realised that its light came not from the night sky but was carried on horseback and that the traveller was searching for someone within the town.

The rider had slowed to a walk, stopping at each house to shine a lantern. The horse, a tired nag, wobbled from side to side, making the figure twitch and jerk like an effigy strapped onto a donkey at the head of a parade of folly and burlesque. Their progress seemed like a procession of some macabre nocturnal carnival—a solitary rite of lantern and jinking hobbledehoy, probing the dreams of the sleepers in the silent houses. They advanced slowly, but with an inexorable urgency—the same deranged mime of her father, when he pretended to creep up the stairs, intoning the rhyme about the candle and the chopper. Opposite their house, the horse stumbled a little, and as the movement passed to the rider, she recognzied the same spasm of surprise that had twisted her father's face as he lay on the ground. But she had misjudged the horse. For all its tics, lurches and laboured gait, it had a grotesque sturdiness.

They passed the house and for about thirty seconds she was deceived into ecstatic relief that the danger had passed. At the foot of the stairs, ready to prepare her husband's bedtime drink, she heard the front door pounded with heavy blows. The doctor, accustomed to the summons of his patients, hurried to answer.

"I nearly rode away. But the moon seemed to shift and shone on your nameplate. My name is Besnik." His relief at finding them was palpable.

She'd seen him at the town's weekly market—haggling over damaged meat and fruit, or scouring the rubbish wagons for stale bread. He was the chief of a clan of nomadic people, who'd set up an encampment, about five miles away, on the fringes of the town and its isolated smallholdings. Tonight, his plight was desperate. His wife was in labour—a painful, difficult birth that he believed was twins. Usually, the women of his camp managed delivery with ease but all were distraught. He'd heard of the doctor's abilities and kindness and begged him to ride out and assist.

The vehemence of Anna's objections surprised both men. She pleaded against the visit, citing the cold, the danger of the ice, the fear of robbers and finishing lamely by protesting that it was his birthday. Besnik misunderstood her anxiety. Accustomed to scorn and rejection, he believed that she suspected his people of being thieves and bandits. Assuming the dignity and grandeur of a tribal chief, he sought to placate her. From his pocket, he produced a ring, engraved with spiralling moons and stars.

"If ever you are in danger, show this ring to my people and you will be protected. I give you my word that I will bring your husband safely back to you tonight."

But his hand trembled as he pushed the ring into her hands and a muscle jerked uncontrollably over his eye. She judged him to be a good man, who promised and meant well but lacked the power and resources to honour his vows. For underlying his bluster and desperation over his wife's plight, was a deeper fear. Her instincts and senses were heightened and she recognized that he too feared the dangers of the night and the perfidious trickery of moon and stars.

From her own country, she'd heard stories of the nobility of his race. Travellers, lost in the forest or wild tracts of moorland, had spoken of their hospitality—of the splendours of their caravans and tents: tables set with feasts and wine for guests, and adorned with golden candelabra. They recalled a quiet calm and the luxury of the wild lands—the smells of woodsmoke, perfume, horses and rain beating down on the wood of the caravan. But this man stank of worry, squalor and poverty. She could picture his cold wagon, stripped of furniture and devoid of food, medicines or wisdom. She saw the dirt and filth of the birthing chamber, where the women fretted and screamed in impotent fear and his family and hangers-on lingered in the shadows, feeble, incompetent or drunk. His word meant nothing. In a crisis, he would fail. But the doctor shrugged, fetched his overcoat, gloves, muffler and hat, and hurried to saddle their pony.

In the stable, the horse whinnied and shook her head—piqued at being troubled so late in the evening. Aleza was a skittish little mare, prone to temper and unexpected bursts of speed. Anna remembered her father's broken neck and imagined Aleza's hooves skidding on the ice and her husband pitched over the reins to his death. She insisted instead that he must use the pony and trap. Its fastenings were loose, where the leather had frayed and the wood was rotting. He had remarked on the damage only yesterday and the knowledge would induce caution and slow him down to a safe trot.

"It will delay us badly. The time taken to fasten the cart and the slower pace on the path may prove fatal," said Besnik.

But she was adamant, emphasizing the dangers of darkness and frost, and the fickleness of Aleza's character. She attached the harness herself, fumbling nervously with the straps and buckles and wasting time by soothing the pony. Besnik paced and fidgeted, barely concealing his anger. Finally, when they set out, her fears seemed foolish. The night was mellow and benign, with patterns of frost and snow on the gates and trees. Masked partly by cloud, the moonlight was soft and enticing. The doctor laughed, insisting that the journey was no more than a midnight ride through the Vienna woods.

As the pair rode beyond the last cottage of the town, the moon emerged from behind a cloud, luring the doctor on—flirting and dazzling him with spectacular displays of light and shade. The track was rough but distinct and he marvelled at the night's beauty: the skeleton trunks of trees, like sculptures; the mountains rising black into the sky, and a frozen lake, with gusts of frost blown across its surface, like a tide of shimmering moths. The two men's breath, mingling with the steam from the horses, came in white clouds—exhalations of moonlight—and they rode as if clothed in silver.

For all the inconvenience of the journey, the doctor's spirits were high. He was still young enough to feel the vanity and hubris of the adventure. He pictured the gratitude of those waiting around the caravan as his deft hands assisted in the successful birth of twins. He imagined the purse of gold, offered by the proud father, which he would magnanimously refuse. Their joyous return journey would perhaps be marked with a gypsy song, a celebration from the wilderness—an ancient folk melody he would remember to impress Anna. He would write to his staid medical friends in Vienna and they would envy his assimilation and acceptance into the romance and culture of unknown lands and peoples.

Noting how the moonlight seemed to clothe the two of them in its whiteness and recalling the rhythm of the tune that Anna had played, he began to sing.

"Four for the gospel makers,
Three, three, the rivals,
Two, two the lily-white boys,
Clothed all in green, Ho Ho."

His voice rose, head thrown back, as if he were bawling out a sports song in a glee club to a group of rowdy medical students.

"I would not invoke those words," said Besnik. "And besides, we know an older incantation. Four is water, earth, fire and air. They are not benign elements but instruments of ruin and downfall. Three are the arrivals—no wise men or magi, bringing gifts, but unwelcome strangers, their identities shadowy and unknown. And the lily-white boys were priests, clothed in the colours of the moon to placate its whims and cruelties. In the secrecy of the forest, hidden by the green leaves, they practised futile rites of blood and sacrifice."

Two miles from the town, the path edged close to woodland and Besnik urged his horse to go faster. Both ponies seemed nervous and hurried forwards. Something moved within the trees and Besnik pulled a pistol from his coat and fired into the blackness.

"A bear," he said. Anna would have recognized the lie in his voice but the doctor was credulous. "You have a rifle in your cart, I hope," Besnik continued.

"I'm a doctor, not a gendarme. Are there bandits in these woods?"

"There are no bandits. Not at this time of year."

The answer was spoken with contempt and a rueful truth. For the remainder of their journey, they rode in silence.

The encampment was no more than a ramshackle group of plain wooden wagons and flimsy tents that offered scant protection against the frost. A fire had been lit and the faces of the men, who leaned into its heat, were haggard with cold and hunger. All the doctor's romantic preconceptions were dispelled. As the flames jumped and flickered, he was reminded of shining a torch on the sleepers in a cheap lodging house in the slums of Vienna—a room crammed with fifty bodies and rife with vermin and disease. Even in the open air, the stench from a communal stew lingered here in the trees and on their clothes—the broth of some crawling animal, unwholesome and rancid.

All were in mourning for they were too late. No attempt had been made to cover them. They had been left exposed for their chief and the doctor to witness as a rebuke for their tardiness. There were two shrivelled things, dirty and white, as if moulded from the clay of the festering moon. Their mother, a girl of about fifteen, lay beside them in all the mess of the botched delivery. In death, her thick black hair and the beauty of her eyes seemed glued on, like a wig and lumps of coloured glass, to hide or mock the mask that was forming. She had been the only spirit of vitality and youth within the camp, their one bright jewel of fire. The men, about six in number, sat in a circle, sullen and numb with drink and anger. The women were huddled in a mass, keening and weeping, their hands kneading their dresses or clawing the air—a single organism of grief. The moon seemed to crane forward, highlighting the scene—an eager voyeur, drinking in each detail.

Besnik crumpled and howled, in despair and shame at their delay—all his previous dignity and hauteur collapsed. Doctor Lahmann, out of guilt and respect, turned his back and walked to the fringes of the camp, distancing himself from the desolation. He had witnessed the carnage of a military field hospital. But its horrors had been balanced by the presence of hardened medics, the imposition of discipline and order, the established routines of dressing and sterilizing gaping wounds, amputating limbs and anaesthetizing the suffering. Here, he was alone. He had attended many dying patients but never had he experienced the silent rage of an entire family or clan. When he dared look, the remains had been taken inside the main wagon. The door was locked and he lacked the courage to knock. The camp was hostile. They regarded him as a failed mountebank or charlatan. He was granted only the courtesy of ostracism. He lingered long on the edge of the fire, trying to keep warm and hoping that Besnik would accompany him home. But realising that the promise of a safe escort was forfeit for his negligence, he climbed into the cart and eased Aleza onto the track that led back to the town.

On the doctor's previous emergency night visits, Anna had been able to sleep easily. often stirring in the small hours to find him in bed beside her. But tonight that was impossible. She'd estimated that with the birth imminent he would be back in about four hours, at two o'clock. Fortifying herself with a tumblerful of brandy, she dozed fitfully in a chair by the fire. She woke shivering and anxious. He was over an hour late. She drew back the curtains and hoped to see the pony and trap in the distance. But all was still and desolate.

The night had given up its pretence of glamour and beauty, its tinsel tricks of moonbeam and sentimental star glow. Little flurries of frost or dirty snow scudded in the air, as if the firmament was swollen with their filth and they dropped like lice from an old mattress. She remembered her father pulling away the roof slats and painted wooden fascias at their home in England. They were rotten and stinking, riddled with the nests of vermin and choked with chewed paper and scraggy tufts of wool. The churning escape of the creatures had sent it all floating down like ash into her hair. Scrape away the cheap veneer, the inky indigo of the sky and it would peel and flake like chewed wood or wallpaper to root out the hiding places of the stars and reveal them in all their monstrosity and malevolence.

The moon no longer played its evasive tricks of peeping and hiding. Brazen and defiant, it shone with a cruel, harsh light.

"Twelve for the moons that wax and wane."

Once, she had known their names by heart. Her father had been gulled by a September moon, swollen and sour like an overripe fruit. The winter moon of February was of cold and deprivation, when the forest creatures were driven by hunger into the townships. Remembering its name, the vertigo returned, its nausea gripping her as she swallowed and retched.

She saw herself reflected in the mirror—a solitary figure with the rooms and corridor gaping empty behind her; the doctor's books, pipe and tobacco pouch, visible through the room's open door, already nostalgic mementoes from a distant past. For her face, creased and white, mimicked the pain of the last child from the dance. It was a widow's face and she knew, with certainty, that she would never see her husband alive again.

"One is one and all alone and ever more shall be so."

The words and symbols of the song might change but always there was the same inexorable reduction and funnelling—a world enclosed and constricted, until only grief remained. All the prayers to the gods—christian or pagan, the saints and apostles—appeals and entreaties to the moon and cosmos, were futile. The towers and beacons tall, the vainglorious swagger of the six proud walkers, were the boasts of posturing fools. The only hope was to cower indoors with the lights extinguished, to hide like small beasts in a hole and hope that the contagion of the night would pass. The rhythm and drum beat of the dance built to a racing heartbeat of pursuit, cornering and kill.

Chastened and buffeted by the scenes he had witnessed and his own shortcomings, Doctor Lahmann guided the pony and trap carefully along the frozen track. He was grateful for the light of the full moon which gave the landscape the sense of a vast amphitheatre. He hoped to snatch a few hours sleep, perhaps delaying his rounds and enjoying a long breakfast. As they reached the tract of woodland where Besnik had fired his pistol, Aleza picked up speed, her obedient trot accelerating to a canter and, finally, to a full-pitched gallop. Conscious of the frayed leather of the reins and the loose wooden fastenings, he tried to steady her. But her pace became more frantic.

Moonlight picked them out, its cold, harsh glow savouring his sudden panic and vulnerability, relishing the tactics and sport of the hunt. A pack of wolves skirted both sides of the path, gradually reducing the ground between themselves and Aleza. Unarmed and helpless, he recalled the discreet cache of rifles that his friends always brought on their winter sledding and walking trips into the woods.

He had always regarded Aleza as a frivolous little show pony, flighty and unreliable. But tonight, her skills and mettle astonished him, in spite of his peril. She seemed to weave instinctively, avoiding the ruts and bumps that would send him hurtling from the trap. A sleek, grey frontrunner closed on her flank but a deft kick from a hind leg sent him yelping and wounded from the chase. To the Doctor's amazement, the main body of the pack was falling behind, as Aleza's speed proved unrelenting. As they approached a humped crossing over a frozen stream, he dared to hope they would outrun the wolves. The trap rose and hit the ground. Its weight and the momentum of the pony's speed snapped the weakest section of the wood, flinging him onto the ground. The impact detached the entire trap and Aleza was able to gallop home, encumbered only by flailing leather and the remains of the fastenings. The moon lit the scene by the bridge, its glow touching and playing with every detail and movement. It caressed each colour and texture—an interplay of bone and blood, tooth and fur.

The Wolf Moon played its last jest on Anna, fashioning the stillness of the last hour of darkness that enabled her to hear from afar the hoof beats of Aleza. Her hopes were prolonged and finally dashed, for a gash in the pony's flanks, made by the fastest wolf, confirmed her fears. As dawn approached, the moon retired, satiated, its sport completed.

In the morning, the town sloughed off the night's siege, blinked, stretched and resumed its customary business with gusto, relieved it had emerged unscathed. The children, belying the priest's prediction, were already skating and sliding on the frozen pond, yelling their greetings to Anna as she hurried to find help.

A search party, armed with rifles, set out to look for the doctor, returning at noon with the bad news. At the bridge, there were sufficient bloodstains and other evidence, which they buried, to indicate that he was dead. Scraps of torn clothing were found and burned. But the wolves had dragged his carcase deep into the woods.

Late in the afternoon, a forlorn procession passed through the town, slowing briefly at the surgery, where no fire burned or lamp was lit. Besnik led them but each wagon seemed locked into its own isolation and grief. The town's children ran alongside, ignorant of the man's tragedy, hooting, pulling faces and dancing in mockery of the strangers. And they gathered, over a month later, with flowers and tears, to wave at Anna's carriage as she left at dawn, under the austere piety of a Lenten Moon, for a solitary apartment in Vienna.

A BLUE DISH OF FIGS

'I saw new Worlds beneath the Water lie,
New Peeple; and another Sky.'
—Thomas Traherne

WORRIED by the folly and impulsiveness of her impending visit, schoolteacher Helen Mathon had dreamed last night of the Arthur Rackham illustration on her classroom wall and the hypnotic and rhythmic simplicity of the quotation.

"She went along, and went along, and went along."

She did not know the story but the heroine strode out barefoot, through a wilderness, fringed with blue hills and the leafless skeletons of trees in early spring, with a boldness and independence that gave her confidence and inspiration.

She had left her car on the edge of a derelict industrial estate, close to the eastern marshes of the Thames, where the shapes of disused pumping stations and outflow pipes loomed from the mud. She faced a long, solitary walk to the waterman's cottage where her pupil lived. Pausing on a bridge over a sluggish creek, where the black water oozed and congealed in oil and garbage, she hesitated. The path forked and she nearly asked directions from two youths who passed, hunched and smirking, but recognising them from school, she knew their answers would be false or equivocal.

As she scanned the horizon for clues, the late afternoon sun broke through the clouds, touching the edges of the straggly gorse bushes with fire. To the west, lapwing were twisting and tumbling; their purple and copper plumage caught by the light as they whirred and thrummed. And a puff of blue smoke from a distant bonfire, in a woodland copse, rose into the sky, masking the trees with its sapphire haze. Driven by a strong breeze, cloud and smoke coiled and mingled, seeming to form the shape of a sailing ship, the foam of the waves breaking against its prow, silver and shimmering. She smiled as she remembered the girl's strange boast.

"I can weave smoke like wool."

Nonetheless, the image confirmed her path. Leaning on the parapet of the bridge, she drew her pupil's notebook from her pocket and read again the opening paragraphs of a narrative that both disturbed and fascinated her.

"I dare not disclose all of the secrets I have learned for I feel my hands stiffening to stone. My limbs cramp and bend back, like the bodies of the hanging ones on the hill of the elm trees. Only by gripping the pen in my fist, like a dagger, and gouging the paper into shreds, can I regain the use of my fingers.

"And when I tell my friends the hidden words in the voices of the trees—their jealousies and lusts—and how their branches ache and strain for the love and cold touch of the moon, my tongue swells and turns to wood and I taste the bitterness of the yews in the grove of Esbat.

"They laughed at first and thought 'Under the Moon' was a clapping song for little girls. But when I chanted the rhyme that is safe to say and whispered the beat of the rhythm into their bones, they became entranced.

"'Stockings red and garters blue,

Shoes laced up with silver.'

"And their gawky, clumsy bodies, that pout and poke to their sterile music, became graceful and solemn.

"I taught them the dance of peonies or 'Snapping Waists', that the girls in the ship from the east showed me, when they came to bathe in the lake. Their hands and sleeves dip like the stalks of the flowers, bending under a strong breeze, their skirts like petals. The peonies have burst their buds and their fingers catch the fragrance like censers. Even the dead stench of playground and dull brick softened and I saw faint outlines taking shape in the tarmac. A crimson butterfly settled on the ghost of a flower and I heard the wing beats of its companions pulse in the woods, a mile away.

"Foolish Miss Hudson smiled and spoke of the charm of folk dance and morris men with sticks and bells. But these are not maypole or fertility rites. They are the ancient dances of trees, rocks and stars—things indifferent or hostile to human imitation. They care not if the corn grows or the women are barren or whelp brats with crow wings and fur like bears."

Helen remembered, as a child, in her parents' garden, watching a silver birch sapling, in its first spring of splendour, in full bud and leaf. The wind caught its branches and the dance was ecstatic and shaman-like; a whirling brilliance of patterns and fleeting colours. But the gyrations and contortions continued even after the wind had dropped. And there was a stillness and sentience in the garden, as if the older trees were aware of her. The young birch had revealed secrets that should not be divulged and, under their censure, it recoiled into itself, shrivelled and died, before the summer came.

Lilian was in her tutor group and about to sit her final exams. But something had happened to her in the Easter holidays that could not be explained by the death of her grandmother. Previously a quiet, mousy child, destined for the drudgery of shop work or unemployment, she had acquired a strange fervency and charismatic eloquence. At first, friendships had intensified and briefly she became the centre of attention, even adulation. But there had been accidents and letters of complaint. The parents of two girls wrote that their daughters had been diagnosed with epilepsy and a boy could not sleep at night for he imagined that the old apple tree in his garden was filled with mouths that writhed and grimaced and spoke to him in his dreams. The girl was shunned and mocked. She spent her lunch hours alone, with Helen as her only confidante, or writing feverishly, sometimes wracked with spasms, in her black notebook, which she kept hidden. Her attendance became increasingly sporadic. And five days ago, in a valedictory gesture, she had pointedly left her book on Helen's desk.

As she walked towards the distant smoke from the bonfire, Helen recalled the next entries from the notebook.

"Even when I was a little girl, looking down from the jetty into the river, I imagined faces and landscapes deep in the water. And sometimes I could hear voices singing, in a language I could not understand.

"There is a spot where the water eddies and shifts back upon itself, where light and shadows merge. One morning, this April, I saw something glimmering in the centre of the whirlpool. It was a fragment of marble and embedded in its grain were mottled colours of purple, indigo and shades of violet that I have never seen before. They twisted and spiralled like the whorls on the shells of extinct crustaceans in the reference books at school. As I screwed up my eyes, the marble seemed part of a huge building—a temple or palace—and each stone was marked with those inky striations.

"Through the arches and columns, I saw a dark blue sky, lit with stars and the outlines of people carrying stone jars brimming with flowers, their petals twisted and distorted like sensuous mouths or locks of hair. And the song that I had always heard became clearer and there were words that I recognised from a long time ago. Breaking through the stench of mud, oil and the filth of the river, came a fragrance of roses, jasmine and other scents that were both cloying and bitter.

"When I walked back to the cottage, I expected the sensation to fade. But it lingered in the air and drew me to the edge of our land, and a disused workman's hut with a locked wooden gate leading to a dense woodland. Long ago, I remember Grandmother wrenching open its bolts and hinges. And when we saw the thickets of impenetrable bramble and thorn, her face seemed to shrink and grow much older.

"As I passed the hut, the perfume became more intense and enticing, and seemed to come from the copse. The gate swung open at my touch and I climbed a grass path that led upwards through an arch of dog roses and honeysuckle.

"Finally, I came to the brow of a hill and the path zig-zagged into a bewildering maze of tracks that I dared not follow. In the distance, I saw isolated houses and towers, with figures of stone gazing out across the plain. And in the direction of the river were ships, with the emblems of eagles, leopards and stars on their sails.

"Some of the paths led deep into the surrounding hills: dark caves with symbols hacked into the stone around their entrances. It seemed that the hills were slumbering, inert creatures, their roots like limbs, spread out and entangled with each other. And I knew that they were dreaming of me—the warmth of my breath and the touch of my footsteps were resonating in their bones and fibres.

"On my right was a thick, pathless forest that stretched to the vanishing point. I peered into its depths and sensed the turmoil of insects burrowing under earth and bark and the heartbeats of countless animals underground, or hidden by the trees. But despite that feeling of motion and the lure of birdsong, there remained a stillness; a secrecy of fur, feather and leaf. That first day, I was a dead, tainted thing, stained and corrupted by all the filth and dirt of the city.

"Gazing into the heart of the wood, I saw a distant flurry of grass and leaves, as if a squall of wind had disturbed the forest floor. Gradually, the outline of an ancient trackway took shape, with the indentations of cartwheels and the hoof prints of cattle. The haze of dust drew nearer and an unseen host seemed to pass. I heard the soft tread of their horses and saw the steam rise from their breath. And voices came, with words that seemed familiar, on the edge of a memory I had lost, centuries ago.

"In the valley below, I saw smoke rise from their city and lights shine from their farmsteads, temples and houses. Fleetingly, I remembered the pavements and columns of marble, its stone ingrained with mottled spirals of purple and violet, and the dancing floors, where they swayed like grass or branches, moving in the wind. All was frozen long under ice and snow and then washed and broken by the floods. In the barren world I inhabit, only echoes remain—buried under hill and forest or buffeted by sea wrack. And there are worlds hidden in the pinpricks of dust, embedded in the glass and metal of the grey towers, the memories of birds and insects encased. The pips from the old orchards lie scattered under the concrete of the airport runways. And I see the figures of giants and horses, once carved in grass and chalk, under the sweep of motorways.

"When the pageant had faded, I found a comb of bone and horn with the same patterns and colours I remembered from the marble. And entangled in its teeth, still warm from a girl's fingers, were strands of golden hair, scented with oils and the musk of her dance."

Helen remembered a conversation about the girl's family with old Mr. Hollowbread, who had taught English and was recently retired.

"They're old London. I have a hunch they've lived by the river since before the Conquest—and I mean the Roman one. There's a strangeness in the girls that comes and goes, and misses generations. The grandmother told stories of madness and disappearances. I taught the girl's mother—she is unimaginative and worldly. But don't underestimate Lilian. She may seem dull and ordinary but once she wrote me a story about a fairground populated with fools and clowns. She called her characters 'Reim', 'Druth', 'Mer' and 'Aesceirdd' and swore she'd invented the names. All of them are archaic figures from Celtic tales."

Helen had read the pages, surrounded by the remains of a mean little supper, in her flat, above the launderette, where shop signs and streetlamps blinked and flickered. The street below, covered in layers of concrete, asphalt, chicken wire and gravel, seemed like a straitjacket or shroud that suffocated and stifled her breath. At night, the moon and stars were blinded by the shop glow, and the murmurs and silences of the darkness were drowned by car alarms and traffic. Sometimes, in the evenings, her doorbell would ring and she would hear the profanities or stifled laughter of disaffected pupils who knew her address.

And she remembered a railway journey, through the back ways of those same London streets, when the train stopped unscheduled at the remains of a disused station. In its yard, overgrown with luxuriant vegetation, on the fringe of a little copse, she had glimpsed a long, tawny animal with a brindled tail. The next morning, she sought the location, manoeuvring through dilapidated gates and railings. The concrete foundations of the old station had cracked and long dormant seeds had broken through and flowered in a blaze of forgotten colours. And she sensed the same wariness and suspicion that she had felt when she saw the silver birch dance all those years ago. Birdsong ceased, a cloud of butterflies dispersed into the undergrowth and the world withdrew into itself. A city fox, sleek and red, trotted into a bush, as if to mimic and confuse her memory of the brindled cat of the wildwood. And in the silence, she spoke aloud the words of the poet:

"They are gone into the world of light
And I alone sit ling'ring here."

But the bulk of Lilian's account had deeply unsettled her teacher.

"In the next few days, when I passed beyond the door, I was careful to remain within sight of the tunnel leading back home. I spent many hours by the side of a lake, near a waterfall, listening to the whispers of the reed beds and the trees. They told me the sacred names of the moons and their colours and perfumes; the dreams of the animals and the secret songs of the birds.

"I learned the slow drip of time—the past stretched out golden and crimson in the dawns and sunrises; the passage of ships, the fall of tribes and peoples and the scourings by fire, in the red earth. And I heard again the music of the river and the long-drowned peals of bells from the fallen churches of the Saxons, the Normans and those of Grandmother's childhood.

"'So sinks the day star in the ocean bed.'

"I spoke those words to her and she remembered the ruin of St. Giles, in Cripplegate, and the blackened bust of the poet, pulled from the wreckage and decorated with a tin hat. There was a knowing undertone of slyness and envy in her voice and I wondered what things she had witnessed, in her youth, and whether she too had passed beyond the door.

"But there are perils beyond the gate—marks of a secret sorcery, more subtle and potent than all the weary flaws and cruelties of the modern world. Amongst the delicate pink flowers of ling, on the rolling heath, I glimpsed bleached skeletons; their bones contorted to the shapes of distant trees and coiled with vines, encrusted with malignant suckers.

"And from the hill, I sometimes see a house on the horizon. By daylight, it is cold and empty; its windows like the sockets in bone. But by moonlight, figures are reflected in the glass, endlessly pacing, like cats in a cage, their faces twisted with visions from a barren landscape. Sometimes, a little caravan, brightly painted with yellow moons and suns, winds up the path to the house. And always it stops and a young man with dark feral eyes waves to me and beckons.

"On the slopes of the river are stone shapes, like ossified tree trunks, with flowers carved deep into the rock, which pulse and vibrate to a soft somnolent rhythm, like a heartbeat. And I know, that if I succumb to their narcotic snares, I will be encased in stone or wood and listen forever to the madness and poison in their voices—an ancient bitterness and hatred for all things of flesh and blood.

"One voice whispered the words and symbols of an ancient depravity—an inward corruption of blood and soul far worse than all the furtive little sins and squalid betrayals our world could muster. It was a rite practised in caves and in the ague-infested swamps of the old world, and the diseased bones of its acolytes have long crumbled into dust. It was an incest of body and spirit—of hands and parts, reaching out into the darkness of slime and rock pool, in intimacy and hideous harmony with things that crawl and bite. Our lizard brains retain an echo of memory in the repulsion some feel for cockroaches, for a snake coiling in the undergrowth or the scaly tails of vermin, scraping on a drainpipe. When I heard the sly asides of my teachers and the chants of my former friends, I tried to speak, to plant its malignant seed in their minds. But my tongue locked. Only beyond the gate, or in the hinterland of the workman's hut, can I weave the spell.

"When I returned home, often in the small hours of the night, my parents made sly jokes and assumed I had been writhing and sighing in the arms of a lover. But Grandmother's wits were sharp and there was jealousy in her eyes.

"Once, she told me a story of things that had happened long ago, when Brandy Nan was queen. A girl from our family witnessed a ceremony by the river, to renew the songs of the boatmen. Figures came from the water, with clothes like the sweep of a willow branch in full leaf, or the rainbow arc of a waterfall, as sunlight catches its spray. They carved a shape from the mud of the river and wrapped it in leaves of hazel and reed. And six girls in white laid yellow flowers onto its eyes and poured into its mouth a red liquid that bubbled and whispered. It was made from rose petals and the leaves and roots of those trees which sing when the wind blows.

"But the coarseness and vulgarity of the world were growing. The songs were fading from memory and the power of speech was dying. Her father, with a voice like a rook, fit only for crude doggerel, forced her to reveal the spells she had seen. He cut a chunk of river mud, knowing it bore the flesh and tongues of the finest singers, wrapped it in dirty muslin and intoned the incantation.

"But although he had no powers, his words attracted the dark spirits from the riverbank and weirs, and the thing twisted and convulsed in his hands. When he poured the liquid into the creature's mouth, it squealed and howled with his voice, for his soul had entered the obscenity. Unable to bear the sound, he broke the neck of the writhing shape, killing himself as its neck snapped. And the world beyond ours retreated and became even more secret and elusive. The daughter passed into the trees and hills and was never seen again.

"One evening, in a secluded part of the lake I had not visited before, I found a red ribbon—twisted and raggedy. And the branch that snagged it had withered. Although bright red, the ribbon's colour was dead—a dyed modern thing—and I knew it belonged to the world of cheap shop counters, fashions and spiteful vanities. I took it back to the cottage. Grandmother pawed at it and begged me to take her back to the grove by the lake. Mother led her to bed as she mumbled and wept. But I sat alone by her bedside a while, and listened. She babbled of a fair, named Ablach, long before St. Bartholemew's, or the ones of the Saxons and the tribes before them. People came from the east with artefacts of gold and silver, fashioned as birds, fish or animals—so sensuous and fluid that they sang and moved, with a delicacy and sweetness that opened the secrets of the rocks and trees. She said that the metal, forged in holy fires, was nourished by the scent of hedgerow flowers and bushes.

"In the morning, Father told me she had died in her sleep. He did not notice that the colour had drained from her ribbon nor did he listen when I said we should burn her body. I visit her grave and hear the wood of the coffin and the worms whispering of the world she forsook. And I sprinkle black nightshade and thorn apple on the soil, to deaden her memory and give her oblivion.

"And I understand why she used to scour the river and its mud to uncover little earthenware heads and grotesque animal carvings. They are crude fairings from a sideshow, pale imitations fashioned in longing and memory for the singing art. These monstrosities adorn our mantel shelves and cupboards. As a child, I imagined them grunting and straining for speech, their eyes popping in their mute futility and sprouting warts and tumours as they mouthed silent obscenities.

"The day after Grandmother died, I returned to the spot where I had found her ribbon and came at last to a clearing, once the site of a great autumn gathering. Although the grass was tall, I could see the outlines where stalls and booths stood at the waxing of the Fruit Moon, and a path led to the sea. The air was heavy with the drowsy perfume of hawthorn blossom, white and thick. Its sourness and sweetness bore the scent of the lust between thorn bush and sun, boulder and sea spray and of the moon for the hills of chalk.

"Nestling in the undergrowth was a tiny hare, breathing and pulsing in the heat of the flowers. At first, I thought it a thing of flesh and blood, but its fur was fashioned from tiny strands of gold and silver thread. When I touched its spine, the fur rippled; its eyes of black opals opened and dilated and it murmured softly.

"I wrapped it in swathes of the blossoms and carried it to school to show my friends its sensuous mysteries and glories. And the stale classroom was filled with the perfume of that clearing: the carnal music of trees, rivers and creatures long departed—the wolf, the bear, the forest cat and the wild white cattle, with ears of red, like the berries of the hawthorn.

"As the eyelids of the hare flickered, the moment of wonder was broken. Someone laughed, another belched and soon the room was filled with their mockery and disbelief. The sweetness of the flowers was corrupted; the air rank with the stench of gangrene and plague. And the living body, fabricated in the sacred fires of the ancient world, became mortal clay and lay rotting and seething with flies and maggots."

Helen remembered the incident well. Together, they had buried the stinking remains of the hare in a quiet corner of the school grounds and the girl had muttered rhymes over the little mound of earth. But it marked her final isolation and ostracism. At a staff meeting, the principal had dubbed her 'Lady Haw Blossom'. The ironic throwaway remark was repeated and the nickname corrupted to 'Haw Bottom' and finally 'Whore Bottom'. Its rumour spread amongst the pupils, who passed her in the corridor holding their noses and making obscene noises and gestures. Her closest friends had been the cruellest, twisting one of her own rhymes against her.

> "Down in the valley, where the green grass grows,
> Dear little Lily, she blooms like a rose."

A letter was sent to her parents, expressing concern for her mental health but, as only days remained before her examinations, expulsion or suspension were considered unnecessary. But after reading the notebook, Helen had spent a sleepless night considering her dilemma. Torn between protecting her pupil's privacy and concern for her welfare, she had, with reluctance, photocopied its pages and shown them to her principal. The response was unexpectedly swift and draconian. Helen had been told that the family would be investigated and the girl taken into the care of the local authority. She was warned against any contact that would jeopardise the success of the operation.

Her visit would be regarded as unprofessional, even treacherous. But she was determined at least to return the notebook and express her gratitude for the gift that had been hidden in its pages. On that last lunchtime, before truanting in the afternoon, Lilian had been engrossed in weaving and braiding a circlet of reeds and grasses. As Helen negotiated the mud and puddles of the long track

119

to the cottage, she imagined the journey by foot of tomorrow's pack of counsellors, social workers and police. She wondered if they would bring restraints or handcuffs, if the girl refused their authority.

But there was another reason that compelled Helen to seek the remote house by the river and investigate the truth of the wooden gate and its hidden pathways. There was one extract in the notebook that she dared not show her principal.

"On Miss Mathon's wall are pictures from fairy stories, of all the golden ones, who endure drudgery and cruelty but walk in splendour through the wilderness or the woods to find wonders. Her eyes fix always on one who escapes the lechery of a false admirer and the dullness of her world. She treads alone through the skeletons of trees, a ridge of blue hills at her back. In the classroom window, Miss Mathon sees her own reflection, her face hollow and lined with crow's feet, like the bruise on an apple that will spread and corrupt the fruit. She mouths the words of the poet:

"'I see them walking in an Air of glory,
Whose light doth trample on my days:
My days, which are at best but dull and hoary,
Meer glimmering and decays.'

"And I see the shabby flat she returns to each evening, sifting piles of paper and growing old in a rented room. Like a million others, she paces the confines of her cell, where the wood is dead, its stone but lifeless dust and its colours reflecting nothing. Every morning, she gulps down her cold breakfast, worries about her weight and dreads the tediums and vexations of the coming day.

"At weekends, comes the sly and greedy lover, with fingers like pudgy worms, and whose eyes are alive only when he soaps his car or watches sports. And when they lie down together, he grunts and squirts, his sweat stinking and the weight of his body suffocating and oppressive. He enacts the tired mimicry of old rituals, grown stale and clammy: desire without beauty, longing without ecstasy. Her curtains are drawn and she does not see the fall of starlight in the far hills. They shine like sapphires under the moon.

"Underneath that classroom picture is a solitary floorboard of hazel wood from the old forests. In the memory of its grain is a fragment of a song from those times. The stone and wood of those buildings have slept so long it is hard to wake them. But I have whispered the secret words and even as he plants a perfunctory kiss, while she sleeps, she dreams of walking the blue hills.

"My own path lies through the forest or to the city of marble, far across the plain. But always the ships in the harbour and the track that meanders to the shore, blue with thyme and violets, reminded me of Miss Mathon and her kindness. As I descended the hill, I saw the familiar sweep of the river and recognised the jetty near to our house. But it was now a long pier, with booths, shops and taverns. And instead of the stagnant ooze of the river, the tide broke on a port and busy market. I sat on the harbour wall, with my feet dangling in the water and watched the dramas of rolling barrels, the sailors with brightly coloured birds and monkeys on chains, and heard the laughter and quarrels from the taverns.

"A ship, with the emblem of a purple leopard on its sails, was unloading its cargo of spices and the air was full of the scent of cloves, cinnamon and nutmeg. But the casks were covered in layers of dust and cobwebs, and weed draped the anchor, as if the ship had been waiting for years. A sailor approached me, bowed very formally and offered me a blue ceramic dish of figs. His fingers were like ivory and dusted with the bloom of the fruit. The flesh was sweet and intoxicating and he pointed into the depths of the dish. And I knew that, hidden in the glaze, was the secret flower of the fig—its colours and fragrance unknown. But my eyes could not conjure it. And the sailor smiled, wrapped the dish in the leaves of the fruit and placed it in my hands as a gift.

"As I passed through the throng of people, I felt I was observing a pageant of shadows or a dumb show. When I studied the playing cards in a hotly contested game, I saw that they were blank. Plates of food and jugs of wine and ale were crammed on huge tables. But when I sampled the bread, it tasted of dried grass and the drink was stale, brackish water. Wagons, loaded with the spices, edged along the roads, as if to distant towns and cities. But when I rounded a corner, the plain stretched out vast and empty, and the roads and carts were gone.

"I do not know if these illusions are part of some malign enchantment—a trickery or sophistry of their art that has deceived me. Perhaps I have been gulled by lies and deception or used as an emissary to ensnare others. Or perhaps the stories in the dumb show were created to amuse and divert through the drowsy years of waiting. For I have seen birds, absorbed in an ecstasy of motion, creating shapes and visions in the dust and light as their wings flicker and glide.

"And when I unwrapped the blue dish, its colours did not fade and the leaves were still succulent and did not shrivel."

The previous night, Helen had fallen asleep worrying about the wisdom of her visit and puzzling over the strange events and coincidences of the girl's narrative. The lumpen shape of her lover stirred a little, grunted, and dripped saliva onto the pillow, and she acknowledged the insight the girl had shown into the squalor of her life.

At first she dreamed that, like the heroine in the picture, she was walking, alone and barefoot, through a wilderness fringed with blue hills and stark trees. In her hand she carried a ceramic dish with the tracery of a flower in its glaze. And on her wrist was a bracelet—a torque of hammered gold and silver—a gift from someone who had rendered her a great kindness. She arrived at the harbour and boarded the ship with the emblem of a purple leopard on its sails. When the anchor was raised, it seemed that thousands of years of weed and sea shells were encrusted on its iron. They shimmered in the sun and spray and briefly she saw glimpses of towns, courtyards and landscapes.

The boat rose and fell as she drifted in and out of sleep. And finally, she dreamed she was walking in an eastern city, amongst its hillside groves of pomegranates and apricots. From her promontory, she looked out as dawn broke on a sea dotted with the outlines of islands, with towers and spires, flashing beacons of fire. The air was rich with a strange overpowering perfume, bitter and cloying. And from a cluster of fig trees, she saw huge pendulous flowers of salmon-pink and violet, their petals curved like lips or drooping like stray locks of hair.

Close by was a tall wooden building that she knew was a library. And in her head were a thousand verses and songs. They were visions that even the strongest opiates could not conjure. They had the power to delight emperors and baffle the wits of philosophers and seers. And forming in her mind was a vast epic—an elegy engraved on bone, to a great city of the dead that she remembered from long ago.

Throughout the tedium of her Monday timetable, she recalled her dream, assuming it had arisen from the girl's narrative. But in the afternoon, when her last class had dispersed, she remembered the floorboard. At first, she saw nothing but a vague outline, as if blue dust had been disturbed by a draught. But amidst the smell of stale food and the tramp of a hundred sweating feet, was the fragrance from the groves of the east. And shimmering in the dust haze was the blue dish. In its depths she could see, like a watermark, the tracery of a hidden flower, salmon-pink and violet.

At the cottage, Lilian's parents greeted her with polite indifference. Their daughter's absences and change in behaviour were attributed to teenage moods and tantrums and they oozed with practised pathos on the death of the grandmother.

"She spends hours moping in the workman's hut. Perhaps you'll find her there," the mother said, anxious to return to her television programme. And Helen noticed the line of ugly earthenware and china fairings, with their warts and carbuncles, their mouths locked, as they eavesdropped and mutely conferred.

The hut was further from the house than Helen had imagined and the path snaked through hedges of gorse and thorn. She had kept the child's gift in her pocket, along with the blue dish. It was a bracelet, closely woven from the yellow reeds and white grasses of that last day, and she considered it too fragile and delicate for regular wear. But as she slipped it over her wrist, the folds rippled and shimmered with gold and silver wire, to form the torque she remembered from her dream. And as the layers twisted and shone, a piece of paper was uncovered, addressed to her. It read:

"I know that next time I pass through the gate, it will be the last. If I vacillate and return, like Grandmother, I will be forever haunted by echoes from its world. I too will scavenge in the mud and be mocked by the tawdry mimicry of the fairings and heave open the gate to find impassable thickets of bramble and thorn. Perhaps I will succumb to the secret evils and lures and enter the caravan of suns and moons or fall asleep amongst the stones that have voices. But the path to the city in the plain shines more brightly with every visit.

"I showed my friends and teachers great mysteries and wonders and suffered ridicule and calumny for my art. And for those that come to wrench me back to reality and the dull sanity of their world, I leave one final act of sorcery. You may glimpse its potency, but like my parents, you are protected from the symbols. If you too pass beyond the door, to seek the mysteries of the harbour, which are hidden to me, search the horizon beyond the forest and remember me."

Helen understood that the girl did not seek the false consolations of companionship, or the cloying reassurances of counsel and sympathy. There would be no tears, no hugs, no reconciliations or lies of compromise. Hers was that most pure of gifts—the selfless kindness shown between pariahs and solitaries who will never meet again.

And the trap had been set. The door to the workman's hut was ajar and there were school bags, books and items of uniform, visible to lure the inquisitive and the predatory. The walls were marked with runes and symbols, both vile and hypnotic—images that fascinated and seduced. From inside came the rank odour of rotting hawthorn blossom and the fumes seemed to coil and entwine with the incantations on the walls, as arsenic in damp wallpaper or spores of mildew can seep into the air and infect the bones and lungs.

The wooden gate was open and the path beckoned through the arch of overhanging flowers. Helen could see the outline of footprints in the grass—some two or three days old. On impulse, she removed her shoes and left them by the gate, the memory of her classroom, the flat above the launderette and her lover, already growing distant. When she reached the edge of the forest, she looked to the horizon, where sun, cloud and wind played with light and colour. And a plume of smoke rose, caught the breeze and formed the shape of the hidden flower of the fig tree, salmon-pink and violet.

SALAMMBÔ AND THE ZAÏMPH OF TANIT

Paris 1866

DOCTOR COLBERT preferred to visit his patients, who lived in the melancholy streets and lanes surrounding the Bièvre river, at daybreak or twilight. The shadows of the crumbling brick walls, encrusted with lichen, the women peeping out furtively from behind broken shutters, and the mournful little river, shaded by poplars, conjured up the landscape of the priestess Salammbô's journey to the tent of Mâtho, the Barbarian, to recover the sacred veil of Tanit, the moon goddess. There was the same desolation and mistrust in the faces of the ragged creatures who scuttled into the wreckage of their houses, and the stench of soot and burning leather from the tanneries echoed the trails of charcoal dust that brushed Salammbô's feet. A silken, watery moon reminded him that the souls of the dead were believed by the Carthaginians to be dissolved there, and their tears created its moisture. Like the Bièvre, with its black, brackish flow, the moon was a place of mud, ruin, darkness and enchantment.

As junior partner in his father-in-law's practice, he was allocated the poorest patients. And during this cholera epidemic, the disease seemed drawn to the Bièvre, where they glutted on cheap shellfish, oblivious to the dangers of contamination. The grey-blue skin and hollow eyes of its malnourished victims reminded him of the Barbarians in Flaubert's story, left to starve outside the gates of Carthage, who gnawed their sword belts and smashed the bones of their mules in their desperation for food. He had grown accustomed to the fishy stink of the rice-water diarrhoea in the infected houses and remembered that Salammbô had refused the fish, preserved in honey from Hippo-Zarytus, as unclean.

He had read the novel a year ago and the historical epic, with its intense imagery, exotic yet precise, had obsessed him. Each chapter, filled with sexual passion, cruelty and death, was like opening a rare and exquisite box, with its own textures and perfumes, and finding lost jewels and wonders. The action of the novel opened up into a series of paintings, vivid and intoxicating, and as he walked the city streets, he played out their scenes in his mind and mouthed the phrases he had memorised. He sought, in the dull, petty monotony of modern life, an echo of the ardour and drama of the novel. In the fall of a woman's hair, the brush and fragrance from her dress and the colours, made by moon and sun, on her face, he hoped to find some memory or trace of Salammbô herself—a beautiful woman, cursed and tormented to the extremes of devotion and jealousy, piety and sacrilege.

And the mystery and allure of the novel's heroine contrasted starkly with the surrenders and compromises he had made, submitting to a marriage of convenience with a woman eight years his senior— a marriage that advanced his career yet brought only material comfort.

He recoiled at the beefsteak-and-ammonia smell of his wife as she sweated in her shapeless woollen dress, hurrying late to church—the black, stubbly hairs on her neck, like the singed bristles on a joint of pork. Intimacy was repellent. She embraced the carnal with the same earthy indelicacy as a farmer's wife, who guides and eases a reluctant bull or ram into undertaking its duties. The mechanics were discharged with roly-poly humour as he was manhandled and mastered. He regarded their bedroom as a cowshed or ringed enclosure, half-expecting the old doctor to saunter in, smoking his pipe, offering observations and grunts and shouts of encouragement.

When her pregnancy was confirmed, he was rewarded with a marzipan cake, as a shire horse is given a pocketful of carrots. His wife ground and kneaded the almonds and sugar, and carefully separated the egg white. And when the yolks nestled in one half of the shell, dripping with little spots of albumen, she swallowed them whole, as if gobbling an oyster. The image summarised their union: a marriage of sickly deceit and slimy coagulation.

Their mealtimes were enlivened with the old doctor's sanguine and graphic accounts of his patients' symptoms. Recently, he had discussed grasping the bloated skin and probing for the inflamed liver of a cirrhosis sufferer.

"Like plumping up a sagging pillow," he had observed, and his daughter had laughed, spluttering food and dribbling sauce down her chops.

But her rough flippancy masked a profound cunning that twenty-six- year-old Doctor Colbert often underestimated. Early in their courtship, he had witnessed his father-in-law struggling with a terrified and intractable boy of twelve, afflicted with a large boil on his neck. His fiancée tempted and mollified the child with sweets, before holding him in an iron grip, whilst the doctor sliced at the carbuncle with his scalpel. The boy yelled with pain and anger at the betrayal and she had smiled, smug and prim, at the success of her trick.

She read ardently the popularist stories of virtue and admired the sentimental homilies and mawkish tales of Berquin, where goodness and wisdom were always reward-ed with sugary treats. She condemned *Madame Bovary* as indecent, yet enjoyed a perverse pleasure at the protracted suicide of its heroine.

❋

Inspired by the vivid imagery, characterisation and bright panoramas of *Salammbô*, the young doctor returned to painting. As a student he had shown some promise, before his medical studies swallowed his leisure hours.

He set up his studio in an outbuilding of the surgery and there he attempted to emulate the great modern art-ists he admired, persuading his wife and servants to act as models. But his painstaking copies appeared as pastiches, laboured and absurd. He exhibited to his medical colleagues and they hooted with derision at the lumpen domestics in fancy dress.

His interpretation of Gustave Moreau's *Pietà* featured a fatuous bun- faced Christ, his loincloth like a grotesque adult napkin. The Virgin Mary, simpering and moon-faced, gripped him as a peasant woman would burp a bloated toddler. His friends entitled the daub, *Indigestion*.

He attempted Millais' *Vale of Rest*, with its distant, enigmatic chapel, looming trees, dark earth, and the tension and fear in the two female figures as they buried or ex-humed an unseen body. The painting hinted at both guilt and a veiled eroticism, as the younger woman wielded a spadeful of earth, her limbs, lissom and seductive, whilst her passive mistress glanced warily away. He spent weeks invoking the latent symbolism and mystery of the scene. When his friends had left, hiding sniggers behind their hands, he discovered the chalked comment, "Planting Rhubarb".

But instinctively, he knew that these pale imitations were but rehearsals, for he sought the model who would embody the enigmas, contradictions and sorceries of Salammbô. Her face would evoke both a fervent sanctity to quieten the rancorous and dampen the passions of the libertine yet also reflect a latent sensuousness that would provoke the hidden lusts of the devout and celibate. Even Saint Anthony, who watched the old Gods falter and fade, sustained by his faith, would scrabble on his knees to catch the scent from her robe and make obeisance before the Goddess of the Moon.

One evening, in the early days of the epidemic, he walked home from a tanner's squalid hut, near the Bièvre, the taste and smell of cholera in his throat. Moonlight fell on the river, making the black water shine, like oil or treacle, and the elms and poplars shimmered in the wind. From a tavern named 'The Blue Vine', where straggly dog roses clustered over the entrance and a flaking sign depicted a bunch of damask-coloured grapes, he heard the notes of a melancholy tune in a minor key.

Inside, a thin young woman with long black hair was singing Gautier's ballad, accompanying herself with a bat-tered guitar.

"I am the ghost of the rose
That you wore last night at the ball."

Blue cigarette smoke rose and curled in plumes, pungent like the incense from Salammbô's devotions to the moon. The candlelight reflected the dark colours of bottles, ranged across the bar, making them glow like stained glass. In the gloom, the singer's hair seemed tinged with purple. He remembered the scene where the priestess of Tanit played an ebony lyre, her hair powdered with mauve sand, as she sang to each mercenary in his own tongue.

Once, he had been taken by a grateful patient to his caretaker's cubbyhole, at the back of the Louvre, overlooking a rubbish dump. And there, amongst peeling plaster, yellow newspapers and piles of shabby tools and paints, was an olive-skinned nude statue, lithe and gamine, rather than the voluptuous full-breasted type of the classical exhibits. It was the work of some forgotten sculptor of the Middle Ages, who had depicted this shy withdrawn beauty— perhaps Armenian or Turkish. The caretaker, a sullen aesthete, had discovered her, forsaken and languishing in underground chambers of the museum's archives. Her presence, in that dank little cave, gave him a chaste solace. The doctor had shared with him a bottle of dark peasant wine. And on that summer evening, from a distant garden, traces of seringa and elderflower had drifted through the open window, more delicate and subtle than the heavy perfumes and sweat that clung to the popular exhibits in the main galleries.

Shyly, he introduced himself to the singer and bought her brandy. She was from an impoverished family of acrobats, dancers and music hall performers. Self-taught and cultured, she might easily have obtained work as a respectable governess or private tutor, except for her air of restrained depravity—caught between purity and sacrilege. There was a fluidity and equivocation in her face that shifted like an image caught in shards of broken glass, or reflected in a moonlit pool or well. In another age, she might have been a mistress of Villon: his muse in exile, lying with him, in the shade of a provincial inn, in a brick-red summer, with the perfumes of thyme and lavender filling the room.

He asked her to model for him and she accepted. When she saw his previous work, she dismissed him as an enthusiastic amateur and dilettante. But it amused her to be paid, well fed and fussed over. Re-reading the novel, she was careful to act the part with delicacy and fastidiousness. She recognised that the priestess of Tanit would not glut herself on pastries, pies and bottled beer—growing fat and double-chinned. She requested fresh cherries, pomegranates and strawberries, and persuaded the doctor to indulge her weakness for shelled crabmeat and lobster.

Faithful to the novel, he dressed her in a sleeveless black tunic, emblazoned with red flowers. Her hair was decorated with ropes of artificial pearls that dropped to her mouth. But rather than piling her hair in a tower, like the Canaanite virgins, he preferred a later scene, where her curls dropped like black feathers in a cascade of black falling on crimson.

Amazed that this beautiful creature had deigned to model for him, he painted obsessively. And to his surprise, his work acquired a grandeur, displaying a fire and passion that silenced the sneers of his friends. His first canvas was sold to a dealer. Neglected as a subject for his art, his wife visited the studio, clutching their son, Bertie, and pretended to humour him. But there was a sulky irritation as she inspected the dishes of cherry stones, pomegranate skins, and sniffed the empty plates of shellfish. And long after his model had finished sitting for him, the young doctor would fall asleep, breathing in the scent of her, and would wake, content, as darkness fell.

Within two months, she became his mistress, living in a tiny room he rented near the Bièvre; snatching clandestine evening trysts, once or twice a week. At first, there was a forced theatricality in their love-making. Accustomed to the husky bawdiness of his wife, who called him 'my little salt herring', it aroused him to hear the elegant, chiselled luxury of Flaubert's prose. As the moon rose and the pungent smells of dyed leather fleeces and scraped hide, hung out on lines in the yards of the hovels below, mellowed in the night air, she quoted Salammbô's hymn to the Goddess.

"Stillness sweeps over the earth, flowers close, the waves die down."

And in time, they grew more relaxed in each other's company. She had assumed that their affair would be a lucrative but transitory diversion that would subside when his obsession with Salammbô inevitably palled. But the art dealer had suggested a series of illustrations for the novel.

They imagined a future where his medical career was abandoned or sidelined. She would become his permanent model, his mistress and muse. They read together Baudelaire's discussion of Delacroix's women, contrasting the opulent Junoesque mythological characters with the more intimate modern heroines like Ophelia, Cleopatra and Desdemona, who displayed "some secret suffering, in the depths of the soul, that cannot be locked away." And they recognised that she too was the embodiment of that modern woman, whether satanic or divine, who could capture both "the odour of sanctity" and the supernatural intensity of lust and desire.

They read *Household Tales* by the Brothers Grimm and envisaged her modelling for 'Ashputtel', 'Briar Rose', 'The Water Fairy' and 'Cat-Skin'. She suggested a canvas depicting Estella, from *Great Expectations*, evoking her cold pallor and emptiness in the ruins of Miss Havisham's house. And when he projected illustrations for *Madame Bovary*, she realised that in considering her for the role of an older woman, he was anticipating years together.

They scoured antique shops and eastern bazaars for props, acquiring a delicate bronze incense burner that curled like the ripples of a serpent's skin and, under candle-light, glowed like smoked gold. He spent a week's earnings on a phallus-shaped vase of black jade that they decorated with blue hyacinths, filling the studio with their intoxicating perfume. And faithful to the novel's final death scene, they stitched and pasted her costume. A net of fine, silvery mesh was draped over her legs, that both glittered as she moved and revealed the whiteness of her thighs. She rummaged through the stock of costume jewellery at the shop her family used for their theatre work and chose imitation rubies, opals and sapphires, which embellished her head-dress of peacock feathers. Contrasting with the darkness of her hair, she wore a second-hand white-satin cloak; rubbed and scuffed so that it seemed layered like swans' feathers.

But one last item was needed—the blue zaïmph of Tanit, the Moon Goddess: a veil so perilous that its touch was sacrilegious and led to death. His finances were almost exhausted but he knew that no cheap or tawdry fabric would suffice. On their marriage, his wife had bought him a gold ring, studded with diamonds, that he seldom wore, for its stones seemed like nails that dug into his flesh, marking his ensnarement. He had secreted it amongst his tiepins and cufflinks, in a bedroom drawer, and when his wife was visiting her aunt, he took it and sold it to a jeweller near the Place Vendôme.

And from a small shop, selling rare fabrics from the east, they chose a mulberry silk robe of midnight blue, with brocade of gold and silver in its weave, that represented precious stones and the faces of the ancient Gods.

"The secret of silk came to Byzantium in the reign of the Emperor Justinian," the old merchant said, kindly. "The eggs of the silkworm were smuggled in bamboo canes by traders from China."

He glanced at their clothes, slightly frayed and unfashionable, and at the worn, greasy patch on the doctor's hat. But there was no contempt or disdain in his smile, as they poured the pile of money onto the table, for he sold the robe at a tenth of its value. It smelled of cedar wood, camphor, myrrh and the breath of fruit groves that overlooked and permeated the bright eastern workshop of its creation, three centuries ago.

In the rented room near the Bièvre, they made love, wrapped in its folds. The cloth shimmered with tones of mauve and violet, creating shapes that changed under moonlight or candle glow, like the scales on the sacred serpent of Tanit. They saw the outline of cats, their eyes mirroring the moon's phases, as they glided between the columns and shadows of the temples. As the silk rippled over her fingers, the blurred stars seemed to pass and he saw the bodies of priestesses swaying, back through time, past the birth of Carthage, to the old rites of hills and forests.

In the twilight of that room, he had listened to her intoning the names of the Moon Goddess, in all her manifestations—Baalet, Tanit, Astarte, Mylitta, Elissa and Tiratha. And he looked out at the silhouettes of the poplars and elms around the Bièvre and the ugly shapes of huts, tanneries and taverns. In his enchantment, they seemed like the temples, cypresses, fishing boats and nets of Carthage, with the shapes of elephants, flamingoes and camels looming in the foreground. He spoke the words of Verlaine's 'L'heure du berger'.

> "Wood-owls awaken now, and soundlessly
> Plough the air with heavy wings.
> The zenith fills with secret glimmerings.
> Venus arises, shining. And it is night."

The doctor's wife was so confident in her world of domestic propriety and pride in her son that until recently she had dismissed this impoverished waif as lacking any serious threat to her marriage; tolerating and humouring her husband's art as an extravagant folly.

But on her thirty-fifth birthday, he had presented her with a plain matronly bonnet, almost as an afterthought. She had seen frowsy wet nurses in the park wearing better. The money he spent on paints, canvases and feeding delicacies to the girl began to rankle. And that morning, foraging in his desk, she was puzzled to find her wedding gift missing.

She knew the story of *Salammbô*, for her husband, in his first enthusiasm, had read the novel aloud to her. Its exotic music, alien and unwelcome, had intruded into her smug world. She would turn aside, laughing at his strange fancies, to feed their infant. And his voice had grown louder, to drown the sound of guzzling lips and cooing mother; her breasts emerging like bloated puddings, copper-tipped and veined like the sickly striations in cooked suet.

When she entered the studio and saw the zaïmph, draped around the girl, in a blaze of shifting and elusive colours, she remembered the chapter on the love between Mâtho and Salammbô and felt that she was an intruder in her own house. Her husband had spoken of sapphire earrings that held a hollow pearl, dripping perfume onto the shoulders of the priestess, inflaming the lust of the Barbarian. And here, in her home, she caught the same fragrance of incense, honey, pepper, rose petals, and another perfume that she dared not acknowledge. Drawing closer, she saw the relaxed faces of artist and model, mirrored and entwined. They communicated silently; two bodies moving in harmony with each other. Neither noticed her thin smile as she inspected the empty plates of food or acknowledged her departure, as she sought an urgent interview with her father.

The next day's sitting was interrupted early. The old doctor was unusually overburdened with patients to visit and needed his son-in-law to deputise.

As his model waited alone in the studio, idly reading Gautier and visualising sketches and canvases, she was surprised by the friendliness of her lover's wife, who arrived bringing gifts of cherries, grapes and a dish of shelled lobster. At her side crawled her infant son, who reached out with his pudgy fist and gaped his mouth wide, like a fat, unfledged cuckoo, when the girl offered him a forkful of fish. With surprising agility, his mother snatched him up, tucking him under her arm like a wriggling piglet. There was a faint patina to the lobster—a rice-water whiteness, like a sheen of egg white brushed onto pastry. But the woman waited impassively for her to finish—a nurse at the bedside of an ailing child. Her gaze was fixed on the zaïmph and its splendour, and the muscle around her right eye twitched convulsively until the plate was empty.

Little progress was made with the painting on the following day, for the girl was listless and slightly nauseous. The doctor watched her leave early, white and shivering, the zaïmph cloaked over her shoulders—a star goddess, fading into the twilight.

When he visited their room after an exhausting day, deputising again for his father-in-law, he received the news, from a neighbouring tenant, that she had been taken ill with cholera, attended promptly by an elderly physician and confined to a hospital. At home, he was greeted by his father-in-law, phlegmatic and full of false bonhomie.

"I'm afraid you'll need a new model for your daubs. A particularly virulent strain of the disease—probably contracted from bad mussels or poor hygiene. You know the habits of the flotsam and jetsam of the Bièvre people. Her family called and asked for you, but you were busy. I did my best."

For an hour, he sat in the desolation of his studio. Footsteps, heavy and deliberate, approached. His wife stood at the entrance, carrying the zaïmph, her fingers wilfully crumpling its folds.

"No point in burying the little trollop in such a fine shroud, although I'm told it matched the colour of her skin at the end," she said. "I'll have my dressmaker fashion me a shawl and there's enough material to make Bertie a pair of pyjamas."

Her other hand held a large paper bag.

"I thought you might want to finish your painting. I'll sit for you. I gave her family a couple of francs for this. It seemed cheap at the price as you seemed to admire it so much. My hairdresser will glue it together."

And from the bag, fell black strands of hair, cascading like birds' feathers.

He locked the door of the studio and sat alone until darkness fell and the moon appeared in the window, casting patterns onto the easels, paints and props. The blue of the hyacinths in the phallus-shaped vase of black jade appeared grey, and their smell was rank and foetid. As he slipped into exhausted sleep, he dreamed of a vast canvas. The bright vibrant colours and panoramas of Salammbô's Carthage had drained and it was a shadow world of nightmare and malice. The Moon Goddesses, in all their enticing shapes and watery beauty, were drowned, for this was a Cholera Moon, and the souls of the dead twisted and writhed in a pale rice-water vapour. The stench of it permeated the Bièvre and its inhabitants emerged emptying buckets of chemical dyes, the carcasses and innards of animals and human refuse into the river, which oozed in streams of mud and filth. Steam rose from the soapy laundry and animal skins, leprous and phosphorescent—a corpse-light tribute to the floating bladder in the sky. Briefly, he saw her face, hollow-eyed and tinged with blue, and the jagged gashes where her hair had been slashed. And a baying rose from the figures around the river; a howl of triumph and obeisance to the diseased white thing that floated balloon-like in the sky. They stretched out their fat sausage fingers as if to embrace it and, in the moist air, their faces and limbs seemed flaccid and grey, like damp suet.

By the river, the trunks and branches of the poplars and elms, encumbered by the tide of sludge, withered and drooped, their leaves the colour of soot. And the air was filled with their soft fall, black like the drift and tangle of birds' feathers and hair powdered with mauve sand.

DREAMS FROM THE APPLE ORCHARDS

1938—A small village in the Banat region of Yugoslavia, near the banks of the Danube, some sixty miles from Belgrade.

I woke to the first fall of snow that winter. The remnants of the summer flowers were black and rimed with frost and grey leaves clustered around the skeleton trunks of the fruit trees. But when I had drifted to sleep, hot and excited by the day's adventure, they had been golden brown and the last crop of apples, russeted and tinged with crimson, awaited harvest. A ladder had been propped against the first tree, ready for Father to climb to the topmost branches, and remove each fruit with a twist of his hand and pass them down to me. I would perch nervously on the third rung and place them gently in the basket, slung over my shoulder, as he had shown me.

But something had happened to me. I had overslept and failed him. And the medlars we had picked, hard as little rocks, and placed on the high shelves to ripen, had bletted and matured. The room was full of their caramel scent. It blended with the chicken soup I'd been spoon-fed, rich with garlic and the hot smoked paprika that seeped into my limbs and warmed them under the blankets.

I remembered fevered dreams of scaling ladders in my delirium, searching for Father in the tops of the branches. I climbed so high into the black sky, clustered with stars, that I looked down and saw the tiny apples, grey and distant, like russeted grapes. And as I swayed, giddy and clutching at falling leaves, a huge butterfly, with wings of midnight blue, had settled on my forehead.

Faces, floating and disembodied, had passed and faded from view. Father seemed older and shrunken, a look of guilt and anxiety in his eyes. And once, the head of the priest seemed to loom over me, predatory and crow-like, droning prayers and incantations.

When I tried to stand, my legs felt as if they were filled with sawdust or feathers, which tingled as they slumped to the floor. It was Grandmother who broke my fall, muttering peevishly that it was fifteen days ago that I had strayed into the forest. I remembered that strange melancholy tune 'Fifteen Years Away From Home', that the fiddler always played on market days and Grandmother's trite little story of its meaning—with the prodigal son returning home from wandering, to a feast and rejoicing. And I realised then, as the dreams and visions of my sickness returned, that all her tales of the people of her childhood and the forest were stale and secondhand. They were but tired homilies to signpost a moral or platitude. Her lessons and warnings of the woods were fables which hid something darker and more potent. They masked her fears of what breathed in the shadows or passed, false and smiling, into our fields, our homes and our hearts.

That day had been auspicious—my coming of age, at fifteen. For the first time, I was entrusted with carrying the fruit to market alone, along the five-mile track through the forest, by cart. It was pulled by Pushka, a pony, over twenty years old.

"Keep to the path, Katya, and avoid straying into the wood," Grandmother had warned me. "There are thieves and brigands in the darkness of the trees. They have grown bolder and more reckless since the war was lost. And anyway, it has never been the same since the old fool betrayed the Grenzer."

Her family had numbered men from the Grenzer—the irregular troops who patrolled the border against marauding Turks. She had never forgiven Franz Joseph for disbanding the force, over fifty years ago, and had not reconciled herself with our village being a part of Yugoslavia. We were citizens still of an empire that once sprawled from Trieste to Galicia.

Her tales of the old frontier were homely and nostalgic. The soldiers brought peace and security with a rough independent justice that seemed both reassuring and comic. She told the story of the elder son of a rich local magnate who mistreated the daughter of a Grenzer captain. He was waylaid, stripped of his finery and dressed in the clothes and bonnet of an old pedlar woman. Strapped to the back of a farmyard donkey, he was sent hobbling home, to the hoots and derision of a succession of villages.

And pride of place was given, in our kitchen, to a grainy framed print of a Grenzer soldier, with limbs and sinews as hard and wiry as an ancient thorn bush. He surveyed our house, orchards and the forest beyond with a cold, ironic detachment. A half-smile played on his lips, as if he relished a secret joke at our expense. But to Grandmother, he represented an era of stability and calm.

She knew of my fascination with the shadowy tracks and bridleways that wound into the forest. They were disused pathways to derelict houses and lost hamlets from the old tales. I was told that they were overgrown with thorns and brambles, and petered out into tangled thickets or woodland glades that confused the senses and baffled any attempts to retrace one's steps. And she discouraged my love of the forest animals, claiming that in the depths of the winter of 1919, in the time she called 'Wolf Month', the packs had attacked the village. The scar on Pushka's flank was caused by their teeth. But Father had taken me aside, reassuring me that the pony's scar had been caused by Grandmother's carelessness with a knife. The wolves were long dead or consigned to the forest depths. Together, since Mother died, Father and I had travelled to market every week for five years, unhindered by animals, thieves or brigands.

Opposite me at market was Peter—a boy of seventeen—and his poultry: a heaving mass of feathers, beaks, sharp eyes and noise. Father and I visited his farmhouse regularly, where the walls seemed impregnated with the smell and texture of goose fat and his four plump sisters clucked and fussed like hens. An understanding was growing between us and his large grey dog, with the coat and sinuousness of a wolf, loped across to guard my growing pile of coins. The fruit sold well and by midafternoon my cart was empty. The villagers and fellow stallholders showed me warmth and generosity, in their kindness buying even the bruised and damaged apples.

But I was tired and on the solitary journey home, the rhythm of Pushka's hooves and the dappled patterns of sunlight in the leaves sent me drifting in and out of sleep. I imagined living in Peter's house—all bustle and chatter: a blur of feathers, fur and the steam and hiss of cooked fowl and apples. And I remembered the story of the star-bear from my childhood. The flecks of colour in the trees, were like the stars falling in gold drops of water into the heart of the wood. Peering into the shadows, I saw the bearded faces from the market blending with the grizzled heads of bears from the story. I curled up, as if in bed, with the dreaming trees growing up to the house and from the roof. And the fur and claws of the cat, who always slept alongside me, merged with the shape of the star-bear, asleep in the forest.

I woke with a jolt. The cart was rattling deep into the woods, down one of the lost tracks. Overhanging tendrils and briars snagged at my hair. But the path was wide and Pushka trotted with vigour, ears pricked, as if the years had dropped from her. The track twisted for miles and through its tunnels and gaps I glimpsed a vast expanse of forest and the slow fall of leaves, copper and golden. And there were strange melancholy clearings, where trees had fallen and clumps of fading purple flowers grew around their crumbling trunks.

Finally, we stopped outside the door of a slumbering and silent farmhouse, surrounded by the remains of its orchards, which stretched to the edge of the encroaching forest. All the mature trees were dead—their trunks black and mouldering—and the branches formed diseased silhouettes against the setting sun. The remains of several ladders, their rungs split and broken, were propped against the skeletons, and these gave the trees the appearance of makeshift gallows, diligently prepared for the morning's proceedings. I inspected the trunks for signs of the canker or rot that had caused such devastation. But each tree had been carefully ringbarked—that slow and lingering death that is far crueller than the woodman's axe.

And in that last strangled harvest, many years ago, fruit had fallen from the choking trees. Seedlings had rooted and created bizarre, misshapen varieties, like the profiles of animal heads, or green skulls, tinged with crimson. Some still hung on the young bushes, ripe and inviting in their grotesqueness. But others, past their prime, had dropped and lay rotting and fermenting on the ground. And in time, as their pips seeded, new strains would rise, more nightmarish and twisted than the parent fruit. Thrushes, blackbirds and a host of wasps and feeding insects, devoured the decaying flesh, and the orchard floor writhed and seethed with their motion. A cloud of blue butterflies, their wings catching the plumes of fading sunlight, gathered and rose from the rot. Attracted by the salt heat of my sweat, several settled on my face and arms, and their delicate touch seemed like the soft caress of blue corpse worms.

The farmhouse door was splintered and broken open. Inside, the rooms had been stripped and a pool of stagnant water remained where the stove had once stood. Vegetation had broken through the windows; branches, flowers and tendrils pulsed slightly, as a sleeper's lips and limbs twitch when dreaming. In the bedrooms was a smell of sickness— subtly different in each room—as if stale fumes from the occupants' sheets had seeped into the walls and were leaking back their poisons to infect the air.

The floor of one upstairs room was littered with the remains of a book, as if its pages had been scrutinized and discarded as worthless by the looters and scavengers. They were from a drawing book and the style suggested the artist was a child of my age. They depicted lurid apple trees, in human form, with faces writhing in pain, and blood streaming from gaping circular wounds in their sides. The trees had been given fond nicknames: 'Uncle Anton', 'Old Daniel', 'Kitty', 'Little Glock' and 'Sweet Jolanka'. From their foliage and fruit, I recognised them as the same varieties from our own orchards. Here were the scented 'Antonovka', the great, bell-shaped 'Glockenappel', the snow- fleshed 'Kitchovka' and the apple of winter, 'Daniel Fele Renet', tasting of wild hazel nuts and spices.

Other pictures showed fields of red earth, barren and arid, scattered with the skulls of farmyard beasts and domestic pets—each with their familiar child-given names. Lush forest vegetation, deep and impenetrable, surrounded the sterile landscapes. In the foreground was the farmhouse, in all its summer glory, with yellow climbing roses, clematis and wisteria in bloom. The foliage was alive with birds, insects and the blue butterflies I had seen in the orchard. But the windows were pale and empty and reflected a cold winter gloom. The inhabitants were gone. Even their ghosts were banished.

The only object left by the thieves was a horse and rider, beautifully carved from cherry wood and stained with plant dyes, its form fluid and abstract. Man and beast appeared moulded together in ecstatic motion. Father had spoken of the history of our people, how we were descended from Thracian cavalry, golden and fearless. Sunlight caught the polished wood, revealing hidden shades of reds, browns and silver—bringing alive fur, flesh and metal. Together they rode, back across the centuries—a gallop across timeless plains and through the wildwood of bears and wolves. I gathered up the carved figure and the pictures, ready to return home.

But in the orchard, a silver twilight glow caught the fruit that still clung to the branches of one bush, like the miniature brass heads of fat, yellow monks, their faces scarred with furry growths of verdigris. The cold air of the approaching night gave the apples a moonlit seductiveness—dream fruit of unknown flavours and hidden secrets. I gripped the largest specimen and its stalk eased from the tree. I bit deep and its flesh released perfumes of such subtlety and strangeness that I picked handfuls to fill a basket.

It was then that I noticed a patch of soft, nettled ground, behind the orchard. In the half-light, carved wooden memorials, shaped like cats, dogs and rabbits, appeared to rise from the earth like totems. Lovingly worked by the same hand that had fashioned the horse and rider, they marked an old graveyard of family pets, and there were older, more austere headstones, denoting human remains. But alongside were the rotting sticks of hastily prepared crosses and their mounds. Carelessly and unevenly dug, their shapes suggested desecration and a crude profanity. I remembered Mother reading me Garshin's story, 'The Bears', and its depiction of faithlessness and betrayal. A government decree required the gypsies of the region to bring their tame animals to town and slaughter them. A hundred animals, from grizzled veterans to young cubs, were assembled—each one a companion and friend, loved and cherished. And there was a terrible hiatus and regret, a prolonged tension and reluctance amongst the older men to comply. But finally, the youngest of the gypsies, impatient and cold, began the massacre. And I wondered what treachery had been enacted here, by the scavengers and looters, under the branches of the dying trees, with their gallows ladders.

As I clambered into the cart, I staggered slightly. Perhaps the sickness was caused by the day's exertions, or the strange adventure at the deserted farm. But I remember very little of the journey home—only the hypnotic sound of Pushka's hooves and the jingling of reins, as she guided me through the darkness. I began to hear whispers and muffled voices in the trees, but the dreams were veiled and hidden. Only later, as the fever gripped me, did they appear in all their terrifying vision and clarity.

But in the smoky oil light of the kitchen, I felt clear-headed and lucid. I handed over the purse of the day's takings and the coins flowed like quicksilver and overspilled onto the floor. I spoke of the deserted orchard and heaved my stash of plundered apples onto the table. But the golden fruit was bruised and tainted, and the basket oozed with corruption. Grandmother's voice, brittle and distant, seemed to echo from the corner of the room where the stove hissed and bubbled.

"The child has gathered windfalls on a fool's errand whilst we feared for her safety in the darkness. The flesh of these apples stinks with rot and maggots."

But Father spoke slowly and kindly.

"The farm you visited was caught between rival forces during the retreat from Belgrade in the autumn of 1915. The head of the family was indiscreet and inhospitable to a request for food. And in revenge and spite, the officer ordered the ringbarking of the orchards. The family struggled on for a few years, scratching a living from the farm, but the wife was not of our people and help was begrudged. And misfortune comes in waves. The influenza of 1919 took them all. Masked against infection, we buried them by the apple trees and the villagers divided their property, amidst much dispute and quarrelling. Pushka was our prize. Your grandmother cut the ropes that tethered her as she fought and kicked. We named you Katya—after the girl who rode her. She was a fey creature—all fire and starlight: one who loved the apple trees, the forest and its creatures."

His voice was measured and patient but I noticed the sly sidelong glances he exchanged with Grandmother. The story had been softened and sanitised, and I wondered what violations my family had committed as the sickness of 1919 spread. The kinship of the Thracian horse had mattered little alongside the deeper brooding resentment, with all its treachery and perfidy, that simmers on the borderland. I felt an affinity with the girl. I held her pictures in my hand but they were soiled with mud and stained with the dampness of apple rot. The bright colours had faded and the clear images of the house and its trees were blurred and indistinct. I squinted and briefly saw her face in the pale winter light of the window, but the lines swam before my face as I swayed and fell. I remember Father carrying me to bed and the figure of the horseman, black against the oil lamp, before the visions rushed in.

I dreamed first that I was riding, not on Pushka, steady and plodding, but a warhorse, fiery and without fear. We scaled treacherous mountain passes—cloud and mist below us and wind in our faces, in an exhilaration of speed—or hurtled blindly through forest tracks, an ecstatic fusion of horse and rider. My cloak of gold and black swept out behind me and I fought in forgotten battles and skirmishes against tribes that rose and fell around the banks of the Danube. Always that grey river, on the hinterland of the disputes and quarrels, formed the backdrop to our adventures. I was part of a proud, warrior people. Our lineage stretched back to Thrace and we fought with a savage insouciance. I witnessed the pageant of our past and understood the fierce independence of the Grenzer—more potent and reckless than Grandmother's homely tales of their exploits. I attended their musters and saw them triumph, brutal and uncompromising, against Ottoman incursion. I looked into their eyes and felt a kinship and loyalty.

But these dreams of fire and ecstasy faded. The chill of the fever seeped into my blood and bones and the visions became ominous and disturbing. I was at market again, but the reckless spirit of the past had invaded and infected its calm. A grey soldiery, their uniforms strange and foreign, moved among us. They were wild and ill-disciplined and ripe for sport and amusement. And sly secret glances were exchanged by some villagers whilst others shrank under the brooding sense of impending violence. I remembered the story of the betrayal of the bears and knew that its horrors were to be re-enacted amongst the stalls of fruit, poultry and vegetables. Opposite, I saw Peter's face, downcast, as if drawn in a cart to execution. It was framed in the bobbing mass of white goose feathers. The birds were agitated and some had broken free, squawking and hissing at the soldiers. As the shots began, my baskets of apples overturned and fell, and the fruit rolled, bruised and shattered. And the pile of money broke, silver coins slipping through the cracks in the cart like fish scales from a knife.

On Pushka's back I fled, seeking shelter in the heart of the forest, where the star-bear lay asleep and dreaming. But the lairs had been ransacked and purged. Trees had been felled, their sap bleeding into the leaf mould and blending with the desolation of fur and feathers scattered amongst the woods. Little curls of smoke were rising from the villages and farms. I flapped at the reins and tried to stop or turn Pushka, for I sensed a new danger, imminent and pressing. There was a prescience and betrayal in the veins of leaves and the call of birds from the depths of the wood. The shapes of branches were twisted and primed like gins or snares. And I realised we were approaching our own farmhouse but the track had been tainted and made strange and unwelcoming, as if years of sour treason had passed. As we rounded the bend, I saw the wilderness of our orchards, scarred and ringbarked. Ladders were propped against the trunks and there were shapes hanging from the branches. I dared not look upon them. The door to our kitchen was splintered and in the wreckage figures moved, fighting and squabbling over our possessions. A woman, her face contorted with greed, slashed at the ropes that tethered our animals. She had bought apples from me at market and smiled and winked at Peter's gallantry. A bonfire smouldered and its smoke blurred the contours of the house. But one face looked out onto the ruin. As the wind blew, the view cleared and I saw myself, older and thinner, before the scene clouded again.

The snow falls fitfully but insidiously, gradually covering the shame of my neglected harvest. Now that the delirium is over, visitors come to my sick bed. The pink, plump little doctor and the ascetic priest fuss and gloat, pompous and confident that their wisdom alone guided me through the worst. And Peter came, all shyness and raw-boned clumsiness, on the pretext of bringing eggs and a fat goose for roasting. His dog nuzzled my hand and curled up beside me on the bed, his fur wiry, like the wolves that are no more.

But on these grey winter evenings, the orchard and the narrow track leading to the village seem sentient and charged with the same tension and foreboding as my dreams. The slope and arch of medlar and apple trees point to the patch of ground where the earth turns easily, and blackbirds and thrushes hunt for slugs and worms. As twilight falls, I see the shape of the mounds begin to form, in the slime trails and spider webs. And there are boughs enough to hang us all and branches to mark our passing.

There are sounds in the wind, and in the mist that rises from the Danube, echoes and voices from Vienna, Bratislava and Belgrade. In the distance, smoke curls up from autumn bonfires, or is it the acrid fumes of burning towns and cities? I hear the sound of carts and waggons, rumbling far away, and watch the dirt track that leads to our orchards. Our visitors are few and familiar. But their approach is slow and equivocal, deceiving the eye into imagining something malign. There is a mockery or design in the creak of a cartwheel or the fall of a barrel, as if the metal or wood conspires to play with our fears. The farmers and the merchants smile. Business is easy and convivial. But behind the teeth of those smiles, some gaze to the branches of the trees, to the windows of our house and to our livestock. There are those among us, treacherous and astute, who wait their moment. All the hollow friendships and fragile allegiances will fragment. And our village will be exposed and prised open, like a hedgepig under the claws of a badger: a thing of little matter; a morning's sport for the passing soldiery, with spoils and plunder for the collaborators and opportunists.

The old totems will fail us. From the wall, Grandmother's soldier, red- cloaked and blue-trousered, like a supercilious minor character from a comic operetta, surveys us all with his fatuous smile. And the glamour and allure of the Thracian horse and rider have palled. Their fluid abstract motion has been withdrawn and the figure appears shrouded, as if the rider's cloak covers them in a deep sleep. The paint flakes and the wood crumbles slightly in my hands. And its colours, that flickered with gold, silver and the fire of its movement, are muted or lost as the grain and lumpen patterns of the old wood return.

VALERIE

SHE came to us, aged nine, as a foster child, in mid-March 1963, when the ice and snow of that exceptionally bitter winter had finally thawed—a bedraggled, dirty creature, wearing a frock cut from an adult's dress, its colours faded and stained from the juice of plants, or even blood. Unlike the other children, who had passed joylessly through my parents' care, she carried no suitcase. And unusually, she was not accompanied by old Miss Gates, one of the clinging stalwarts of Father's dwindling congregation, who gushed and fretted over the children, invariably reducing them to tears and silences, which brought out the worst in me.

Her escort was Miss Broat, a woman known to me only by whisper and innuendo at church and school. Her orphans were rumoured to be fey, manipulative little things, wilful and dangerous. It was said that they understood secrets about the adult world that were best forgotten and that their presence within a family was fleeting but destructive.

Miss Broat's manner was firm and perfunctory. Valerie was directed to her room with a carrier bag and told to change her clothes. And my parents were flustered and angry that Miss Broat had stipulated that I should be present as they discussed her background.

"Girls like Valerie slip through the system. Their births are unrecorded, their fathers unaware of their existence," she said. "They are kittens born in a hedge—the product of squalid liaisons in sheds, woodland or alleyways. And like kittens, many are smothered or drowned."

Father sighed and shook his head, his public face composed in a mask of oily piety.

"Has little Valerie suffered recent neglect?" he asked. And I noticed Mother's lip curl with familiar contempt at his affectation.

"She has not been well," said Miss Broat. "She has been confined in a cold, poky room—quite isolated. In her delirium, she has lost track of her past. Her memories are confused at best. The coming spring, warm weather and having a girl of her own age as companion, will transform her. But her time with you is limited. She will return, on her birthday, in October, to be reunited with her mother, whose identity is withheld. At school, she will be registered under your name."

As she spoke, the folds of her black dress rippled like the wings of a giant bird of prey. The image triggered a long-distant memory that once, during a time of suffocating discomfort and anxiety, I had seen her before. I had spluttered and choked, perhaps during the act of baptism, or swaddled under thick clothes in my pram, and her body, predatory and enfolding, had loomed over me. And I sensed that Mother recognised her too. Her face was now white and cowed and her fists were clenched, the fingers digging into her palms.

Summoned by Miss Broat, Valerie appeared at the top of the stairs, clutching her dress of rags, embarrassed and incongruous in her new frock.

"Let me burn that old dress," Mother said, glad of the distraction. "It's filthy and beyond repair."

"No," said Miss Broat. "It is of great sentimental value to her mother. In its lining is sewn a remembrance—the sole reminder of Valerie's father. It is a token of love and a bond between parent and child."

Valerie handed her the bundle and, with surprising delicacy and reverence, she folded it and held it like the shrouded corpse of a beloved family pet.

My parents adopted children with a cold, missionary zeal, devoid of love, fun or affection. And like Caddy Jellyby, in *Bleak House*, who 'hated Africa', I despised the pageant of pale waifs who fidgeted and sniffed at mealtimes opposite me. Although we could afford to eat well, Mother relished the sparse utilitarian cookery of cheap cuts, without seasoning or variation. The grey, greasy food was spooned onto our plates with the same solemn ceremony as that with which Father dispensed the communion wine and wafers. Both parents lacked the courage and imagination of medieval flagellants, who mortified the flesh with thorns and whips or squatted on poles. Instead, their pale asceticism was practised by chewing and grinding mutton gristle and swallowing gobbets of pork fat. Towards me, Father maintained a distant clerical pose of intellectual and spiritual detachment. But Mother never troubled to hide her physical revulsion, shuddering if we inadvertently touched, as if she had brushed against vermin or the skin of a snake. Their indifference or disgust meant, at least, that I was left to my own devices and allowed to wander the town unsupervised.

They despised each other with an impotent fury that found release only in silence and withdrawal. They slept in separate bedrooms and maintained defined areas of the house, marking their territory with locked doors and poisonous glances. When forced together, by social convention or at table, they resembled two toothless, warring mongrels tethered to the same post, in a back yard. Their duties and responsibilities to the children they adopted were punishments to be visited upon themselves and upon me. And today, prompted by Valerie's arrival, or some bitter memory associated with the season, there was an added venom and acidity in their loathing.

I had resolved to hate and torment Valerie as I had teased and harried her predecessors. She had been allocated Grandmother's old room—far superior to mine with its cornices, Art Nouveau wallpaper, curious little recesses, oriental rugs and delicate mid-Victorian furniture. The exotic décor, beloved of the old woman, was retained despite being anathema to my parents' tastes, probably to spite me and encourage my jealousy.

Grandmother's company had been a solace and relief in my early childhood. I spent many hours in her room, hearing tales of the romance and glamour of her youth. We rarely discussed my parents, but then her fingers would toy nervously with an ugly grey scarf she used as a comfort blanket. Once, when I remarked on its dowdiness, she said, "There's a story I'll tell you about that scarf, when you're old enough to understand." But illness came and death took her before its secret was revealed. I missed her desperately and was surprised and embarrassed when Miss Broat turned to me as she left and said, 'A pity for you about the old lady—a kind woman and a brave one, too.'

My first ploy against Valerie, as I knocked on her door, feigning friendship, was a practised lie and often resulted in nightmares and bouts of bed-wetting. And I would sit up in the darkness, relishing the tears, the tired sighs, the irritated reassurances and frantic searches for clean linen and pyjamas.

"My Gran died here, in this bedroom. You can still see the outline where she lay," I said, shaping my hands, to add to the effect. "Sometimes, I think I hear her still, creeping and moaning in the night."

And without mockery or malice, Valerie heaved herself from the bed and tottered to the chair by the window, where Grandmother used to sit, miming her stick-ridden movements exactly.

"She smelled of jasmine, lavender and talcum powder, to disguise the stenches of old age and illness," she said. "There's a mustiness here, like finding a pressed flower in a book and sensing the woodland where it was picked. And there are other sensations here—fainter and more distant—of those who died in this room, long ago. But the house is very old." She shrugged as if stating the obvious, speaking without art, guile or intention to shock. And I realised for the first time that many must have died in my own bedroom, choking and retching as Grandmother had done.

Valerie saw my surprise and was quick to reassure me.

"They are barely shadows and almost impossible to see. The memories of the dead won't hurt us. But I am afraid of Miss Broat. She knows something terrible about my mother that she refuses to tell me. And I don't want to go back there. I know that at night I dream of those times before I was ill. But I wake cold and shivering and remember nothing."

She brightened, pointing out of the window at the drab vicarage grounds.

"But there are deeper secrets and enchantments than the weary dead, both in this house and its gardens and in the town. Will you help me and we can explore and unravel them together?"

To me, the vicarage was a gloomy monstrosity; a place of monotony, enforced virtue and needless privations and duties. Season followed season; bringing only the varying discomforts of intense cold or sweltering heat. But already, Valerie had revealed one of its mysteries that had eluded me in my dullness and sullen self-pity. Silently acknowledging her superiority, I welcomed her friendship and love and we became allies and confidantes. I promised to help her and hoped that together we might unlock her memory and solve the mysteries of her past. Valerie was fascinated by my own memory of Miss Broat and our shared fears of the woman strengthened the bond between us.

The lingering presence of Grandmother and the others was never mentioned again. We accepted them like the impress of footsteps, wearing down the treads on the stairs. But in time, I too became aware of her benign echo, as under Valerie's influence my heightened senses understood many of the wonders, terrors and glories of the town.

I had always been allowed to explore the vastness of the vicarage; its lumber rooms and abandoned bedrooms, where dust and cobwebs gathered on discarded furniture. It was as if to prove that by scouring every cupboard, recess and cellar, I would stifle any lingering hope of romance and colour.

When Valerie insisted that we investigate these rooms, I was sceptical. But in one of the attics was a huge battered trunk. It was not locked but had been strapped, buckled and roped with the same savage fury I recognised when Mother tied our token Christmas presents. In the past, I had made desultory attempts to unfasten its clasps but my strength was insufficient. But with Valerie's help and strong nimble fingers, we gradually released the bindings.

Inside, strewn in an untidy, creased bundle, was a collection of Mother's old clothes. But instead of the drab greys and browns she wore, like hair shirts, were elegant party frocks, ball gowns and pleated tennis skirts and blouses. Several were unwashed and it seemed that, long ago, her entire wardrobe had been gathered, discarded and buried here. We took each item out separately, shimmying and posing in front of the mirror. They still retained the traces of perfumes, sophisticated and subtle, but also the lingering fragrances of dance halls, sports pavilions and the grass of summer picnics.

At the bottom of the trunk, with scuffed corners and dislodged photographs, as if it had been hurled against the wood in anger, was a scrapbook containing the memories of my parents' marriage, before I was born. I retrieved a postcard, dated 1951, addressed to them both and read aloud.

"Dear Simon and Beth,

"Head still a spinning, spinning, spinning from the party. Caught a couple of hours sleep on the train to work. Your 'Fred and Ginger' dance at dawn—a bravura treat with the bacon, eggs and claret. Heigh-ho. Love, Binkie."

Tucked into the back of the scrapbook was an oil painting of the vicarage, signed by Mother and dated 1949. But she had embellished its bare façade with mythical creatures and flowers carved into its brick and stone. The leaves of a creeper—either imagined or long destroyed—shone with crimson, gold and russet. Father stood in the doorway, his leg curled around a pillar, smiling provocatively—a knight in a sunlit courtyard, enticing his lady. And inside the house were the outlines of couches and bedspreads, decorated with moons and stars. Its eroticism, playful and voluptuous, showed that my parents' lives had once sparkled and glowed and been touched with magic.

And there were other, more prosaic memories, indicating the variety of their social activities. Clippings from the local newspaper—a broadsheet which documented all the minutiae of the town—included Mother's numerous horticultural triumphs, with flowers and fruit, at gardening shows. There were grainy snapshots and reviews of concerts and amateur dramatics, where both had played leading roles. A photograph, headlined 'The Volleying Vicar', showed Father, youthful and exuberant, winning the town's tennis tournament. Mother's hair was rich and luxuriant—a stark contrast to the clipped pudding bowl cut she now wore.

The vitality and sense of fun in my parents' lives were unrecognisable to me as I glumly sifted through the pages with Valerie. A cruel child would have voiced the obvious reason for their fall into embittered puritanism. But Valerie was anxious to reassure me.

"When were you born?" she asked.

"December 20th, 1953," I said.

She counted back on nine fingers.

"There are no photographs of you as a baby or toddler. The last entry is March,1953—about the time your mother became pregnant. Something terrible must have happened. Something unconnected to you for you were planned and wanted."

And she proved to me that the book had been compiled with humour, delicacy and affection. For amongst the ephemera of parties and local triumphs, were intimate personal confessions, describing their hopes for starting a family. Valerie's gesture of love and conciliation towards me was typical. For in those short seven months, no unkind word passed her lips.

It was in the lumber room that I first noticed the ugly weeping sore on Valerie's thigh, which I assumed was the result of her mother's neglect. But it remained throughout her time with us—an intractable, heart-shaped wound, impervious to Mother's iodine or calamine lotion. During times of anxiety, Valerie's fingers would reach out automatically to claw and pick its surface, inflaming and festering the broken skin. Our class teacher, Miss Round, who understood my character well, suspected at first that I had deliberately scratched and infected Valerie. And only my friend's impassioned denial convinced her of my innocence.

Those early revelations about the secrets of the vicarage and my parents' past made the small pleasures and escapes I had contrived seem banal and false. On our first Saturday together, I took Valerie to the recreation ground, to meet my school friends. But there was a hollowness in our play, as we clambered over the earth mounds of Second World War air-raid shelters, their entrances sealed over. The concrete had weathered and broken and, peering into the depths, we always imagined them to be ancient barrows, hiding the bones of a king, surrounded by gold and defended by a sleeping dragon. In our adventures, princesses and knights, rogues and clowns, battled, loved and died. But like my malicious tales of Grandmother's ghost, the stories seemed flat and stale. In the gloom of the shelter, I saw only the shapes of old sticks of discarded furniture. The twitch of the dragon's tail was but the scuttling of spiders. And my friends fell into the parts assigned for them in classroom and playground, with the same taboos and pecking orders. I saw their sly, eager faces, urging me to torment and humiliate Valerie, as I had bullied her predecessors. As the game subsided into silence, the pair of us stood apart from the others.

"Look at them pouting and sulking—Tweedledum and Tweedledee," one said.

Bored with these charades, I led Valerie to the high street, enthusing on the whirl and bustle of the shops that fascinated me. In the window of a toy emporium was a huge farmyard where the colours and textures of the animals rippled like those of live beasts. Inside, the models were displayed in glass cases and I would linger as if selecting a cow or sheep with its own character and distinctive markings. And the shopkeeper would run her finger over the animal's back, as if she stroked or scratched living fur and hide. But with Valerie, I saw the identical daubs of factory paint, the plastic moulding and the maker's trademark. The displays seemed fraudulent and cheap and the patter of the shopkeeper was rehearsed, like the face of piety Father assumed when he pulled on his cassock. Valerie made me aware of the vast spaces behind the shops, the stairwells which rose to rooms of shadow, and the passages which led to strange courtyards and walled gardens.

She put her finger to her lips and, as we listened intently, whispers and muffled voices came from the depths. Some babbled in fevered excitement, as if talking in their sleep, whilst others intoned rhythmically, like monks chanting in a distant chapel as dusk fell. Naively, I asked whether they too were ghosts. But she laughed and shook her head. She told me that behind the thin facades were secret lives, vivid and intense, hiding both miracles and depravities, virtues and sins. The shopkeepers spoke quickly to ensure a sale, casting veils and shapes to fool us, for they were anxious to hurry back to their dream worlds inside.

Only once before, by accident, had I experienced that feeling of secret worlds behind the veneer of the town. The previous summer, I had visited the annual circus, alone, expecting the excitement of crowds, performing animals and the slapstick of the clowns. But I had mistaken the dates and walked through a deserted field of canvas, cages and locked caravans with their curtains drawn. Sneaking through a flap in a tented enclosure, I entered a silent arena filled with the circus horses. They stood in pairs, their tails swishing the flies from the faces of their companions. And for a moment I was part of that strange, communal intimacy of mane, bone and flesh, sharing their reveries and dreams. I slipped away, feeling an intruder, as if I had eavesdropped on a rite or ceremony of great sanctity. And as I passed the cages of the tigers and panthers there was a darkness more potent than all the contrived snarling of the ring, with the whips and sham theatre of the lion tamers. I mentioned the incident to Valerie.

"Of course," she said. "But why haven't you shown me the paths behind the orchard gate at the vicarage? There are many similar wonders and secrets to be seen there."

I was puzzled. The orchard was a dank wasteland, dotted with sheds and outbuildings that backed onto neighbouring properties. I knew of no footpaths or bridleways.

"But it was down that lane that Miss Broat brought me to you after I had been ill and forgotten everything about my past. We didn't come down the drive to the front door."

Back at the vicarage, Valerie led me through a clump of ragged bushes, to the tall privet hedge that seemingly bordered our neighbour's property. But blending into its branches were the outlines of a gate. It opened into a narrow lane lined with high fences and foliage, overhung with huge pendulous buds that even in early spring seemed charged with latent perfume and colour. The lane skirted the back gardens of our avenue of detached houses and each had its own door, the locks and bars heavily rusted and out of reach. But as we hastened past, brief images, beautiful and unattainable, were revealed through the cracks in the fences. I glimpsed a towering sculpture of a human figure, modelled from red clay or wood, the hollow sockets of its mouth and eyes, straining with ecstasy or pain. Another garden revealed a network of perilous walkways and stilted pagodas rising like shaved bone from an expanse of silver water. They were works of solitary obsession—shielded from the eyes of the town. And from the gardens we could hear the murmur of voices like a hive of bees. Some seemed half-familiar, of people that I knew well, but transformed by excitement and passion.

Eventually the path forked and I realised we had entered a labyrinth of side alleys that snaked through the heart of the entire town. Buildings were visible and I thought I recognised landmarks, but they seemed distorted and mis-shapen, as if extra rooms and balconies had been grafted on, like jewels or tumours.

"No, not that path," said Valerie. "I remember coming that way with Miss Broat, from the hospital. The trees seemed to pulse in the wind. And there was a rawness in its sound, like flesh stripped open with a razor. I saw things moving in the hedge: giant shell-like creatures of slime and mud, some with horns, and with their bones and skulls laid bare. I was wearing the only dress I can remember. It clung to my limbs like scaly, stinking skin and the things with pale, lamp-like eyes craned forward, their mouth sockets wet and drooling and their teeth clenched. We turned the corner into cold, bright sunlight. The buds were opening and dripping with dew and I knew then that all would be well."

She paused and led me down a different path.

"Miss Broat pointed me in this direction and said I might find adventures and brief happiness in one of the houses, where there is a room filled with dust and song."

Here, some of the fences were broken and it was possible to peep into the gardens. In a tumbledown stables we saw an antique fire engine, immaculately preserved and polished, its brass bells gleaming in the sun. Alongside, were two shire horses, their plumes and harness laid out ready. And for years afterwards, whenever the siren sounded throughout the town, I expected to see the fire engine roaring down the main street like some ancient carriage or chariot hauled back from past ages.

The pathways and lanes were more magical and strange than the pale flitting of the vicarage ghosts. My senses became alive and receptive and we saw deep into the souls of the townspeople as the veils and curtains hiding them were peeled back. But in some houses there was a malevolence and enticement to linger and even climb the fence to explore. One gate had a spyhole, carefully placed, so that a child could see tantalising glimpses into the garden. There, with all its booths and attractions, poised on the edge of motion, was a miniature fairground, with carousels, swings and coconut shy. A colourful wooden merry-go-round with the carved heads of elephants, horses, black panthers and camels, needed only a touch to send it swirling into life. And facing the lane was the life-sized effigy of a circus ringmaster, beckoning with his yellow finger pressed close to his face, as if he warmed his hand with his breath.

Almost hidden behind the fairground was a row of sheds. In the darkness and shadow, I could see the shapes of caged or tethered animals pacing and could smell their bodies and hear their murmurs and squeaks. Briefly, I caught the glimpse of a polecat or ferret, its body sinuous and lithe. And I desperately wanted to hold it, to stroke its fur and forever watch it coiling around the vicarage trees and darting into holes and burrows.

Before Valerie could stop me, I climbed the fence, straining to get a closer look. And the eyes of the ringmaster became sentient with recognition and understanding. His wooden body quivered a little, as if sap pulsed again in the dead timbers, and the yellow paint on his finger glistened, for it seemed his mouth had sighed in some sweet, languid reverie.

It was as if a tripwire had been sprung. The merry-go-round heaved into life and from its depths came an hypnotic waltz tune. I stared, transfixed and enchanted, as the wooden animals rose and fell. Valerie pulled me down and motioned for us to hide in one of the bushes bordering the fence. And as we waited, we knew that someone was coming, their slow footsteps lightly brushing the grass, moving rhythmically in time to the music. The fence creaked a little, as if bearing a heavy weight, and my name was called, very softly, as a sleeper speaks in their dreams. The shadows within our hiding place darkened as a head craned into the lane, tasting the air with its tongue and sniffing the leaf mould and vegetation. When the gate opened, we recognised the toyshop owner. Cradled in her arms was the ferret, its compliant body soft and rippling, like a purring cat, as she stroked the fur on its back. She whispered to the creature and I knew she was speaking of me and that she could sense us crouched in the undergrowth. Finally, with the same slow, inviting gesture as when she opened the glass cases of miniature farmyard animals, she touched the catch of her gate and was gone.

For days I dreamed of the ferret. Together, our minds moving as one, skin and fur in perfect harmony. We hunted rabbits in the hills above the town, alone amongst the grass, the trees and the dark, teeming burrows, until the moon rose and stars filled the sky. Valerie told me that the dream had been implanted to bring me back to the garden—its lure was as potent as opium. To succumb once was to be ensnared forever.

Valerie hurried me onwards down the lane, past the hidden worlds behind the main street, to an area that backed on to the detached houses of the wealthy.

Finally, attracted by the sound of a piano and a sweet melancholy voice, we came to a house that I recognised. It was washed in a pale eggshell blue—the colour of the expensive silk lingerie in the ladies' dress shop where Mother bought her crisp linens and dull flannelettes. It belonged to Miss Crick—a woman in her mid-thirties who affected Bohemianism and dabbled in art, music and theatre. She was a louche, forlorn figure in the town, her clothes frowsy and stained, and she was often the worse for drink. She reminded me of the dotty eccentrics in the 'William' stories: rich adults who are childish and self-absorbed in their hobbies and obsessions. But I found her unnerving and always crossed the road to avoid her, for in her cups she singled me out for maudlin and sentimental attention—ruffling my hair and sighing as she stared at me, mooncalfed and fatuous.

There was a wild, unkempt beauty to her garden, with a mysterious pond, its surface like a black mirror, where huge, golden fish swam. Clumps of silver grass folded and bent in the wind, like plaited skirts on a tropical dancer. And the skeleton branches of her trees overlapped and jostled into each other like the contorted limbs of lovers, gripping and embracing.

Miss Crick was visible, alone in a long drawing room, seated at the keyboard. The song was plaintive and old-fashioned but her voice was simple and melodic, untainted by the heavy, plum-pudding richness that fine singers often affect.

> "With a garland of straw, I will crown thee, my love,
> I will marry thee with a rush ring;
> Thy frozen heart will melt at my love,
> So tenderly I shall sing."

Remembering the malevolence and dangers in the garden of the fairground, I was worried that our faces peeped over the fence. But Valerie, enchanted by the voice, ignored my tugs and protestations, and even clapped loudly when the song was ended. Miss Crick saw us and approached, her mouth gaping, as if we were beings from fairyland or sprites from the surrounding woodland. She barely recognised me and spoke as if trying to recall some distant memory.

"It's many years since I walked in the lane. I thought it lost or overgrown with brambles. And sometimes I even doubted its existence. In nightmare, I remember its magic and wander lost through the garden, unable to find the gate."

And her hands fumbled blindly amongst ivy and dust and her face became petulant and on the verge of tears, as wide awake, in bright sunshine, the door again eluded her.

When Valerie opened the wooden gate, snapping the tendrils of clinging foliage and showering us with leaves, bark and resin, Miss Crick stumbled into the lane, like someone emerging into the daylight after years in a cave or pit. Valerie held her hand to steady her, for she seemed overcome with vertigo and emotion. But breathing deeply the scent of the overhanging buds and leaf mould, a shudder of pleasure rippled through her body. And she craned her neck to explore the labyrinth of paths and dream worlds, shielding her eyes from the glare of the sun. Unused to visitors, she babbled and chattered, insisting that we should come inside to hear her play. As Valerie and I passed the pond, I saw our reflections—two identical dryads, hair draped in leaves and flowers, and surrounded by reed.

There was a faded glamour to her house. Her curtains were rich and heavy but thick with dust, and their tassels were strung with cobwebs. The walls were brown with tobacco stains and the plaster on her cornices and decorated friezes was cracked and flaking. As the piano echoed, little plumes of grey powder dropped from the cherubs and goddesses, corrupting and distorting their faces. The walls were covered in a gallery of male actors in Edwardian clothes and matinée idols from the silent film era. I recognised only Rudolph Valentino, sleek and alluring, as 'The Sheikh'. They stretched back into the distance, a captive audience of the lustrous dead.

But she was a courteous host, interested in my father's welfare, and she listened wide-eyed to Valerie's account of her illness, nodding earnestly when she confided her fears of Miss Broat.

"That woman has been in my house. Many years ago, I too was sick, alone, in great pain and confined to my room. And once, she was there with me—a nurse perhaps, but stern and terrible. She passed down my garden and stared back at me from the lane, like one of those snake-haired Furies. When I was myself again, I dreaded meeting her there and avoided its paths."

We snuggled deep into her armchairs, their stuffing oozing through the fabric, dunking our stale biscuits into weak milky tea. Comfortable and relaxed, we readily agreed when she begged us to call on her again. And as an afterthought, she picked a bunch of violets, black and glistening, which she pressed into Valerie's hands.

We visited her weekly and the gift of flowers became a ritual. The daffodils and primroses of spring, the marigolds, roses and mignonettes of high summer and the melancholy chrysanthemums and Michaelmas daisies of the dark anxious days of autumn, chronicled the brief months of Valerie's time with their vitality and decay.

On our return, I expected to see the vicarage, glowering and dark in all its familiar constrictions. But the scene from the lane revealed a section of the garden, unseen from the house, whose magic I had never before realised. I viewed it as a stranger, or one returning home from years of absence, to find the landscape transformed. We saw the remains of Mother's orchard, neglected and overgrown, but with its trees in bud and shining with moisture. And the air pulsed with the flight of birds, the nests and clouds of teeming insects and the sap pumping through the trunks and branches. The gooseberry and currant bushes were rampant with suckers and a pair of bullfinches, their plumage, little flashes of red, as they perched and balanced.

Almost hidden under brambles were two statues: a classical male nude offering a bunch of grapes to his companion—a shy nymph, who glanced coyly back over her shoulder. The vegetation and weathering of the stone made them appear furtive and ashamed, as if time and old age had withered their desires.

Passing through the gate, we found a secluded arbour. Valerie pointed at its wrought-iron bench, whose tracery of flowers had turned to rust; its flakes falling like little drops of blood. And we both pictured the impress of bodies, entwined and sensuous, in the lines of its decay. For the arbour retained an intimacy of adult secrets. Once I had blundered into the shelter at the recreation ground expecting to find my friends, but I had disturbed a courting couple, their clothes dishevelled and their faces hot and pink. Giggling sheepishly, they had hurried away, but the draughty hut still held the clinging aura of their stealthy pleasures.

When the vicarage came into view, we realised it was the scene from Mother's painting. We remembered that she had added fanciful embellishments—Cupids, flowers, goddesses and leering fauns—and we tried hard to imagine them taking shape on the walls again. But the house refused to give up its old secrets. Its flowing hair, once opulent and golden, was tied and bonneted in black. But leaves and twigs, and the sap from the broken tendrils of the lane, stuck to our clothes, and the musky smell from the arbour lingered in our hair. We passed Father, self-absorbed and despondent, on the stairs. He stopped, breathed deeply and stared, as if we were strangers, or changelings, bearing rare gifts from a forbidden land.

Moved by the memory of Miss Crick's singing, we investigated the vicarage piano, which throughout my lifetime had remained locked. Together we searched through the piles of music stacked in the piano stool, hoping to find the ballad we had heard.

Valerie found the lyric in an 1883 collection entitled *Panpipes—A Book of Old Songs* by Theo Marzials. Inscribed on the title page, in Mother's handwriting, was the humorous dedication: "To the Reverend Simon Halkyn, on his ordination. A gift from a nymph, to a faun." And there, in the first illustrations by Walter Crane, were languid full-breasted sylphs or dryads, enticed by the pipes of a satyr. Every song showed pastel depictions of drowsy eroticism. Knights, shepherdesses, cavaliers and their mistresses courted and dreamed. Love prospered or turned to melancholy and death. Each page was decorated with the ornate swirling shapes of flowers, like hair drooping on a pillow. And we knew that for all the courtly formality and stylized beauty, the twisting of the foliage mimicked the writhing of limbs and the secret ecstasies of the lovers. The worn stone and brickwork of the gazebos where they whispered reminded us of the neglected arbour of the vicarage orchard—a faded afterglow of my parents' former happiness. And what sprites and ghosts entered the bowers and groves after the bright maidens and their swains had departed or been banished?

But Valerie purred with delight at her find and pressed one of the violets into the page of Miss Crick's lyric. And with each weekly visit, a new flower was added, until by autumn the book heaved with colour and perfume.

Opening a page, fragrances rose from a woman's dress or hair, and from wild garlic and hawthorn blossom came the astringent male scents of beards and leather jerkins. The figures came alive and we identified the progress of their affairs with the passage of the seasons.

We returned daily to the orchard and its arbour, for Valerie was fascinated by the gradual blossoming and flowering of the trees and bushes. And when the fruit ripened, selecting the most perfect specimens, she left them, like a votive offering to Pan, in an ornamental gilt dish on the stone sundial that was visible from Father's study. For weeks, her tributes of strawberries and raspberries were untouched, and patiently the tarnished flyblown fruit was discarded and replaced afresh. But one morning, in July, we found the dish of blackcurrants empty and stained with purple juice. The next day, we spied from her bedroom window and saw Father, like a wary town fox who is tempted at last from cover, take the dish and seek the solitude of the arbour. Thereafter, the daily ritual continued, but not a word of our shared secret passed between us. But Father's aloof manner thawed perceptibly. He would stop us, on the stairs, or in the garden, and make laboured attempts at humour. Towards Valerie, in particular, he was ponderously avuncular and the frostiness of meal times was relieved by botched conjuring tricks with coins that danced briefly across his fingers before dropping onto the table. His old triumphs from amateur dramatics were hauled from memory, as he recited long narrative poems like 'The Road to Mandalay' or the comic "Abdul Abulbul Amir'. Valerie listened politely with genuine attentiveness and interest, as he stumbled over the verses and finished lamely, the rhymes lost or blundered. But Mother remained unmoved, icy and ramrod-straight in her chair, and the line of her mouth turned paler and thinner as the monologue progressed and faltered.

※

"You might almost be twins," observed Miss Round, our class teacher, one afternoon, after watching us work together, our minds and bodies intuitive and complementary.

"Valerie's over six weeks older than me," I said. "And cleverer by far."

Miss Round dismissed my unaccustomed self-deprecation with a raised eyebrow.

"Some tribes believe the wisest and dominant twin is the second born. For it is she who sends the first out into the world, to assess the dangers and perils of birth," she said.

She paused, perhaps remembering Valerie's troubled and uncertain past.

"Forgive me, I spoke my thoughts aloud, clumsily and tactlessly. Nevertheless, I am pleased at your friendship."

She was a lumpen, ungainly woman, in her mid-fifties, who dressed in mannish tweeds and wore a cap, even indoors, to hide her alopecia. In class, she had the reputation of a tartar and strict disciplinarian. But in hindsight, I cannot remember a cruel word or deed. However, in the playground, before Valerie's arrival, we had sung:

"Granny Round, Granny Square,
Granny Oblong has no hair."

We passed her house once, in the lane and saw her dressed in a crimson ballgown that sparkled with flecks of gold. She was dancing, with an imaginary lover, to 'Begin the Beguine'. She wore a luxurious auburn wig that she flicked from side to side to the rhythm of the music. Sometimes, with a delicate mannered gesture, she grasped the hem of her dress, pouting and curtseying. There was a poignancy and elegance to her dance that belied its absurdity. We told no one of what we had witnessed. That was the unspoken etiquette of the lane. Occasionally we would glimpse people we knew, hurrying ecstatically to assignations and trysts, or seeking the solitary glories of their crazed dreams. But we never spoke. And we never betrayed their secrets.

Those days of spring, leading to high summer, were idyllic, magical times, as we investigated and wondered at the mysteries of the town. The shadows of autumn and Valerie's enforced return to the mother she could not remember seemed distant and unreal—for seven months is an eternity when you are nine years old. We hoped and pretended that her stay would be permanent. But sometimes, in the early morning, I would slip into her room before breakfast and catch her sleeping. She was always curled in a foetal position, her fists clenched and gripping the bedclothes or pillow—wracked with the dreams of her past. She seemed locked in nightmare, unable to release herself by waking or screaming. And when she finally stirred, the sound of my voice or the sunlight through the window caught her by surprise. She spoke of the return to her mother with dread, for some nameless fear lingered from the night's terrors that she could never recall. I, who had learned so much from her about my own past, longed to help unlock those memories, and I felt powerless and weak.

Mother resented our friendship and I realised that she had fed off my past jealousies and resentments towards the previous orphans, to censure, punish and forbid. When I freely shared toys or sweets, there was an angry intake of breath, for she begrudged any vestige of happiness or affection.

※

One curious stipulation that Miss Broat had insisted upon, during her first visit, was that on Sundays the pair of us would explore, by bicycle, deep into the surrounding countryside. Father had opened his mouth to protest, but she had said:

"Her time is short. She is not to endure the unmitigated drabness of your sermons."

And Father, admitting defeat, had sulked and pouted, resembling a whipped altar boy, with his pink, chubby face and straw-coloured hair.

Every week she arrived, bringing an intricate hand-drawn map and food to last the day. And there were rare delicacies—later shared—which she gave only to Valerie. I realised my role was only that of an attendant child to provide companionship—a foil for my friend's thoughts and revelations.

The remote landscapes we toured were numinous and unforgettable but their solitary magic contrasted with the strangeness of the town, which teemed with the fevered or lonely dreams of its troubled inhabitants.

On a dark autumn day of lowering clouds, we came to an ancient forest of silent, black trees. It was a woodland of intense sadness and beauty, with the soft fall of leaves like flakes of soot. High in the canopy, curling like bonfire smoke, wheeled little flocks of birds—flimsy shadows before the storm broke. And sheltering from the rain, on the fringes of the wood, we saw rows of spider webs—skeins of silver thread in a dark maze, pathless and impenetrable. There was a primeval stillness here, untouched by man, and I sensed that we were the first and last witnesses to its melancholy.

I remember a June day of brick-red heat—finding a secret heathland lake, hidden in a vast wasteland, alive with dragonflies. Once, we climbed a hill, clouds scudding above us, to the remains of a cairn, where one stone had been hollowed and was stained purple as if with the dregs of wine. The faint outline of dancers, veiled and mysterious, was scratched onto its surface.

Rarely did we glimpse another human. The exception was when we cycled down a canal towpath, secluded in the midst of an industrial landscape, where the roar of the traffic grew faint and finally disappeared, past isolated cottages, shuttered and basking in the afternoon heat. On the waterside, a group of children was playing ball and one said, pointing to us:

"Let the strange sisters join the game."

Someone beat a rhythm on a drum and a song was started.

"Queen Anne, Queen Anne, she sits in the sun,
As fair as a lily, as white as a swan.
We bring you ten letters, can you read one?
We cannot read one, unless you bring all."

As the ball was thrown and caught, the pace of the game increased to a dance. The rhymes interwove and twisted and I found myself, threading through the column, inventing lines and images that blended perfectly into the verse. Words and pictures came in an ecstatic trance of movement and imagination. I remember only that fragment.

Many years later, in my nostalgia, as an adult, I tried to find again those woods, groves, hills and lakes—the lands of my lost content. All were buried under motorways, shopping centres or housing estates. I found their echo only in Victorian maps, which hinted at their forgotten beauty—wild, secret places or country estates, sold or broken up.

It was as if Miss Broat had been greedy for Valerie to experience those pleasures and sensations, cramming a lifetime's colour and adventure into a few months. But never once did we visit the coast, with its stark cliffs and lonely storm-tossed beaches, littered with shells and sea wrack.

We called on Miss Crick every Saturday afternoon, when my parents assumed we were playing in the town. She began with a selection from Theo Marzials' *Pan Pipes*, highlighting a new song each week, which Valerie commemorated at the vicarage with her pressed flower. And then there were parlour games, charades and frantic rounds of rummy and snap; French cricket and sun-bathing on the lawn. We acted comic sketches, using the wealth of theatrical costumes she had accumulated, laughing at ourselves in outsized dresses and hats. The afternoons ended blissfully flopped on her armchairs, talking nonsense and eating too much. We did the commonplace lovely things a normal family would do, happy and relaxed in each other's company. Modern sensibilities will view Miss Crick's motives with deep suspicion. But she never hurt us, touched us or made us feel uncomfortable. And she did not drink in our presence. She was a lonely woman, ridiculous and out of place in the town, finding comfort and solace in childish things.

Only once did something uncanny happen. She had sung 'The Seeds of Love', a strange, ambiguous lyric of beauty, loss and death. In Walter Crane's illustrations, the luxurious creams and reds turn to blues and greys as the heroine wallows in the scents and colours of her loneliness. The flowers of spring displease her and only the rose is favoured.

> "I told him I'd take no care
> Till I did feel the smart
> And still did press the rose so dear
> Till the thorn did pierce my heart."

She derives a wilful pleasure in her unhappiness. There is a masochistic embracing of pain and sorrow as she enfolds herself in flowers and thorns, breathing the perfume even as the briars grip and tear her flesh. And I remembered the iron tracery in the vicarage arbour, with flakes of rust like drops of blood.

The tension and emotion of the song, as Miss Crick wrapped herself in the character of the heroine, made the atmosphere heavy and charged. To break the silence that followed, I suggested a game of hide-and-seek. Miss Crick closed her eyes and began counting.

Valerie, whose instinct was always for fresh air and open spaces, motioned me into the garden. But instead, I headed for the lure of the dark flights of stairs leading to the attics and bedrooms—places we had never been invited to explore.

By the top landing was a lumber room, filled with the discarded canvases, easels and dusty colours of her abandoned art. Her paintings were half-finished smudges—all greys, browns and greens—where nature turned to slimy decay. And the shelves and floor were covered in a chaotic accumulation of huge shells, tree trunks and roots, and the skulls and antlers of a range of creatures. It seemed like a seashore washed with the flotsam of a thousand tides, where the relics of an ancient civilisation poked through the mud when the tide withdrew. There was a stench of decayed weed and salt, as if crabs and ragworm might ooze through the floorboards to feed on the marine corruption.

In the middle of the room, like a rock surrounded by little pools of seething matter, was a dark wooden chest. Inside, like a deep mattress, were layers of old frocks and dresses, once freshened by potpourri. The perfume, heavy and narcotic, contrasted with the rankness of the exhibits. And positioned as a pillow was a blue silk cushion—the colour of the woman's dress in the illustration for 'The Seeds of Love', when passion had soured and turned to madness and pain. There was an ingrained stain, as if someone had dribbled in their sleep as they dreamed. But I pressed it to my face and it was warm and comforting, like Grandmother's bed. Here was the perfect hiding place. The lid of the chest folded over me and there was a spyhole, through which I could see only a monstrous shell and the twisted horns of a deer or antelope.

Snuggled into the cushion and breathing the scent of dried flowers, musty linen and something earthy and sweet that puzzled me, I shut my eyes and fell asleep—perhaps only for a few minutes. But when I woke it seemed like an age had passed, for the light in the room had grown darker and the horns of the antelope were grey and in shadow. My hands gripped the pillow tightly and I felt cold and numb, like an animal waking after months of hibernation.

I began to worry whether the lid had shut tight and that my hiding place would never be discovered. But then I heard Miss Crick's footsteps on the stairs. As she explored the other rooms, she was crooning 'The Seeds of Love', her voice, relaxed and melodic. But the tone became fretful and impatient as her search for me proved futile, and as she entered the lumber room her song stopped.

Several times she circled the trunk as if prolonging the game, and I remained curled and silent.

"Turn around three times, little kitten and fall asleep. Hidden in the farthest recess where no one sees," she said to herself, her voice sly and odd.

I flung the lid open and said brightly, "Here I am."

She was flustered and surprised, her expression dull and imbecilic, like Alice's White Queen.

"So you are, little puss—all tucked up tight—wrapped in silk and darkness."

And I realised that I too had dribbled into the pillow as I slept, my saliva darkening and expanding the old stain.

When school finished, at the end of July, with a party and prize-giving, I looked forward to the long holiday, anticipating weeks of adventures. But in mid-August Valerie's mood changed from exhilaration to impatience, and fear of the encroaching darkness of the nights and of inevitable autumn. Despite the heat, summer had exhausted itself. The strawberry leaves were yellow and wizened under the baking sun and the soil in the orchard was marked by cracks and fissures like crow's feet on an ageing face. Valerie grew more introspective and her insights into the characters and souls of the townspeople were dulled. She seemed ordinary and vulnerable, and to compensate I became protective and quarrelsome in her defence.

During those dog days of August, we set up a tent in the garden and spent the nights on the shrivelled grass. We slept curled together, like twins in the womb, or seeds enclosed in a pod, hands and feet interlocked. One night, as we drifted into sleep, our faces touching, I wondered whether we would share the same dreams and whether, on waking, I might penetrate the mysteries of Valerie's night terrors.

It was the end of term party and all the class were there. But it was held not at school, but in Miss Crick's house, as she smiled and gushed and dispensed prizes to every child from the old trunk I had discovered during our game of hide-and-seek. I was given a book, beautifully scented and wrapped in gauzy muslin-like paper that was almost transparent. Valerie was given a huge bunch of waxy dahlias, their dark petals of purple, indigo and crimson, intense and hypnotic. But some blooms were frost-blackened and there was a cold, unseasonal chill in the air.

As the trunk emptied and Miss Crick's hands delved deep to find the last presents, she became flustered and angry, circling the box three times.

"One of you has come here as a liar and imposter," she said. "By stealth they have planted something foul, that is alive and monstrous, to make me sick and in great pain. By back ways and covert paths they have brought the terrible secrets of their house to corrupt and bewitch my home. Tuck them up tight and straiten them. Let them be bound up and forever kept in darkness."

And I realised that, like Valerie's flowers, all of our gifts were tainted. Some girls held dolls with broken or palsied limbs, or with faces marked by scars or harelips. Worms and maggots oozed from the boxes of chocolates and cakes that had been immaculately wrapped and tied with ribbons. And the cover of my book was bruised and its colours stained my fingers, as from a moth roughly handled and vainly struggling to fly.

Finally, in shame, we were dismissed, and formed, in pairs, a long crocodile line that passed into the lane that snaked through the back gardens of the houses. We moved in slow, ceremonial progress, silent and fearful. The wonder and enchantment of the lane had been replaced by a sinister malevolence and I remembered Valerie's remark about "flesh stripped with a razor".

But one by one the gates opened and the relieved children were swallowed up by the embraces and hugs of their parents, until only the two of us remained. We shivered, partly from fear, but also from the increasing cold and the onset of darkness. Leaves and flowers fell in great swathes from the trees and we trudged through them, knee-deep, our feet floundering in their sludge and rot. Our summer frocks were flimsy and unseasonal, and Valerie clawed at the sore on her thigh until it bled down her leg. She stumbled and sank, drowning in a quicksand of petals and leaf mould. Her hand rose above the slime, but in cowardice I dared not linger to help her.

In time, the ground became more firm, for the trees were bare and snow was falling. The colours in the book I clutched seemed to be draining from the pages and leaking through the sodden wrapping, staining my frock. Ahead loomed the vicarage, unlit and funereal in the cold aftermath of Christmas. I recognised and knew well the sour and poisonous remnants of that festival, for Christmases and birthdays were drear occasions, more wakes than celebrations. But there was something especially raw and toxic about this one. Its remains had been butchered. All the tired props of hypocrisy had been discarded with a savage rage. A bedraggled tree, its trunk still clinging to its dead lights, had been wilfully torn to shreds in the yard. The dustbins overflowed with unopened or smashed presents and ripped cards.

Inside the house, the ashes of a mean little fire remained in the grate, the chill and damp of early January permeating the rooms. From the attic, I could hear Grandmother, muttering and complaining. But otherwise, the house was empty. Overcome with exhaustion, I settled down in an armchair to sleep.

But through the window I saw two figures, hand in hand, who had been following me. Their faces pressed against the glass. Valerie's eyes were shut and her mouth overflowed with blue petals and dribbles of saliva, but Miss Broat stretched out her free hand, inviting me to join them in the cold.

I felt constrained and helpless. Something was tightening around my neck and I struggled and gasped for breath. As I nearly slipped into unconsciousness, Miss Broat was in the room, her arms wide to gather me up.

But the door opened and the constriction and choking eased. I heard Grandmother's voice, angry and shocked, and I was swept up in her grip. Miss Broat acknowledged her with a slight bow. Valerie's eyes opened and rolled in disappointment and she waved forlornly before Miss Broat manhandled her, screaming, into the lane. I was carried to the warmth and comfort of Grandmother's bed. And from her waist, dangling like a noose, was the grey scarf.

The dream was a disappointment. I had hoped to conjure up the people from Valerie's past—and in particular, the shadowy figure of her mother. But she listened fascinated, trying to recall her own nightmares, as I related its events.

"I remember my leg bleeding," she said. "Something cold and metallic pressed down and burned into my thigh until all was numb. And there was a book, full of colour and perfume, like the Theo Marzials songs, but it was given to me as a present. But I dared not or could not open it. It lay under my pillow as I slept and I could hear the characters moving inside and doing terrible things, worming themselves into my dreams and dragging me, screaming, into the pages. But I have no recollection of Christmas or snow falling. I'm sure those memories belong to your past."

As summer faded and the evenings darkened, Valerie's dread of the return to her mother and the coming winter intensified. The insidious cold and damp of the vicarage seeped into her bones and she begged for the forbidden luxury of a hot-water bottle. Father relented and heated house bricks in the oven of our sooty cooker that choked and spluttered to warm the draughty bedrooms. He wrapped them in old rags and Valerie clutched and hugged them, scorching her pyjamas.

From her window, she watched the trees in horror as the greens, reds and yellows drained from the leaves until they fell and rotted. And she imagined her hair dropping in swathes onto the pillow, dead and grey. A wasp, drowsy and drunk in its death throes on a decaying apple, sent her running indoors in despair. There was something almost pagan about her rage against the darkness. One cold morning, in half-term, she coaxed Father into lighting a bonfire. She stood hunched, close to the flames, her teeth chattering, soaking up the heat, like a creature from the Stone Age in fear of perpetual ice and darkness. An old newspaper from the previous bitter winter, showing bleak street scenes, with cars half-buried under snow, seemed terrifying and alien to her. And I tried to picture the horrors and privations of her home life and the cruelties of her mother.

Only our weekly visits to Miss Crick and our cycling adventures offered a temporary respite. She pedalled furiously, as if to escape and hide in the solitary landscapes. And the flowers of autumn that she pressed into the last pages of the song book seemed elegiac and sombre.

As a diversion from the cold, I persuaded her to revisit the scrapbook we had discovered on that first day of magic and wonder. The memory of her enthusiasm and vitality seemed a lifetime away. But it was there that we found a photograph, scrunched and pulled from its hinges, of a theatrical review, dated February, 1953. Mother sat in the foreground, almost unrecognisable—playful and flirting with the camera. And in the back row, glowing and resplendent in the costume of a Victorian flower girl, was Miss Crick. Around her neck was a locket, heart-shaped and silvery. Her fingers toyed with its chain and her eyes were fixed on Father, who returned her glance with the same provocative pose that Mother had captured in her oil painting.

Valerie's tenth birthday fell on a Sunday and Miss Broat arranged to collect her at four o'clock in the afternoon. Father had written to her, against Mother's wishes, earlier in the week, enquiring about the possibility of permanent adoption. But the terse letter of refusal arrived on Saturday morning like a rejected appeal for clemency to a condemned cell, complete with its solemn clergyman conveying the bad news. And our final visit to Miss Crick was even marked by a sombre game of cards. The poor woman was distraught, almost tearful, as she picked the last bunch of flowers from her garden—the rimy dahlias my dream had predicted. At the vicarage, the last flower was pressed into the back page of the song book, glumly marked by the signature, 'Valerie Halkyn—October 1963'.

To compensate for our missed cycling expedition, Father persuaded a retired curate to lead his Sunday services and announced he would take the pair of us to the coast as a valedictory treat. It was the prelude to a day where the hopelessness and misery of Valerie's enforced departure were made more cruel by farce. Secrets and bitter resentments, nurtured and cosseted for over a decade, were exposed with a toxic mixture of vindictiveness and horrible burlesque.

It was a cold day of swirling mists, as we wheeled through mud flats and climbed a gravel path to the sea wall and surrounding cliffs. The tide was out and there was a foul smell of rotting seaweed and decaying marine creatures. Father was reinvigorated, relaxed in an old sweater and scavenging for shells amongst the wrack, holding up his more grotesque finds for Valerie's approval, his fingers slimy and covered in filth.

But, struggling to slough off ten years of sanctimony, his cheeriness was forced and clumsy. I recognised only the tired ghost of the man I'd seen in the scrapbook. And there was something surreal and nasty about the landscape. Valerie and I sheltered under a breakwater, shrinking from the vast expanse of stinking mud and the cliffs that loomed above us, shrouded in fog. Father, babbling excitedly about soil erosion and the exposure of fossils, dinosaur bones and ancient tree roots, failed to notice our unease and explored the undercliff alone. He returned, clutching some hideous relic of bone—perhaps the skeleton of a swan, thrusting it towards Valerie. Her legs buckled and she seemed overcome by vertigo, curling up in a foetal ball amongst seaweed and all the flotsam and jetsam of the beach. Jollied along by Father, pushing two bicycles whilst I steadied Valerie and my own machine, our procession limped home early, where Sunday dinner threatened us with its smells of cabbage water and mutton fat. Accustomed to our packed lunches and the delicacies provided by Miss Broat, the food stuck in our throats. And Valerie, anxious and distraught, gagged and dribbled an ooze of saliva onto her plate.

Miss Broat's knock and heavy footsteps came with the punctuality of the hangman, and she carried her own grim little bag of accessories. It contained Valerie's old dress, crumpled and unwashed. She was sent upstairs to change and emerged, close to tears, offering her frock to Mother.

"You might as well burn it," Miss Broat said. "She won't be needing it again."

She spoke without cruelty and her tone and expression held a bleak implacable honesty. As an adult, it's a face I've learned to respect, from doctors and vets who convey the worst news without sentiment or duplicity. Smiles and false reassurances are deceitful and cowardly. But any dignity about Valerie's departure was banished when we heard singing, wild and tuneless, from the direction of the orchard and its arbour.

> "My garden is now run wild;
> When I shall plant anew,
> My bed, that once was filled with thyme,
> Is now o'errun with rue."

Mother, who had been subdued and silent in Miss Broat's presence, started to her feet and sprinted to the garden. In a shambolic, gawky tangle of bodies, like the slapstick of two inept female clowns, the two women shoved and clawed their way to the house. Miss Crick was drunk, maudlin and whining and she carried the remains of a birthday cake, damaged and smeared in the tussle. Simpering with self-pity, she offered it to Valerie, whilst Father fussed and flannelled around her in embarrassment. There was a failed attempt to light the candles and the pair fawned over Valerie, pleading with her to write and visit. Miss Broat viewed the scene with stony detachment before gripping Valerie's shoulder to frogmarch her to the door. I reached inside the piano stool for the song book we had embellished with seven months of flowers. Some were already powdery and smelled of dried spices but others still retained the freshness of their perfume. Quickly, I thrust it into Valerie's hands and whispered, "I'll find you." It was an empty promise. But I meant it.

Miss Broat frowned and hesitated but permitted the gift—a last cigarette or swig of brandy from a kindly jailer to deaden the sight of the noose and the trap door. And clutching her book, Valerie was dragged away to the lane, her screams prolonged and bitter.

Too distressed to remain in my parents' company, I hurried to my room and shut the door. There was a brief altercation downstairs and I heard the door slam, and from my window, I watched Father shepherding Miss Crick to the car.

Mother's approach to my bedroom was silent and insidious. Her sudden appearance at the doorway frightened me. But she spoke coldly, honing every word to wound and humiliate.

"I hope her mother, whoever she is, locks her up and punishes her. You won't see her again. That's for sure. You are as deceitful and faithless as your father—siding with that strange, wicked girl against me to visit and consort with his whore. I caught them, together, in the arbour, all those years ago. We wanted you so much and were so happy together. But he crept from me, the milk and sweat of our bed that spawned you still on him, to be with her. I came downstairs into the garden and spied on them through the bushes. And a strand of my wet hair wrapped itself around her as they grunted and squirted, their bodies writhing and contorting on the seat. And he slunk back to me, sly and obsequious, the reek of her on him and in him. All the magic of those years turned to ash and filth by their treachery. But you're more her child than mine. The wrong one whelped and I hated you from the moment you infected me. I should have choked and smothered you. And I nearly did, little afterbirth as you are."

I accepted Mother's admission with cold resignation and a strange relief. Her loathing for me had always been obvious. Now I knew that it originated from my conception rather than anything I had done. And I felt that I could behave as badly as I wished, without guilt or regrets.

There was one more hasty adoption, to atone for the fiasco of Valerie's last day. He was a plump, nervous boy called Mervyn, Malcolm or Martin—I forget the exact name. And I bullied him cruelly. My awareness of Grandmother's presence and the vicarage's older dead, made my ghost stories real and potent. I turned those benign shadows into malignant revengeful spirits and the visions I created tormented him. I remembered the circus ringmaster and planned to lure the unsuspecting boy into the lane, speculating on the nature of the evil and its outcome. But even Miss Gates, unquestioning in her loyalty to Father's dog collar, sensed the rottenness and malaise of our household and removed the child.

Valerie's name was expunged from the class register and my former friends revelled in my distress. Only Miss Round's discretion saved me from serious trouble when I responded to one of their taunts with scratches and blows. I searched diligently at weekends in neighbouring towns and villages, pedalling my bicycle to rundown estates and hostile shopping precincts. I learned from Miss Gates that the adoptions arranged by Miss Broat were unconnected to the church, the local council or recognised orphanages. And the cottage hospital, where I had assumed Miss Broat held a position of authority, politely searched their records in vain.

Finally, I resolved to brave the path that Valerie feared after her release from the hospital, remembering, from her delirium, 'creatures that craned forward, their mouths wet and drooling'.

It passed through a derelict area of the town, of waste ground and the neglected, overgrown banks of the canal. Visible through both sides of the broken fence were abandoned ornaments and pieces of furniture. It was the time when families embraced the modern and discarded the ornate and the antique. Once, from my bedroom window, I had seen an unwanted piano, exotic with its gilded candelabra and textured panelling, strapped on the back of a lorry and destined for the scrapyard. In nightmare, I imagined its systematic destruction—the shattering of wood, the splintering of ivory and the snapping of its strings. And here, in the desolation of canal mud, piled high, were pianos and harmoniums, grandfather clocks with their hands broken or askew and their innards exposed, and Victorian fireplaces with scrolls of floral tracery in their wreck. It was a graveyard of the old and beautiful. And wedged prominently in the towering heaps were curious little bundles, some split open and rotting. I dared not look at them for it seemed that it was animal fur that peeped out. In my cold family, the simple joys and companionship of dogs, cats and rabbits were anathema. I remembered with bitterness each missed opportunity—the offers of puppies and kittens, dismissed at breakfast: one of the only times my parents were united in agreement. Each mean little bundle, in this wasteland, recalled some rejected creature from my past.

With each step, the images became more intimate and personal, and the urge to turn back seemed overwhelming. But my nerve and determination held and, finally, I came to an isolated building, austere and forbidding, like an abandoned workhouse. I passed down a tunnel of intricate fencing, like the interior of a long birdcage. It led to a network of chambers that seemed to combine mortuary, laboratory and clinic, with all the stenches and apparatus of each.

On a table, wrapped in rags, was a bundle that stank of ponds and the lonely dumping pits of the canal, with all its sins and secrets. Alongside was a pile of clay or wax that glowed and throbbed with a soft yellow light. And it seemed that hands had worked and moulded a layer of this living tissue onto the dead thing that lay shrouded in dirty cloth. An aromatic scent, like tree bark, or honeycomb fresh from the hive, contended with the ooze of filth and decay.

An open door showed a tiny room, like a hospital ward, with a single occupied bed, still and cocooned, as if in hibernation and bathed in the same yellow glow. The figure, sleeping in a hunched foetal posture and clutching a thick blanket, was a girl of my age. My first thought was that it was Valerie and I pulled aside the pillow. But the hair was dark and lank and the eyes were empty in the ashen face of some strange, inert child.

The room overlooked an unkempt garden, enclosed by a high brick wall and the overhanging balconies and cavernous chambers of the clinic. I remembered Valerie putting her finger to her lips and showing me how to listen for the secret voices and dreams of the shopkeepers. The breathing of the sleeper faded and in the stillness I heard a babble of distant murmurs and echoes as if a host gathered far beyond the wall.

And as a parent bird can locate the cries of its young on a vast expanse of beach, in a colony of noise and motion, I picked out familiar whispers.

> "Gold and silver, by her side,
> Lead her across the water,
> Give her kisses one, two, three,
> And call her a lady's daughter."

It was Valerie's voice, amongst many, by that remote canal, as the dance shifted and interwove. And I sensed her footstep, also, in the solitary forest, as she held her breath to listen to the music of skeins of spider webs, stretched and pulsing, as the branches dipped in the wind. And I heard my name called across woods, mountains and rivers, as a falcon hovered on the hillside where we had found the cairn of wine-coloured stones.

"This futile search will destroy you and consume you with longing and regret."

Miss Broat stood in the doorway. But her voice was soft and not without sympathy.

"Where is Valerie?" I asked, angry and pugnacious.

"She is with her mother. Always, she had led a sheltered and constricted life, although with an understanding and awareness of esoteric matters. You helped her gain confidence in the world and experience wonders unknown to her. You were her ideal companion. And nine years old is the perfect age—the time of both magic and mystery. It is the time I would wish to revisit myself. Together you discovered escapes and freedoms most can only dream of. But now, allow your friend her secret places and her solitude, away from the narrow and straitened world, where she was confined."

All the strange memories and dreams I had experienced about Miss Broat confused and baffled me.

"Who are you and how did you know my parents?" I asked.

"There are some things that must remain hidden about me, for the truth would break you. But I will tell you as much as I can. And I will speak candidly, for with Valerie you have explored the depravities and duplicities of the adult world.

"Your father was a fool—intoxicated with his own charm and conceit. Even in the harems of Eastern potentates, it was considered inauspicious to lay with two women, as he did. The offspring from those frenzied couplings fare badly. The women recoil and loathe their pregnancies, breathing the stale smell of their rivals, even as the children grow inside them. They react with revulsion, as your mother did. Many, as I told you, are smothered or drowned.

"Against the odds, I hoped your mother might have forgiven or laughed off your father's infidelity, for there was much love in their marriage, deep and sensuous. But it was not to be. Your grandmother fought hard for you on that bleak January evening, you barely remember. She watched over you and protected you for many years, until you grew, hard and bitter, and able to fend for yourself.

"Do not ask what happens in these rooms. If you wish, I can wipe its memory from you with a draught of forgetfulness—such Lethe water as I administer to all who lie sick here. But no, you are able to withstand such imaginings. The visions you saw in the lane are illusions to deter the curious. The animals you imagined, bundled and rejected, did not die and rot through your negligence. Valerie, too, saw her own demons and was terrified. Few can bear them as you did.

"But you are your mother's daughter—despite her protestations. You have her fault lines, as you know well. And Miss Round's powers to intervene on your behalf will not extend to adulthood. You would not wish to know me as your mother and others do, and suffer the dreams and visitations that I bring. I am a cold and implacable Fury, as someone once observed. Remain single and childless. There are solaces and consolations in that state. And therefore, I hope, for your sake, this is the last time we shall meet."

Taking my arm, she led me to the lane and, with a slight bow, bade me farewell. My return to the vicarage was uneventful, for the nightmare landscape was gone and I walked slowly through scrub and woodland.

Remembering Miss Broat's last words to me, I never visited the lane again, fearing its crazed dreams and ecstasies. But for a short while, in my late teens, I attended parties held in Miss Crick's house. Craving company as she entered middle age, she affected the fashions and habits of the late sixties, revelling in the society of people twenty years her junior. Curiosity and the persistent desire to wound and shock my parents, made us brief friends again. Through the fug of dope and acid-haunted fantasies, she would stare at me, confused and befuddled, calling me by Valerie's name. And sometimes, in the lassitude and inertia, after the drug-fuelled dreams had palled, she ventured into her garden, as if sleepwalking, to return with bunches of flowers, which she pressed into my hands. The Marzials tunes were often played to a background of guitars, bongos and muffled voices, infecting the songs and their characters with the narcotic haze of that era.

Both of my parents died in their mid-forties, when I was at college. Beneath that rigid exterior of pruderies and self-righteousness, there was a surprising brittleness and vulnerability. Left alone together, at the vicarage, they crumbled easily—to stroke and cancer. After their deaths, they seemed more alive to me, in the photographs and diary entries from the scrapbook, than in my own memories. Their lives had effectively ended when I was conceived. The old house was sold for development by the church authorities, the modern clergy shoehorned into the same anonymous estates as their absent congregation.

I never forgot Valerie and long into adulthood I hoped and expected that she would return. In hindsight, it was the determining factor that made me stay in my home town. At all the crucial moments in my life, I saw her in my dreams, not as any supernatural figure or premonition but as someone I had known and loved a long time ago, whose insights into people were wise and intuitive. Once, despite Miss Broat's warning, an affair, in my early twenties, nearly precipitated me into marriage and motherhood. But waking one morning in his flat, drowsy and contented, as he dressed quickly for work and answered the telephone, a stillness fell in the bedroom. I had dreamed of our visit to the toyshop, when the owner's mind was preoccupied with the visions and cruelties of her garden where the ringmaster waited to warm his fingers with his breath. And I understood that for all my lover's passion and eloquence, our conversations were prosaic, our gropings and fumblings routine and forced. I heard his voice, animated and transformed, and pictured the young woman who had telephoned and captivated him in ways I could never achieve. All the jealousies, infidelities and bitterness of the coming years played themselves out in dumb show, both clownish and tragic. And so, bolstered by a well-paid but undemanding job, I settled into a life of contented independence, surrounded by an ever-changing menagerie of domestic animals. The town's population expanded. New estates, drab and identical, mushroomed in the fields and waste grounds. And sometimes I speculated whether the labyrinths of paths, with all their dreams and magic, had been swallowed or disinfected.

But Miss Crick endured. Beneath her fragile veneer, with all its layers of eccentricity and weakness, was a hard centre of self-preservation and survival. When my old home, that had appeared so solid and formidable, was smashed by the builder's bulldozer, her house prospered in its dust and flaking plaster. She drifted into a faded gentility, bending and bowing with each wind. I saw her in the town from time to time and we would wave or nod, but rarely speak. As she grew older, she exuded a distressed and distinguished glamour, writing impassioned nostalgic letters to the local newspaper—quite moving in their evocation of the lost people and places of the 1940's and 1950's. She even mastered modern technology— contributing observations, photographs and reflections to the pages of Facebook. And in that unlikely setting, the early years of my parents' marriage, shining and untroubled, were viewed and remembered. I was well into my own retirement when I realised I had not seen her for several months and I heard later that she had died, comfortably, in her sleep and in her own bed.

※

I knew that the figure, confidently striding down my drive clutching a thick briefcase, was no saleswoman or religious canvasser. When her knock, firm and decisive, resounded through my bungalow, bringing my two Jack Russells to my side, growling at the door, I guessed correctly that she was a senior policewoman. She introduced herself as Detective Inspector Dresh and referred casually to the death of Miss Crick. Her manner was relaxed and informal but I saw the hidden tension in her face as she studied my reactions carefully.

"I know it's a lifetime ago, but do you remember Miss Crick from your childhood?" she asked.

"Once, I believe she was a close friend of my parents. I visited her house a few times," I replied.

"Whilst cataloguing the contents of her house, the executors of her will discovered an old trunk in an art studio. Hidden under many layers of clothing was the body of a female infant—born prematurely and aged about seven months, give or take a few days. It was wrapped in one of her old dresses—very badly stained, as you can imagine. We've dated the birth to the early 1950's—perhaps 1953—the same year that you were born. There's some doubt whether the child was stillborn or smothered—although blue fibres in the mouth, from a silk cushion, point to the latter conclusion. Sewn into the dress was a keepsake, like the remarkable things that distraught mothers hid in their child's clothing before handing them over to Coram's foundling hospital. Over time, it pressed down into the thigh of the body. It was this."

And she held up the silver, heart-shaped locket that Miss Crick had worn from the photograph of February, 1953. Opening its clasp, it revealed a miniature image of Father, together with some strands of his straw-coloured hair.

I managed to retain my composure for I dared not tell the truth to this woman. Dissembling, I feigned my shock and sympathy—oozing the same false piety my Father had perfected.

"My parents were always rather aloof and distant with each other," I said. "But this revelation surprises and saddens me."

And when Inspector Dresh asked me to provide a DNA sample to confirm the parentage of the child, I volunteered, willingly. I imagined that the interview was over and relaxed, dropping my guard. But from her briefcase, she pulled a wrapped parcel.

"The discovery of the body—sordid and tragic as it is, holds an enigma. For the child gripped this book—a gift to your father—so tightly that our pathologist had to prise the fingers apart to release it. And the last page is signed and dated 1963—ten years after the unfortunate birth. Who was Valerie Halkyn? I understand that you were an only child."

"Valerie was a foster child. We never knew her mother's identity. She took our name," I said, trying to be offhand and indifferent.

"Yes, I'm aware that your parents gave respite to a number of children— how very commendable and public-spirited, they were—through the agency of a Miss Gates. But there is no record of a Valerie."

"I think it was a Miss Broat that escorted Valerie," I said, pretending to scour my memory for her name. "But she was middle-aged or elderly. Of course, she'd be dead now, wouldn't she?"

I made the question teasing and provocative and I noticed a muscle around her mouth tighten. In her brief-case was a loose stack of files, some yellowed with age and marked with spidery, old-fashioned handwriting where the ink from fountain pens had smudged. But others were pristine, with the colours and fonts from modern printers. And I knew that Miss Broat, shadowy and elusive, moved through the pages of each one. I desperately wanted to hear the other stories, to know the secrets of those mys-terious children—their lives, their deaths and the imprint they made on those who remained to remember them. But neither of us dared to confide, to be the first to speak of wonders. Instead, she gave a disappointed smile, nasty and knowing, and said:

"The silver locket must pass into Miss Crick's estate. But the book appears to have belonged to your father and there-fore is now yours. Its contents may divert you—perhaps recalling happier times. Incidentally. my own father was very briefly the beneficiary of your parents' care. His name is Melvyn and he remembers you for your kindness."

And closing her briefcase and gathering her coat, she was gone.

Unwrapping the brown paper that masked the book, I found that it was also tightly sealed in transparent plastic. I had expected its boards to be loose and its contents faded and crumbling. However, it seemed sturdy and intact as I scissored at its coverings, anticipating the nostalgic scents and memories of the pressed flowers. But the stench that rose from its pages was rank and foetid, as if it was doused and stained with human filth and corruption.

The songs and Walter Crane's illustrations are unrecognisable. The stalks and petals have absorbed and blended into the text and pictures, transforming and distorting them into hideous caricatures of the scenes and people from my childhood. The faces of a cavalier and his young maiden grimace and scowl, as my parents had confronted each other throughout my life. Words twist, elongate and concertina—contortions of language, enunciating old curses and obscenities. The patterns of print coil and snake, or become pale shadows, like worms, slimed and white, that probe and intrude into their bodies.

A shepherdess, her features crumpled and broken, resembles Miss Crick as she flounders in the wreck of her art studio. Her face is hollow, her lips curl back and her teeth are bared, as if the image captured the agonies of her last convulsion.

And the pictures change subtly on each viewing, as the plant juices shift and flow. For page after page, they reenact and reprise their old lusts, hatreds and solitudes. The smells that emanate recall the rooms and gardens of the vicarage—the sour reek of mutton, the carbolic soap of the lavatories and the musty fall of rust, like drops of blood, from the seat in the arbour, with all their secrets, bitterness and squalor.

Curiously, the scrolled, decorated borders, where the sylphs and dryads disport, remain intact and separated from the main pictures. And it seems that the figures of my parents and Miss Crick are locked forever in their frames, where, like captives or tethered beasts, they fret and pace their cells, as day follows day.

But the last few pages, where the heavy, melancholy flowers of autumn were pressed, are a sea of abstract colours that ebb and flow, devoid of text or human deformity. And the stench of adult vices is purged, for the fragrance of the original blooms rises occasionally as a draught of wind or patch of sunlight catches the book. Only Valerie's signature and the date remain fixed.

At first, drawn morbidly to the earlier nightmare depictions of folly and corruption, I paid scant attention to any hidden mysteries, within its colours. Instead, I remembered Valerie's dream of a book lying under her pillow with the characters moving inside and doing terrible things, dragging her screaming into the pages. For days, I searched those restless and churning images, fearful that I would find her trapped, endlessly enduring her suffocation and confinement within the trunk. And gradually I understood the despair and tortured isolation of the imprisoned adults as they writhed and searched their cells. Valerie had eluded them.

The day had been sultry and hot, bringing thunder clouds and the relief of rain. I sat, with the windows open, engrossed in the Art Nouveau patterns of the book's scrolled borders, where swirls and spirals twisted like the labyrinthine paths of the lane, with all its dreams and secrets. A sudden squall blew the pages to those last sweeps of abstract colour that I had neglected.

There was a watermark glow, faint and indistinct, of trees, stretching to the distance, in that forest of primeval stillness where Valerie and I had sheltered from the storm. And from its depths came the scent of rain on fallen leaves and the wet bark that rubbed our summer clothes.

The images change with every compulsive viewing that I make. A few are the hidden places we visited by bicycle. But most are unknown to me: fragmentary scenes of people and places, beautiful and strange, as if in the long years since 1963 she has crossed seas and explored worlds and continents. And voices come, sometimes familiar, but also intoning rhymes and songs in languages that I cannot understand. The landscapes haunt my dreams and I wake, struggling to recall their shapes and echoes. And I wait, becalmed and in limbo, my body bound to the clay of this earth, impatient to know their glories.

THE ABDICATION OF THE SERPENT

TO sailors, far out at sea, the Temple appeared part of the cliff face, its columns and towers blending into rock and ocean. The honeycombed network of libraries and archives, housing the books of ritual and precise religious observances, seemed like holes for colonies of nesting birds. Even the great bronze serpent that curled around the central spire might have been mistaken for a path of golden sand that wound its way to the trees on top of the hill.

But on this spring night, the landscape appeared fluid, with swathes of gorse and grass swaying in the wind. Under moonlight, the scales on the huge statue to the deities of the water glinted silver and ultramarine. Its coloured minerals, glass and gemstones had been fashioned to give elusive glimpses of light—like giant fish seen in deep water from a crow's nest high on the mast. The statue's eyes were hooded and shaded from view, like those of a crustacean. From under its lids, it peeped out, following the night wanderings of a thing, furtive and timid. First, it had sought shelter and solace in the rock pools, where molluscs pulsed on the stones and seaweed covered its fear. Fleeing landward, it lingered too long, weakening itself, in the Street of the Glassblowers, where the front doors of the shops comprised dazzling mosaics of thick, coloured glass, individually crafted to form whirls, bull's-eyes and spirals. It never dared to venture into the Quadrangle of the Artists, where boisterous shouts, music and the glare of torches extended into the small hours under the auspices of the Styrax family—the arbiters of religious art for generations. Always, soothed by the lazy smell of old incense and the coconut scent of the gorse, it drifted towards the Temple. And like a huge moth, its wings flattened and camouflaged against the darkness of the ivy, it rested outside the sleeping quarters of Porzano, the High Priest. Fastened to the stone, it seemed to attune itself to his dreams, whispering of snakes, old orchards, the brightness of birds and secret passages that were lost under cloister, nave and choir.

Porzano had served in the Temple for over forty years and on his election to High Priest, three years ago, had looked forward to the privilege of climbing the stone stairs in the Tower of Sapphires to light the night beacon and sing the designated hymns to the changing constellations. But instead of savouring each moment and relishing the sound of his voice, enunciating every syllable as it echoed in the chamber, he found himself hurrying the words, longing for the task to be over. The ritual and order that he loved seemed stale. He laboured up the steps worn down by the tread of dead predecessors, to chant the plodding progress of the night sky. It seemed that he mouthed prayers to mere algebra and calculus, as school children learn to chant their tables by rote.

And yet, whereas the established routines had palled, he found that the Temple had the power to surprise and delight him, in opening up its hidden ways and secrets. It was as if the buildings were mischievous and deliberately diverting him from his duties. At night, the ivy outside his bedroom window trembled and rustled and he fell asleep immediately. He woke with curiosity and restlessness, knowing that in his dreams, he had visited uncharted corridors and chambers deep within the Temple. A companion walked beside him, their voice soft and measured, explaining the lives and histories of forgotten inhabitants: priests, musicians and artists. But when he woke, he could remember nothing—only the feeling that he had witnessed wonders. He did not even know if his guide had been man, woman, bird or animal. Often, he dreamed that in the recesses of the archives, he had located a document, intrinsic to the founding of the Temple, that unlocked the language and codes of plants, animals, insects and the surrounding landscape. As he carried it to his room, the manuscript cracked. Folds and fissures began to form; the inks smudged and ran. Trying to gather the pages as they slipped from his hands, they broke and flaked into dust. He woke, his fingers clawing at the pillow to retrieve the imaginary fragments.

Spurred on by these tantalizing glimpses, he resolved to explore and map the Temple's neglected cloisters, derelict lands and underground passages. He was rewarded with many unexpected pleasures from the natural world and the history of the site. A heavy oak door, locked for a century, opened onto an abandoned orchard, with vast hedges and rampant fruit trees. And for a whole morning in June, he had watched fascinated as a brood of five red-backed shrike fledglings were encouraged by their mother to hunt the large beetles that clambered in the high grass. It amused him that the adult bird had heard and mimicked the choir practising at vespers for the Temple's feast of the summer solstice. Even their errors and false starts had been remembered and imitated.

The orchard became a favourite retreat from his duties and a place where he sat alone, watching the passage of the seasons. One winter day, studying a landscape bare of leaves and foliage, he was intrigued by a loose barrier of bricks and stone that, when uncovered, led to a subterranean passage. There, he discovered the old chambers and living quarters of the nuns and monks, before the current bedrooms were built, five hundred years ago. The tiny cells were intact, their sparse furnishings and ornaments fresh and vibrant, as if the inhabitants were about to return from breakfast. And the walls had been painted and illuminated, according to the tastes and religious passions of each resident, with birds, flowers and landscapes. Here, he found lost minor deities of woodland orchids, tiny mountain springs and curiosities of weather whose beauty had endured for a day and faded. Each was depicted with diligence and awe. And there was humour too. The resident of each room had been caricatured by a cartoonist of some skill. Their most prominent traits and eccentricities had been lampooned with affection. A nickname identified each one: Miss Wiggletoes, Hogsnorer, Corker, Lord Flutebottom, Redlegs, Dogspit and the Lobster. The artist had signed herself as Slyfingers and it was in her room that he found a bottle of pale rose liquor, with a message, consciously ornate, each letter coloured and embellished with spikes and distortions. It had been left on the day that they departed to their new rooms.

"For an unknown guest—
from those who are now dust and soot,
under tree and stone."

To honour them, he brought the bottle to supper, to share with the High Priestess and other senior clerics. It was sour and stale but did not make them ill. But briefly, in the aftertaste, was the hint of a summer five hundred years ago. He dreamed of them that night: their devotions, their art and their bad jokes. And he wondered what end they had made and what age their bodies had been burned on the pyres of yew wood, scented with oils and flower petals.

There were other successes. In a cellar, beneath the nave, he found a cache of antique musical instruments, manuscripts and drawings. Some had been gnawed by the little rodents—a cross between mice and hamsters—that were unique to the area. But the Temple craftsmen were able to reconstruct them and dances, forgotten for hundreds of years, were performed again.

His discoveries proved so fruitful that he contemplated a book entitled *Voices from the Old Temple*. It would be his legacy and ensure his fame and reputation beyond the performance of mere ritual. He pictured it on the most prominent shelf of the priests' library, alongside such classics as *Theories on the Wolf Carvings in the Idesian Hills* by Cotinus and *Cynic or Visionary: the Stone Sonnets of Bubulcus* by Nuphar.

Its composition filled the quiet night hours of his leisure and he sat up late, writing in a notebook, honing the phrases and priding himself on the music of his prose.

Always, he woke feeling that there were discoveries that he had missed. In his dreams, he felt prompted to more energetic searches and chivvied if he dithered too long, as if his unseen companion grew impatient. And one morning he found that he had risen in the night and scribbled in his book.

"Eyes still gaze, their stare unbroken,
Where fumes of nightshade linger still.
Strange serpents weave, in dream encumbered,
Where web and hemlock sigh as one."

The references to narcotics reminded him that at the end of the old residents' quarters was a chamber, wedged shut, that he had disregarded in the excitement of finding the cartoons and bottle. Weighing up its function, he judged that it might be a medical room or sick bay. Here might be a treasure more remarkable than any he had yet uncovered. In an anatomical treatise was a footnote hinting that long ago, snake venom was gently squeezed from the vipers that inhabited the rocks around the Temple's foundations, to treat epilepsy and the tremors of senility. It suggested that the doctors had the ability, through the timbre of their voices, to handle the snakes without being bitten. It further speculated that these practices were part of a lost canon of knowledge relating to communication, in both speech and thought, with the natural world.

The underground rooms were his secret and, absenting himself from his duties with an excuse about his arthritis, he worked with chisel and hammer to prise away the door. As he hacked an opening, scented wafts of herbs and tinctures encouraged him. He imagined himself leafing through the medical texts, uncovering wonders.

Finally breaking through, he found his conjectures about the room's purpose were correct. A few empty bottles of commonplace medicines remained, surrounding a plain bed for the sick. But wedged in the corner of the room was something that punctured all his daydreams. Its banality and squalor destroyed his childish vanities of historical research and literary glory. It was the remains of a young woman. Her neck had been broken.

The external wall of red rock had cracked and its fluid crumbling dust had leaked into the chamber and onto the corpse. The room had the atmosphere of stone—part of the cliff face itself—perhaps ensuring that the body remained uncorrupted. Pale and cobwebby, she stared at him reproachfully, as if he'd dallied and was late for a lovers' tryst. And he realised that he'd been duped and led here like a pig whose task was to root for buried truffles. The honeycomb nature of the rock, with its holes and channels, was a familiar nesting place for the vipers. Several had squeezed into the room. There was nothing predatory or malign about them. He had the absurd idea that they had been guarding the body prior to his arrival. Having recognized his authority, they made a stately retreat to their holes.

Cobwebs draped the room, like dark, floral robes, heavy with the dust of the rock and with a thick overpowering perfume. He recognized the smell and an amulet around her neck confirmed that she belonged to the Dwale—the exclusive order of Temple courtesans. Her clothes were patterned with the purple, white and yellow flowers of the varieties of nightshade, indicating the order's skill in the use of the herbs both to enhance their attraction and to intensify the visions and pleasures of their clients. The young men and women of the Dwale were as revered and honoured as the priests and artists of the Temple. Many argued that their status was greater as they represented the transience and mutability of human beauty. They were permitted to retire at the age of twenty-five, with a generous lifetime annuity. Known for their serenity and wisdom, they were sought after as marriage partners, although most chose to remain single. A date mark on the amulet indicated that she had been dead for forty years.

Amongst the detritus of dust and the husks of insects, were tiny scraps of thick paper or card, marked with black or red ink. A closer inspection suggested that once they had formed a drawing that had been scrunched and ripped in anger. Meticulously, he gathered them up and placed them in a leather satchel.

The murder, from its occurrence to its discovery, encompassed his years at the Temple, from novice to High Priest. It soured and negated everything he had worked for and made empty all the obeisances and devotions. His tenure of office would be remembered and scarred by this single dishonour.

Of course, there had been quarrels and jealousies that simmered within the cloisters. Furious disputes raged over spiritual and liturgical doctrine and the resultant bitterness and sulking often lasted years. Blows had been struck. Once, the north wing had accepted the gift of a sun bear from a traveller in the east, and kept the creature as a totem. It had plundered the bee hives, outraging the priests who devoted their worship to the insect gods. The two factions had brawled openly in the quadrangles, wielding their ceremonial staves as weapons, inflicting broken bones and concussions. But never since the early years of the Temple's foundation had there been a crime so secret and wicked, committed within its walls, as this sordid murder. It would be lazy and hypocritical to assume that the culprit was an outsider—a pilgrim to the site—perhaps a rich sea captain or merchant, intoxicated and driven wild by the potency of the nightshades. No stranger had the knowledge of and access to these remote underground chambers.

He located her portrait in the galleries devoted to the Dwale. Her name was Myrica. No artist was accounted fit to undertake sacred work unless they had first captured the beauty and spirit of the courtesans. Some priests, both men and women, became dangerously addicted to studying these images, shunning the warmth and perfumes of the living. Theirs was a febrile nostalgia for the ivory pallor of the nubile dead. Their fishlike presence infested the galleries until they pined away or succumbed to self-slaughter. Studying her face, with its pert, aloof eroticism, he tried to recall his own youthful debauches. But the memories were blurred by nightshade, strong drink and the twilight atmosphere of the Dwale, where candlelight made everything shadowy and equivocal. Perhaps he had lain with her in those years. He did not know.

He almost hoped that her parents were dead for it would have spared him the duty of breaking the news. But he found them, frail and stick-ridden, in the Street of the Glassblowers. As they welcomed him, he noticed the same bone structure of the dead girl, through the parchment-like skin of the dying mother.

Their respect for his status embarrassed and shamed him. They had not reported their daughter missing as they had assumed she had committed some sacrilege against the Temple and been banished. When he asked of her character they fetched, almost apologetically, a thick portfolio. It contained a bundle of juvenile sketches, in charcoal, together with more mature paintings. The quality and imagination of the work amazed him. It comprised a mythological flora of the native shrubs and trees, highlighting aspects of the divine in each leaf, branch and root, that more esteemed artists had neglected. And dotted around the room were thimble-sized offcuts of the unique rose-red stone, used for the carving of the deities. Its scarcity meant that only the most established Temple sculptors were given free access to the mined rock. Wealthy amateurs, dilettantes and dabblers paid exorbitant prices at the quarry face.

"Myrica chose to seek service in the Dwale to earn the pension at the age of twenty-five to buy the red stone," her father said.

Each piece was a perfect miniature: the filaments of an ivy leaf, a single cat's claw, a yellow and black beetle—the colours enamelled so that the pink rock shimmered and glowed with a ghost echo.

The stone was notoriously difficult to master. It was predominately pink and fleshy but with coloured layers, some of a spongy, almost blood-like constituency. Other sections were hard and dry. When hammered, they produced slivers of sharp needles that broke into crimson dust. Moulded by a great artist, it could become luminescent, or resemble the textures and tints of the human body. The sculptor needed an instinctive, versatile touch, both the hands of a surgeon, manipulating delicate veins and sinews, and also the strength of a blacksmith, to smash the more intractable segments.

All the major statues were currently undertaken by the twins of the Styrax family. The pair functioned as a single unit but with contrasting skills. Calluna, with her huge fists and muscles like whipcord, carved the frame. Crinum was a subtle colourist, who breathed life and detail into the raw stone, manipulating glass and jewels to blend with his brushwork. On large structures, the twins seemed embedded into the rock, like two climbers straddling and embracing a cliff face. Crinum also worked on the friezes and smaller icons that adorned the churches. They were the same age as the High Priest and for two generations their work had epitomized the soul of the Temple, as their ancestors' art permeated the history of the site.

"My daughter used to watch the artists at work from this window," the old man said. "Rock hackers and paint throwers, she called them. She described the style of the recent statues and friezes as eyebrow dancing—tricksy and false."

The window was small, its green glass corkscrewing like a peppermint humbug. It looked into the distant Quadrangle of the Artists and gave magnified views that were distorted and broken. He saw a flurry of nuns in the rich livery of the peacock worshippers. They had been buying brushes and paints. Their images fragmented, as if they had been badly assembled using wires and shiny marbles. Bits of body lagged behind and then rejoined the rest, only to dissolve again in a rainbow shower of light and colour. Other figures, gathered around the ornamental pond, flickered like human insects, dragonflies capering and dancing over a lake. Finally, he spotted the Styrax twins. They were known in the Temple for their grace and elegance. Dance partners said that Crinum glided across the dark varnished floor like a swan on a black lake. But through the sly trickery of the green window, they moved like a goose and gander out of water: clumsy and gawky. And there was a pomposity in their waddle, a brooding temper tantrum, as if they were about to peck at the legs of strangers who neglected to give way. As the glass mocked and played with them, their faces changed colour from the purple of raw meat to the sickly blue of apoplexy or a choking fit.

In the bitter satire of the window, the High Priest recognized the age old hostility and resentment of the glass workers, who felt that their own skills were undervalued by the Temple hierarchy. He remembered Crinum's aside when he heard of their complaints.

"The Glassblowers are but artisans and labourers, at best. They are the pencil sharpeners and glue boilers for the sculptors and poets."

Requesting their silence, on the pretext that he could investigate covertly, he assured the old couple that he would work to expose the truth of their daughter's death. His motives were equivocal, for he knew that his authority and reputation would be undermined if news of the murder were circulated.

He confided only in Caltha, the High Priestess, a practical, hearty woman of his age, with an earthy sense of humour, whose jokes and innuendos at table made him giggle and splutter his food. For two days, gravely and meticulously, they consulted old lore and documents for advice. But there was no precedent for this treason. Their only guidance came from an incident, three hundred years ago, when a vintner was found dead at the gates of the Temple. The priests had speculated and aired their suspicions on the cause of his death. It was ruled that the body should be burned, together with the seasonal flowers, shells, soil and leaf detritus of the surrounding landscape. Only when the corpse was entirely consumed by the flames were they satisfied that its spirit did not linger in malice and revenge.

It was early summer and the shingle banks were bright with the pink sea thrift that filled the shoreline. Together, they gathered the blooms in sacks, their fingers often snatching at air as the flowers billowed and drifted from their grasp. Their joints stiff and aching, they stooped and groped in the rocks at low tide to collect the fallen petals.

"We are chasing clouds," Caltha said. "Like two old paupers scavenging for flotsam in the mud."

In the dead of night, they constructed the funeral pyre, the shape of the body appearing absurdly pretty and winsome, like a giant iced sponge cake, under its canopy of pink blossoms. The intensity of the heat would have consumed a herd of oxen. The flesh burned quickly but the bones, white as milk in the candlelight, and the sticky residue of rock, seeped together. Both of them knew that the spirit lingered, bound to the Temple and its surrounding streets. With his hands, he collected the remains. His body shook and the smaller bones slipped through his fingers, like pearls, to drop on the stone floor. Finally, they carried her to a fissure in the cliff, a place sacred to the presiding serpents, and watched as the little heap dropped into the rock.

✳

The murder, the visit to the old couple and the failed atonement of the funeral pyre, challenged his faith in the Temple. It felt like a sin of blasphemy to question the beauty and sanctity of the art but the girl's remarks seemed accurate. The recent statues, lining the cloisters, appeared contrived and flyblown, depicting muscle-bound heroes and blowsy goddesses. The frescoes which illustrated man's place in the cosmos, reminded him of the faces of the nuns and monks he knew, smug and contented, who had sprinted to the refectory to bag the best seat at table, to grab the first helping of mushroom and dumpling stew. Ritual seemed tired and forced. It was lip service and a lip music, profane and vulgar, blowing raspberries to the moon and stars.

His entire life had been spent under the auspices of the Temple. But always he had sought out travellers and listened to their tales of other divinities and mythologies in distant lands. His mind was open and generous. In one country, the landscape had been flat and neutral, a bland wilderness of sand stretching to infinity. But beings had come—animals, plants and humans—creating and destroying, to form rivers, forests and mountains, filling them with life and colour. From another land, he learned that the stars were sentient and carnal, seeking brides and husbands. The evening star fell in love with the lynx, whose leap into the air was so fiery and mercurial it seemed to command sunlight and twist gold and crimson to its own will.

An explorer, made mellow and expansive after lovemaking in the twilight haze of the Dwale, told him of his sense of awe in the bleak tundra he had visited. Travelling alone, without sight of humans, for three days, he noticed strange symbols that were visible only by moonlight, carved on rocks and earth. Following their track, he came at last to a lake, still and watchful. On its shores, under a towering cliff, were caves, extending deep into a mountain. Similar runes had been hacked over the entrances. He did not know whether they were warnings, invitations or the final messages from a dying civilisation. His courage failed and he retraced his steps, always regretting his cowardice and dreaming of what he had missed.

These religious variants had moved him and he'd asked about the majesty of their temples and whether their archives matched the learning of his own library. And the travellers had smiled gently at his naivety, explaining that there were no buildings and no written languages. The stories, they said, seeped into the inhabitants from the landscape, the animals and the cosmos.

As these merchants and sea captains departed, he watched from the shore as their sails disappeared over the horizon. Vicariously, he shared their adventures, delighting in the diversity and truth of the stories. But he had never been jealous of them. Now, as he climbed the Tower of Sapphires and watched the lights on the ships fade into the distance, he felt parochial and insular. And he trudged down the moonlit stair to his rooms, feeling that he entered a cramped cell that he had knowingly built for himself. His books and his ritual were but diversions to pass the long hours and nights.

✳

He was sure that the torn scraps of paper, found at the scene of her death, were significant. They matched the colours and brushwork of the illustrations from her portfolio. He spent hours piecing them together, trying to recreate the original image. But the tiny fragments were mottled with mould and stains of red dust, which seeped into the lines of the drawing. He fabricated eyes and faces, sometimes whole bodies, deceiving himself that the picture was forming. They seemed like the broken limbs of sculptures, riddled with the holes of insects or vermin, making the stone corrode and flake. They toppled into each other, in obscene couplings and embraces: a copulation of rotting rock and dying statue. But always, the secret of the young woman's art eluded him. The scenes he had created both disturbed and unsettled him. But he knew they were but hints of something worse: a nightmare of charcoal and shadow, moonlight and marble.

At night, he battled against sleep, judging it slothful when faced with his crisis. He became conscious of sounds that once he had blocked out or disregarded. The sea roared, echoing in the caves and channels under the Temple that the tide and decay had fashioned over the centuries. With each storm, the predations of weather and subsidence grew. He could hear the small rodents burrowing further into the crevices and foundations. Their colonies were breeding and quarrelling, growing inexorably.

Despite his resolution to keep awake, the soft nightshade whispers from the ivy soothed him to sleep. He was rewarded with dreams of spectacular beauty and ecstasy. He strode on the cliff path or on the beach, his old limbs and lungs rejuvenated. He felt he had the energy of the gymnasts who entertained in the Courtyard of the

Tumblers and Acrobats. With great clarity of vision, his eyes adjusted to view distant objects in precise detail. It was as if he peered through the peppermint witchcraft of the telescopes in the Street of the Glassblowers. He saw caterpillars gnawing the leaves high in the foliage of oak trees; the scurrying of mice and voles in the fields and the quiver on a kestrel's wings, as it hunted, hovering in the air. In the cliff, he discerned the outline of bone and fossil, each ancient feather and scale illuminated in stone. And once, standing on the shoreline, with the waves lapping at his feet, he heard a voice, soft and enticing.

"And here, by this shingle,
Between the ocean and the sand,
In the turmoil of shell, mud and weed,
Stone crumbles and breaks into flesh."

He woke, remembering every detail, knowing that he had been allowed these visions as the successful pig is handed an apple for digging out the truffles. But the verse troubled him. It suggested some foreknowledge or deceit concerning the most popular festival in the Temple's calendar.

Despite the pantheistic nature of the Temple's worship, with its almost infinite and expanding roll of minor deities, the most anticipated ceremony celebrated the creation of humanity. Believed to be born from storm clouds, as thunder and lightning animated the churning mud, salt, shells and carcases of sea creatures in a river estuary, the first person was represented by a statue, set high in the cliffs, overlooking the ocean.

On a hot July morning, Porzano led the opening procession of senior clerics, as they mimicked the ascent of a giant serpent. Every sinuous twist and deviation of the column was choreographed and rehearsed, their robes and headdresses coordinated for the green, yellow and black markings of the viper. As the tongue of the reptile, he made passes with his stave at significant rocks and bushes on the path—a shaman, summoning the magic of the stone. The crowd below roared their admiration. They did not see the retinue of helpers, guides and robe carriers who sweated and scurried beneath the heavy cloth of the priests. Many could scarcely walk unaided to supper, let alone climb a steep rocky path. Sticks, wheelchairs and walking frames were hidden from view. There were several falls and stumbles and a few had to be hoisted on the shoulders of muscular aides. It was a carnival parade of the infirm. He expected a keen observer to spot the absurdity, hoot with derision and the ritual to collapse forever. But today, the illusion was maintained.

As the musicians, singers and dancers gathered, he observed the statue coldly, through a telescope. Nearly a thousand years old, it had not weathered well. Bird lime had corroded the pink rock and its face appeared pocked with blotches and scabs. The hollow eyes gaped inanely. It reminded him of the empty faces of the senile priests in the infirmary, whose bodies leaked, stank and squirted. It perched on its pedestal of rock as they squatted on the heavy wooden commodes. It seemed to embody the sloth and atrophy he had noticed recently—an inertia of spirit, soul and sanctity. Alongside it, the statue of the Insect God shimmered in the heat. Its amorphous nature suggested, by turns, a swirl of bees, the bright sparkle of beetles or, at night, the cold, dark beauty of a moth colony. At its right, stood the grandeur of the God of the Sea Creatures.

Wealthy pilgrims and observers from foreign lands added gold to the coffers of the Temple for the privilege of observing the ceremony. The rooms of the Dwale were heavy with the scent of the nightshades, long into the small hours, as the courtesans satisfied the heightened lusts of visitors, artists and the younger, more nubile, clerics.

In spite of his cynicism, the power of the spectacle drew him in. It began with a single drum, reverberating in the Cave of the Musicians. Gradually, other percussion instruments were added until a primal throb, like a collective heartbeat, pounded. The bass voices of the men were answered by the rising skirl of the women. The musicians and choirs, hundreds strong, affected the listeners physically. In past years, some had been moved to such ecstasies by the pulsing beat that they claimed the statue itself had become animated, its muscles moving or its eyes filled with tears of emotion.

The heavy back beat lodged in the core of his solar plexus, like a hammer blow, whilst the higher notes made his spirit soar. The sound echoed around the arena, filling it with a shared warmth and joy. His body shook with pleasure as he watched the communal dance of townspeople, temple dwellers and the rich merchant women and high ranking soldiery from overseas. The doubts about his faith and the spiritual health of the Temple were dispelled.

Groups in the crowd were pointing at the statue, cheering and yelling that it had come to life. Trembling, he located his telescope. The stone twitched and convulsed, its facial expression contorting. It seemed to gape or yawn, a pantaloon woken from an afternoon nap by a sudden noise or a playful tickle from a cheeky grandchild. Taking in the landscape and the crowds, it acquired a dignity and resolution. Its last act was to twist irritably on its plinth, causing the surrounding cliffs to shake and rumble. Its fall was a humiliation, for it dropped like an old man toppling from his commode, still straining and labouring. Rocks and gravel followed it like a shower of its own dung and diarrhoea. It broke on the jagged cliffs below and mixed with the sea water in a mocking parody of the myth of its creation. It oozed a thick, coagulated blood, a sickly body fluid, diseased and distempered with senility.

※

The qualities that had enabled Porzano to rise through the ranks of the priesthood clicked into place. He addressed the assembled worshippers, who fell silent when he raised his arm. He spoke of the mutability of rock imitating the mortality of man. It was a brief speech, politic and soothing. The festivities resumed.

But he knew that the statue's fall was linked to the body he had found. The jigsaw of torn scraps of paper continued to elude him and he believed himself to be teased and goaded by the confused images. The sanctity of the cliff face had been desecrated. The rock seemed to bleed—the red gap in the line of statues like a missing tooth punched out in anger. It would have to be replaced in time for next year's ceremony.

He consulted with the High Priestess on the subject for the new sculpture, the treason of the murder foremost in their consideration. They chose an incident from the birth of the modern Temple that defined its principles and ethos. Over a thousand years ago, the original clergy had ruled the neighbouring townships with fear. Sacrifices were required of the most beautiful youths and young women, to placate the giant serpent or dragon that inhabited the hill. For two generations, parents were compelled to deliver their children to an appointed door. It opened and the young disappeared forever. One couple rebelled and resolved to confront the snake, barging through the gate with concealed swords. There was no dragon or giant reptile. Instead, they encountered a cabal of priests, corrupt and depraved. Grown old and wicked with power and status, they preyed on the youths. A swift and bloody revenge was exacted. But the benign serpent, native to the rock, was exonerated. It became the symbol of the Temple's enlightenment. The new statue would depict that original couple, who stood against murder, secret and treacherous. And despite his reservations about the art of the Styrax twins, they, as the most accomplished and acknowledged artists, were assigned the commission.

On the cliff face, the two deities of sea and insects straddled the chasm in the rock where the statue to humanity had stood for one thousand years. Sunlight flickered on their glass and gemstones and the pair seemed to be breathing in harmony, sharing the dreams and reveries of damselflies, water fleas and sand beetles.

Their tongues had tasted the black smoke from the sorry little funeral pyre and they had seen the heap of congealed rock and bone as it was cast into the hill. Wind stirred it and rainwater carried it deep into the cliff. There, snakes guided it through the caves and channels under the Temple, where sea and storm encroached. It rested finally in the quarries of the sculptors, its fragments blending into the blood-red stone.

The pair had watched the preparations for the Creation ceremony with amused cynicism, for their companion had been locked in comatose slumber for three centuries. As the choirs assembled, a shadow touched his rotting stone. Perched on his leg was the forlorn spirit who had scuttled from bolthole to sanctuary and battened on the walls of the High Priest. Her powers and confidence were rising. She sang and whispered to the statue and, remembering her wiles from the Dwale, caressed his ulcered thigh. And her voice and touch roused him, stirring old blood to course again through diseased channels in his rock. He babbled of the days of his pomp, the water dribbling from his lips as his tongue trembled. There was one last moment of coherence, a searing memory of what he once was and a final spasm as he flung himself from the rock, exhaling relief at his oblivion. Her work done, the creature acknowledged them both and departed.

For over forty years, she had whispered and pleaded, trying to insinuate herself into the dreams of the High Priests. All had been deaf to her arts. Lampranthus thought only of the young men from the Dwale, smiling in his sleep, as his fingers stroked their thighs. Amerula worried herself to an early grave, obsessing over spurious hierarchies of the soul in birds and insects. Gentle Isatia loved only the poetry and music of the litanies, whilst Picrasma, the grey celibate, devoted all his time to the colonies of wasps and hornets. Only Porzano, with his cat-like curiosity and willingness to follow his whiskers into unknown areas of the Temple, had been susceptible.

A month after the fall of the statue, they observed her again, when the drey horses sweated and heaved the mountainous lump of rock from the quarries to the Quadrangle of the Artists. She sat astride the head of the unformed statue like a general entering a broken city after a prolonged siege. It was a triumphal progress and her gaze lingered long on the thriving workshops and galleries. Finally, her shadow passed down the stone and entered the studios of the Styrax twins.

Calluna Styrax was enjoying a lunch of hard-boiled goose eggs and rough rye bread when a servant brought the news that the stone was being delivered. Wiping stray pieces of shell from her fingers and brushing yolk from her mouth, she quickly supervised the unloading, matching and surpassing the obscenities of the carters and quarrymen. When the statue had fallen, she had been with her brother, Crinum. The pair had purred with hubris and joy even before it had smashed on the rocks below. The distinction of undertaking a sculpture for the pedestal overlooking the sea, occurred perhaps once in five hundred years. Their names would be honoured in the same pantheon as the great artists of antiquity.

At formal religious and social ceremonies, she mustered a stateliness, like a weather-beaten flagship of the fleet. But at home, she was dishevelled and unkempt. Clothes flopped loosely around her huge frame and her long thick hair was rarely washed. Her mother had described her appearance as 'a turkey cock, surprised by thunder'. A solitary child, ungainly and socially awkward, she sought solace in the hidden areas of the Temple, where she delved and explored. Aged twelve, she discovered the secret of the old residents' quarters. And by her late teenage years, she had uncovered enough forgotten outposts of the buildings to have thrice written Porzano's *Voices from the Old Temple*.

By contrast, Crinum was a dandy and wit. An habitué of the Dwale, he spent many silver merulas on expensive philtres and powders to maintain his flagging virility. When the stone arrived, he was finishing a portrait of a rich merchant's daughter and contemplating her seduction.

The twins' skills complemented each other. Calluna's strength and prowess in hewing the raw stone gave the statues a sense of majesty and awe. Crinum had learned from his father the knack of crowd-pleasing. His lines and careful combinations of colour exploited a sentimental popularist taste. Myrica had seen the deception from her window in the Street of the Glassblowers. His art resembled the slobbery public embraces common to the Quadrangle. In the galleries and exhibitions, artist and viewer sighed and simpered, congratulating each other on their taste and erudition.

The twins shared a genuine affection. They kept separate houses but socialized in a communal set of rooms. Together, they were a powerful force, a phalanx that guarded all sides, anticipating trouble and uniting against criticism and enemies. But Calluna was sharper and more astute, with an almost instinctive awareness of danger.

It was the largest chunk of rock she had ever attempted to work, a slab of raw cliff face that towered over her apartments, obstructing the light from her windows. By day it loomed, red and formidable. But on the first night, she felt hemmed in, as if encased in stone. A crimson glow leaked in, a contagion of moonlight filtered through the wounds in the rock where the quarrymen had hacked it free.

She fell asleep disorientated, the familiar night shadows of the Quadrangle obliterated. She dreamed of an earlier time, when as a gawky child she had sought out the hidden Temple. It had been her practice to ease herself to sleep by imagining visits to the rooms in the old residents' corridor. She viewed them as comic characters, jibbering grotesques, whose clumsy art she humoured and patronized. Each chamber had its own distinctive smell and the occupants paid homage to her by offering little bunches of wild flowers. But tonight, in dream, uncontrolled by her will, they rebelled. They smirked and giggled, party to some joke at her expense. Bowing and curtseying in mock humility, they dropped posies at her feet that were rotten and stinking. Each one gestured towards the sick bay at the end of the corridor. Finally, the fat, red-faced monk, nicknamed 'the Lobster', who sweated and wheezed, said,

"Our drawings are only the daubs of clumsy rustics. But our latest guest can catch a likeness. We call her Jinny Jynx, for she has a wry tilt to her neck when she works."

Usually, the sick bay was dingy and drab, but now light flooded from within. The door was open and an artist was busy, covering the walls with murals. Calluna could only see her back as the scenes began to take shape. They depicted a murder, sly and secret, from the act to the concealment of the body. The outside stone of the sick bay had crumbled and the whole picture was visible to anyone who passed the window. A crowd was gathering, pointing at the horror and whispering the names of Calluna and Crinum. Her work finished, the artist turned and smiled. A face, broken and lopsided, that she had forgotten for forty years, jolted Calluna awake.

It had been a day of triumph. On her twentieth birthday, she had secured her position as a Temple artist, giving her free access to the red rock. Her successful sketch was of a tulip-mouthed youth from the Dwale—a favourite of that old satyr, Lampranthus, the High Priest. Portraiture was never her strength and Crinum had secretly executed the picture. She had passed it off as her own. The good news had come late at night and she'd hurried to the Dwale in the small hours to inform her brother.

Its bedrooms were spacious and homely, with the same comforts provided as in the studies of senior clerics and academics. Many of its buildings resembled small detached cottages. Some clients preferred their revels to be convivial, with music and poetry, whilst other guests liked their pleasures to be taken quietly. The thick stone walls and heavy draperies ensured that the most noisy and energetic liaisons did not disturb their privacy. Calluna had often visited Crinum in his favourite suite of rooms. The courtesans were discreet and accommodating, fetching her food and wine in the lazy aftermath of love-making.

Quietly, she had pushed open the door. Her brother was groggy, splayed across the bed with little bubbles of froth dribbling onto the pillow. But the girl was sober. She was perched on a stool, sketching, appraising the supine form of Crinum. Calluna tiptoed closer to inspect the drawing. It was a wicked caricature of the twins that exposed the fraudulence of both their art and their character. She recognized the brilliance of the satire and its threat. If such works were circulated, the twins' reputation, social position and wealth would be undermined. The Temple would laugh at them. A new dynasty of art would supplant them.

A slight noise made the girl turn. She was unknown to Calluna. Her expression was of amused contempt, almost indifference. There was a struggle in which Calluna wrested the drawing from her hands. The rest was not an unfortunate accident—a moment of anger that turned to tragedy—it was a calculated act to ensure that their careers would prosper. Both heresy and heretic had to be destroyed. Her strong arms gripped the head, twisted it as she would wrench a stubborn segment of rock, and the deed was done.

She shook her brother awake. At first he grumbled and blathered. But a succinct summary of their position and a quick study of the drawing. brought him to his senses. Guided by the glow from a muted lantern, they picked their way in the darkness, Calluna carrying the body through the forgotten quarters of the old Temple, to the abandoned orchard. And in the sick bay of the old residents' corridor, they left her. Calluna intended to burn the drawing but her brother, still heady with the fumes of nightshade, crumpled and tore it to shreds in the tiny room. They wedged the door shut and, using what fallen masonry and bricks they could find, disguised the entrance to the old rooms.

For a week, they fretted and worried. But the courtesans were independent, free to leave their calling without question or notice. Months and years passed. There were no feelings of guilt or conscience. In time, Calluna recalled the incident as if it had happened to someone else. Her skin, blood, nails and hair were no longer the same fibres and drops of liquid as had inhabited her body all that time ago. She had not discussed it with Crinum for over twenty years. He had laughed and was more concerned that an astute critic would recognize her portrait of the tulip-mouthed youth as his forgery.

✳

Calluna understood that the initial work promised to be arduous, back-breaking, physical labour as she hewed the rock into shape. Her stamina was great and she relished the task. On days of leisure, she strode miles into the surrounding countryside with a restless energy. But now her sleep was troubled with the memory of the murder. She dreamed each night of carrying the body through the grounds of the Temple and straining with brick and stone to cover the entrance. And the girl was difficult to lift. Calluna's shoulders bent under the weight. In life, the girl had seemed as light as gossamer. Calluna woke each morning already exhausted. The blows she struck with pick and hammer vibrated back into her bones and muscles. Within minutes, her limbs ached as never before.

And there was so much dust. It swirled around the lump of rock, blotting out the sun and sky. It seemed also to deaden all the familiar reassuring sounds from the galleries and studios of other artists. She felt isolated and vulnerable. Her world became narrow and confined. The parties and night entertainments diminished. Her friends were vexed with the choking fumes that lingered in every corner. They excused themselves, prevaricating that her work, vital to the Temple, demanded solitude.

By early September, she had made inroads, excavating channels into which she could burrow, shinning up the holes, using her elbows and knees like a chimney sweep's boy. As she stumbled to work each morning, her home, with its thick layers of dust, and the rock, seemed one vast network of tunnels.

It was Crinum's practice to allow his sister free rein on the statues before they worked in partnership to finish the sculptures. Irritated by the noise and dirt and bored with the lack of company, his time was spent in the Dwale and its surrounding taverns. Cursory inspections of her progress pleased him but he was surprised at how much weight she had lost.

When he began work with her, the wind and autumn rains arrived. The dust became claggy and stuck to their skin and clothes. The sleek luxury of his apartments became slimed with red mud. He scrubbed himself raw to be rid of it, and his baths and wash basins clogged and backed up, leaving pools of stinking water.

Back in the summer, they had made detailed sketches of the two figures for the sculpture, accentuating the bathos and sentimentality of their heroism. The townspeople would empathize with the pair. They would hug their babies and children, imagining their own deeds of valour and protection. Crinum worked with glass and paint to enhance this effect. He staggered to bed, coughing and fatigued, but content with his progress. In the morning, he surveyed the statue with the sense that someone else had been working the stone during the night. His tricksy artifice had been smudged and eliminated. Something more potent peeped from the rock—luminescent and ethereal, beyond his powers. And some of the coloured glass had been changed. When he studied it, images skewed and fragmented, offering subtle changes of character in the eyes of the two figures.

Their labours consumed them. All other activities ceased. No visitors came. Their servants understood the magnitude of their art and discreetly withdrew, leaving food and changes of clothing outside the studio.

As winter advanced, the cold wracked them. Their corridors and rooms felt like the caverns and passages of an underground network of dank caves. And the close contact with the blood-like stickiness of reddish sections of the rock caused skin rashes that mimicked the striations and textures of the stone. When they rubbed ointments and balms onto the infection, their skin flaked, merging into the dust that clung to the furniture and mirrors.

Waking and sleeping became blurred. Sometimes, lying immobile, their limbs heavy and their flesh numb, it seemed that someone pushed and guided them down the corridors and onto the rock. Unsure of their surroundings, as exhaustion worsened, they knew not if they were carving, painting or dreaming.

And yet, there were periods of fevered intensity in which their perceptions were heightened. They were conscious of the sentience of the rock, the stolid silence and endurance of ancient things around them, millions of years old. They felt themselves merging and assimilating with these things. The cuts of knife and hammer and the applications of paint and glass were made on living tissue. They felt that they were working their own flesh. Always, it seemed that they were artisans and labourers, sweating under a master. The very last time they looked at each other, they stared at the stone figures they had been modelling and understood they had themselves been hewn, painted, chipped and manipulated.

On the first sunny morning of spring, the other artists opened their windows with surprise and relief. The pall of dust that had hung over the Quadrangle had gone. The twins had not been seen since the turn of the year. A week's food supply remained uncollected. Gingerly, they investigated. The rooms were deserted but pristine. Rumours had circulated that rivers of dirty water and dust contaminated the houses. But these were obviously false. The statue was complete. It was a masterpiece and they ran to Porzano's study to break the news. Instantly, he recognized the style, how shadow and light shone from within the stone with a technique beyond the skill of the twins. There were multiple aspects of the divine in the flowers, insects and birds that surrounded the human figures. Even the rock appeared to breathe and dream.

Back at his rooms, remembering the completed statue, he solved the mystery of the torn scraps of paper found at the murder scene. Water, grit and rust had corrupted and changed the original drawing. Now, he saw the twins in the last throes of their transformation on the rock. At the end, they had worked naked, as their grey limbs and faces merged into stone. He wondered whether they still thought and dreamed, retaining any hint of memory or consciousness. And he recalled the strange green glass that corkscrewed and whirled in the pupils of the eyes on the human figures.

His work was done. There had been both justice and atonement. But he had resolved not to preside at the statue's unveiling. On the eve of the ceremony, when the senior clerics were at supper, he entered the rooms of his friend, Caltha, the High Priestess. Outside the window, he could hear the flocks of wildfowl as they gathered and made ready for their migratory flight to the summer breeding grounds—teal, wigeon, pintail and brent goose. Over the bed, he draped his robes, marked in the colours of the serpent, and left his stave of office. On her study desk, he arranged Myrica's portfolio of drawings and her stone miniatures, retaining only the cat's claw that he particularly admired. These would serve as models for the art of the Temple in his absence. Hearing the birds, he wrote, as an afterthought.

> "As the geese fly north,
> So abdicates the serpent.
> Old skin is sloughed aside,
> The fraying silk of discarded robes."

In a leather bag, he packed a few clothes and necessities. He carried no literature—only a thick notebook and pencils to record his travels. After a salutary visit to the Street of the Glassblowers, he met, as arranged, the sea captain, whose adventures had long enthralled him

The next evening waves bore him, under the roar of sail. The Temple grew smaller and faded from view—a child's toy, beautiful but fabricated and over-elaborate. The stories would come now, seeping into him from the hills, trees, animals and birds; unknown lands, peoples and stars.

A PARTIAL LIST OF SNUGGLY BOOKS

LÉON BLOY *The Tarantulas' Parlor and Other Unkind Tales*

S. HENRY BERTHOUD *Misanthropic Tales*

FÉLICIEN CHAMPSAUR *The Latin Orgy*

FÉLICIEN CHAMPSAUR *The Emerald Princess and Other Decadent Fantasies*

BRENDAN CONNELL *Metrophilias*

QUENTIN S. CRISP *Blue on Blue*

LADY DILKE *The Outcast Spirit and Other Stories*

BERIT ELLINGSEN *Vessel and Solsvart*

EDMOND AND JULES DE GONCOURT *Manette Salomon*

RHYS HUGHES *Cloud Farming in Wales*

JUSTIN ISIS *Divorce Procedures for the Hairdressers of a Metallic and Inconstant Goddess*

VICTOR JOLY *The Unknown Collaborator and Other Legendary Tales*

BERNARD LAZARE *The Mirror of Legends*

JEAN LORRAIN *Masks in the Tapestry*

JEAN LORRAIN *Nightmares of an Ether-Drinker*

JEAN LORRAIN *The Soul-Drinker and Other Decadent Fantasies*

CAMILLE MAUCLAIR *The Frail Soul and Other Stories*

CATULLE MENDÈS *Bluebirds*

LUIS DE MIRANDA *Who Killed the Poet?*

OCTAVE MIRBEAU *The Death of Balzac*

CHARLES MORICE *Babels, Balloons and Innocent Eyes*

DAMIAN MURPHY *Daughters of Apostasy*

KRISTINE ONG MUSLIM *Butterfly Dream*

YARROW PAISLEY *Mendicant City*

URSULA PFLUG *Down From*

JEAN RICHEPIN *The Bull-Man and the Grasshopper*

DAVID RIX *A Suite in Four Windows*

FREDERICK ROLFE *An Ossuary of the North Lagoon and Other Stories*

JASON ROLFE *An Archive of Human Nonsense*

BRIAN STABLEFORD *Spirits of the Vasty Deep*

BRIAN STABLEFORD (editor) *Decadence and Symbolism: A Showcase Anthology*

TOADHOUSE *Gone Fishing with Samy Rosenstock*

JANE DE LA VAUDÈRE *The Demi-Sexes and The Androgynes*

JANE DE LA VAUDÈRE *The Double Star and Other Occult Fantasies*

RENÉE VIVIEN AND HÉLÈNE DE ZUYLEN DE NYEVELT *Faustina and Other Stories*